"We ha   **r**
shouted.

Lila pointed to the left. Smoke covered the back entrance and they couldn't see. The fire alarm screeched in their ears. Carter grabbed her jacket and blouse and his jacket and then took her hand and ran into the hallway. "Maybe we can get out the front door."

Flames clawed at the front entrance like an angry monster, roaring and destroying what it touched. Carter, still holding her hand, rushed into her office. He looked around. "No windows."

There was one long window at the top, but it wasn't a potential exit. The gallery was fully secured. Without a key, there was no way to get in or out.

"Wrap the blouse around your face to protect it and put your jacket on to protect your skin," Carter said as he wrapped his jacket around his head and covered his mouth. "Try not to breathe too much of the smoke. I called 911, so someone should be here quickly. Just stay calm."

"Yeah, right." Her hands shook and she tried to do as he'd asked, but that was impossible. The fire was all around them and no help was in sight.

* * *

Colton 911: Chicago—Love and danger come alive in the Windy City...

* * *

If you're on Twitter, tell us what you think of Harlequin Romantic Suspense!
#harlequinromsuspense

Dear Reader,

I'm the new kid on the block and I'm so excited to participate in this new continuity from Harlequin Romantic Suspense, Colton 911: Chicago. I spent weeks researching and reading Colton books to get caught up. My character is Lila Colton, the only girl of the second Colton family in Chicago. I could identify with that as I'm the only girl in my family.

Lila owns an art gallery and she's found her niche in the world until Carter Finch, a handsome insurance investigator, comes to town and informs her that she might have a forgery in her gallery. Before he can authenticate the painting, her gallery burns to the ground. And all eyes are looking at Lila...

It was an absolute pleasure to write this book and to be among the talented authors writing the series. I hope you'll pick up a copy to learn more about the Coltons of Chicago.

You can email me at Lw1508@aol.com, send me a message at www.Facebook.com/authorlindawarren or www.Twitter.com/texauthor, write me at PO Box 5182, Bryan, TX 77805, or visit my website at www.lindawarren.net. Your mail and thoughts are deeply appreciated.

With my love and thanks,

Linda

COLTON 911: FORGED IN FIRE

Linda Warren

HARLEQUIN

ROMANTIC
SUSPENSE

Special thanks and acknowledgment are given to Linda Warren for her contribution to the Colton 911: Chicago miniseries.

Recycling programs for this product may not exist in your area.

ISBN-13: 978-1-335-75941-2

Colton 911: Forged in Fire

Copyright © 2021 by Harlequin Books S.A.

This edition published by arrangement with Harlequin Books S.A.

For questions and comments about the quality of this book, please contact us at CustomerService@Harlequin.com.

Harlequin Enterprises ULC
22 Adelaide St. West, 40th Floor
Toronto, Ontario M5H 4E3, Canada
www.Harlequin.com

Printed in U.S.A.

Two-time RITA® Award–nominated author **Linda Warren** has written over forty books for Harlequin. A native Texan, she's a member of Romance Writers of America and the RWA West Houston chapter. Drawing upon her years of growing up on a ranch, she writes about some of her favorite things: Western-style romance, cowboys and country life. She married her high school sweetheart and they live on a lake in central Texas. He fishes and she writes. Works perfectly.

Books by Linda Warren

Harlequin Romantic Suspense

Colton 911: Chicago

Colton 911: Forged in Fire

Harlequin Heartwarming

Texas Rebels

A Child's Gift
To Save a Child

Harlequin Western Romance

Texas Rebels

Texas Rebels: Egan
Texas Rebels: Falcon
Texas Rebels: Quincy
Texas Rebels: Jude
Texas Rebels: Phoenix
Texas Rebels: Paxton
Texas Rebels: Elias

Visit the Author Profile page at Harlequin.com for more titles.

A special thanks to the gracious and super nice Patience Bloom for including me in this series. And to the wonderful Kathleen Scheibling for her steadfast guidance. Thank you, ladies!

Chapter 1

The sweet feeling of success was empowering. Lila Colton's tummy bubbled and fizzed as if she'd downed a bottle of champagne. She wanted to dance, sing or run across the street and kiss that good-looking guy who'd winked at her this morning. That would put a smile on his face. Maybe hers, too.

She tapped a key on her laptop and the printer responded with a soft clicking sound. It belched out the financial report without a problem and she held it in her hands for a moment. She'd made it. All her life she'd wanted something of her own. A dream in her silly head, but she'd made it happen. The gallery was finally making a profit. She folded the report neatly and tucked it into her purse.

It had been six months since she'd opened the Weston Street Gallery in North Center, and the first two months were lean and hard as she had to chase down artists and beg them to show their work in her gallery. It had been a monumental task since no one knew her.

Tomorrow she had a show featuring the work of Homer Tinsley, a modern artist who was popular. When she'd first seen a Tinsley, it looked as if someone had thrown paint at a canvas. She'd hovered around it to get a better view; all the colors flowed and meshed together in a way she couldn't explain. She just wanted to step into the painting and experience the feeling it had generated in her. She had three paintings in the show, and usually every Tinsley sold quickly and would bring in added capital.

Now she was going to go see her mother and celebrate. Her mother had been her biggest supporter and Lila would never forget that. She might pick up a bottle of wine and they'd dance around her mom's kitchen. Her father didn't care what she did and that hurt at times, but she tried not to let it show.

She reached for her purse as she heard the bell jingle at the front door. Who could that be? They were closed for the day. She stepped into the hallway that went to the front door to see who it was. A man stood there in a two-piece suit, looking around. By the cut and the way it fit him, she'd guess it was a name brand. He had an air of confidence and self-assurance. His dark brown hair was cut short like an executive. She couldn't see his eyes from where she was standing, but from his broad shoulders to his lean body encased to the max in the suit, she knew she could really go for this guy. What was she doing? She wasn't used to falling for guys at first sight, but there was something about this one.

She cleared her throat. "May I help you?"

He swung around. "Yes. I'm looking for Lila Colton."

"Why?" She didn't understand why she was being defensive. He wasn't a threat to her. Or maybe he was. Once she looked into his gray eyes, she was mesmerized. They were light with hidden nuances that suggested he could laugh in an instant. Or they could turn as dark as a thundercloud if the occasion arose. The man was very striking.

"Oh, I'm sorry. I forgot to introduce myself." He reached inside his suit pocket and pulled out identification. "I'm Carter Finch, an art insurance investigator."

"You mean like fraud?" Why did the good ones come with baggage?

"Yes. I hear you're showing some of Tinsley's work tomorrow."

"We show Tinsley's work a lot lately. His agent is very forthcoming with pieces."

"I'd like to meet the agent and Mr. Tinsley. Do you think you can arrange that?"

Lila thought about it for a minute, and that sweet feeling she'd experienced earlier disappeared like foam on a beer. That meant the Tinsley paintings in her gallery could be fakes and worthless. And that made her bottom line a little shaky.

"Do you think I have forgeries in the gallery?"

With one easy movement, he slipped his ID back into his pocket, as if he was taking time to answer the question. "I haven't looked at the paintings, but that's what I'm here to investigate. Namely, the Tinsley paintings you're showing. Do you think you can arrange a meeting tomorrow?"

"Walter Fox, the agent, will be here. I haven't even met Tinsley. I've asked Fox several times for Mr. Tinsley to show up for the viewing, but he tends to ignore me. I'll introduce you to Fox and you can take it from there."

"That should work. I'd like to see the paintings."

"Now? Everything is locked up and I have plans. Can we do this in the morning?"

"What time do you open?"

"At ten."

"What time is the viewing?"

"Two."

"I'll see you at ten."

"Are you going to seize the paintings?"

"No. I told you, I'm here to authenticate, and if they are forgeries, you'll probably have to give the buyers their money back."

"Oh, lovely. Do you know what that means for me?"

"I'm sorry. That's just the way it is." He strolled out the front door and she released a long breath. One minute she was floating on a cloud and the next a whole lot of bad had been dumped on her. What if Tinsley's paintings were fakes? It would bankrupt her. Good heavens, how was she going to survive this?

Carter was at the gallery at ten o'clock as promised. Ms. Colton was busy in the gallery with another woman as they were checking to make sure every piece, every painting, was perfectly hung and displayed. While she was busy, he took a moment to look around. The gallery looked freshly painted and bigger than he'd expected. Gorgeous hardwood floors and the walls were a delicate ecru. Intricate carved dark mahogany trim highlighted the room but didn't take anything away from what the room was displaying. There was a case for jewelry from foreign countries. He wasn't aware she sold jewelry.

He watched her as she talked to the woman with her back to him. Her dark hair was up in a twist and two decorative combs held it in place. Several strands had come loose and dangled by her face, giving her a soft feminine appeal. From out of nowhere he had the urge to remove the combs and let her hair flow free. She really was a beautiful woman and he hated what he had to do. In other circumstances he might have even asked her out.

She finally spotted him. "Oh, Mr. Finch, I didn't realize you were here."

"Do you mind if I look at the paintings, and please call me Carter."

"Mr. Finch, I don't think we'll be close enough to call each other by our first names. Let's leave it business."

"Yes, ma'am."

The Tinsley paintings were displayed on one wall and he stared at them for a long time. The bright colors always seemed to jump out and send a message that he could never figure out. Tinsley was a genius, but these paintings were not. Carter knew without checking further that they were forgeries. But somehow he just couldn't tell her. He'd notify Neil Dunning in the office and he would be here tomorrow. They would make a decision on the paintings for authentication, and if they agreed, the forgeries would be seized. That would take time. So he saw no reason not to let her have her show. She was aware of the risks.

"Thank you," he said as he walked away from the paintings.

"That's it?"

"No, it's just the beginning. I have another expert coming to look at them. It's a long, twisted road and a lot of paperwork, but I hope we can put the forger out of business."

He could almost read those beautiful green eyes. *And me, too.*

"I'll be back later," he said and then paused. "Wait. I need to get your phone number in case Fox or Tinsley shows up early." They exchanged phone numbers and he left feeling as if he was getting all wrapped up in Ms. Colton's affairs. He had made it his motto to never get involved with anyone he investigated, and he planned to keep that record clean.

The rest of the morning Carter went over information trying to piece together Fox, Tinsley and Ms. Colton's connection. Why was Fox offering the paintings to a small gallery in Chicago? His paintings used to show in Paris, New York and Washington. But now all of Tinsley's work was in small galleries and sold quickly.

Carter had hired a PI to see if he could find Tinsley. A little over a year ago, Tinsley's wife had passed away, and he'd become a recluse and no one had seen him since. That was puzzling since his paintings kept popping up everywhere. There was no connection between Fox and Ms. Colton. The only interaction they had was at the gallery.

He called for room service and then talked to Neil in the office. It was after three when he headed back to the gallery, and the showing was in full swing. She had a good crowd. People were looking at paintings, drinking champagne and talking. Ms. Colton was in the middle of a group of people asking questions about a sculpture.

A waiter offered him champagne and he took a glass while watching Ms. Colton. She was styling for the night with a below-the-knees black skirt and a white silk blouse. The short jacket had a beaded collar and beads down the front. Her high heels were adorned with tiny beaded straps around the ankles and over the toes. He had to blink to make himself look away.

When he found her alone, he walked over. "Has Fox or Tinsley been here?" He had to be all business.

"No, or I would've called you."

"Is that different? Doesn't Fox usually show up?"

"Yes. I called Mr. Fox when the paintings sold and he answered, but when I called him with some questions the buyer had, he didn't respond. And he still hasn't. I don't know what's going on."

People started to leave, and Ms. Colton went to the entry to say goodbye and to thank everyone for coming and supporting her gallery. Something very suspicious was going on and Carter's first guess would be Fox was alerted that he and Tinsley were being investigated for fraud. That was the only reason he wouldn't show, but Carter was betting he'd show up for that money.

A blonde with blue eyes walked over to him and shook his hand. It was the same woman Ms. Colton had been talking to earlier.

"My name is Savon. I'm Lila's assistant."

"Nice to meet you. Seems as if the showing went well."

"Yes, it did. I'm happy for Lila. She's worked very hard to make this gallery succeed, and then a con artist like Fox comes in, and you…"

"Savon, please," Lila said as she walked up to them. "I was very naive."

"Do you want to clean up tonight or wait until tomorrow?"

"You can go ahead and go. I know you have a date. I'm going to package the items that were sold and have them ready to go on Monday morning."

"I'll stay," Carter offered. "I need to ask more questions, if you don't mind."

"I don't think I have a choice." She hugged Savon. "Have a good time."

Carter followed her to a back room full of shipping materials. She sat in an old chair, undid the straps and kicked off her heels. "Aw, that feels so much better."

"Why wear them if they hurt your feet?" He took a seat on a bench that was against the wall.

"Said like a man." She lifted a dark eyebrow at him.

"What?"

"I don't see you kicking off your shoes."

"They don't hurt my feet."

"Aha." She pointed a finger at him. "Exactly. Do you know men's shoes are made for comfort and women's are made for style and to accent the feet and legs?"

He leaned forward, resting his forearms on his thighs. "This is an interesting conversation."

"Sorry. Sometimes I get carried away, but it bugs me that it's a man's world."

"I don't know about that. All you have to do is put on those heels and you can be in control of every man on this planet."

She laughed out loud, a soft, melodious sound that warmed his heart, and whatever tension there had been between them disappeared. "I believe you're a charmer, but I have to warn you I'm very good with charmers."

"I bet." He smiled and knew beyond a doubt she could charm him out of anything. They worked for the next hour together. He held things when she asked him to. He took paintings down to be shipped. And he carried things to the large safe to be stored for the night. She also sold two sculptures and she had a big bag with Weston Street Gallery emblazoned on it. It was like a big clothes bag. It would keep the sculptures clean during shipping. She placed tags with names and addresses on the items sold. They sat on the floor in the storeroom as she went over everything she had to do. He had come out of his jacket a long time ago, as she had hers.

She fanned herself. "It's getting hot in here. Do you mind if I take off my blouse?"

He leaned against a box, one arm over his raised knee. "I don't think anyone would say no to that."

She made a face at him and undid the pearl buttons on the blouse. Beneath was a white tank top. His disappointment was similar to an eighteen-year-old whom he thought he'd left behind a long time ago. But beauty was beauty even if you were eighteen or thirty-four. It was to be admired just like a painting.

"You said you had more questions. Fire away."

"Huh…" He was lost and hadn't heard a word she'd said. That was the first time that had ever happened to him.

"Okay, I'll ask some questions. Where are you from?"

He recovered quickly. "I was born and raised in New York. My dad worked on Wall Street and my mom worked at the Metropolitan Museum."

"That must've been an interesting life."

He moved uncomfortably against the box. He never liked to talk about his life. "Not as interesting as you'd think."

"What do you mean? You could go to the Metropolitan anytime you wanted."

"It wasn't like that. When I was small, Mom would take me to school and someone would drop me off at the museum. And I had to sit in my mom's office and do my homework. It was boring. It wasn't until I got older that I started to roam around and I found the nudes. They became my favorite paintings, but my mom became concerned and wanted my dad to find a psychiatrist because she thought it was unseemly that a boy my age would enjoy looking at naked women. My friends and I laughed about that a lot. And there was an influx of teenage boys to the museum."

"That's funny."

He brushed dust from his pants. He wished most of the stories had been like that, but they hadn't. "Ever since I was ten years old, all I ever wanted was freedom from the small space of the apartment. It was confining living in New York, but like all things, you get used to it."

"But it didn't keep you from still wanting freedom?"

"You bet it didn't."

"How did you get into the art business?"

"Due to my dad's insistence, I attended Columbia University because he went there. I was eighteen and could go where I wanted, but I didn't want to disappoint him. I stuck it out and was thinking about leaving when I met an art professor, Neil Dunning. He taught a class once a week and I was lucky enough to get into his class. He knows everything about art—the good, the bad and the forged. I learned so much from him. When I graduated, he asked me to work on his team and I've been with him ever since. I've traveled all over the world, and my home is now out of a suitcase, and that's just fine with me," Carter said.

"Do your parents still live in New York?"

He shook his head. "When my dad was turning sixty, he started talking about retiring, and my mom insisted that they weren't. They were too young. I don't know what happened. I was doing my own thing by then. When I came home for a visit, they said they had something to tell me. They were retiring and moving to Southern California. And that was it."

"Do you see them often?"

"No. I usually spend the holidays with Neil and his family."

Her face creased into a frown.

"Why are you frowning?"

"I think it's so sad when a child loses touch with their parents. That's a bond that shouldn't be broken. My dad is dysfunctional, but I still talk to him and check on him every now and then because he's my father."

"I knew you would be like that."

"How?"

"Soft and kind." He shifted again. "You know, it is getting hot in here."

Lila sniffed. "What's that smell?"

Both jumped up and ran into the gallery. In the right corner, flames licked toward the ceiling and smoke billowed toward them.

"Oh, my God! My gallery's on fire!"

Chapter 2

"We have to get out of here," Carter shouted. "Where's the exit?"

Lila pointed to the left. Smoke covered the back entrance and they couldn't see. The fire alarm screeched in their ears. Carter grabbed her jacket and blouse and his jacket and then took her hand and ran into the hallway. "Maybe we can get out the front door."

Flames clawed at the front entrance like an angry monster, roaring and destroying what it touched. Carter, still holding her hand, rushed into her office. He looked around. "No windows."

There was one long window at the top, but it wasn't a potential exit. The gallery was fully secured. Without a key, there was no way to get in or out.

"Wrap the blouse around your face to protect it and put your jacket on to protect your skin," Carter said as he wrapped his jacket around his head and covered his mouth. "Try not to breathe too much of the smoke. I called 911, so someone should be here quickly. Just stay calm."

"Yeah, right." Her hands shook and she tried to do as he'd asked, but that was impossible. The fire was all around them and no help was in sight.

"What's on the other side of this wall?"

"It's the exit that goes out into an alley."

Carter tapped on the wall. "It's drywall." He picked up a stapler from her desk and started hitting the wall with blunt-force blows. The drywall splintered and he pulled away big pieces with his hands.

She reached in to help him until they had a big hole. He kicked the two-by-four out with his foot, taking most of the outside office wall. "Be careful of the wires."

"You first," he said. "Fast! The smoke is building in here."

With the blouse wrapped around her head and over her face, he pushed her through the hole and she tried not to breathe. He tumbled through after her and they faced the big exit door, which was locked. Carter reached up and hit the security pad, and the door opened. They fell out into the alley into a fireman's arms.

Other firefighters charged into the building. "Anyone else in here?" one of them asked.

"No," Carter shouted.

An ambulance backed into the alley, and within seconds, she was lying on a stretcher, thanking God for her life and Carter's.

She looked at him sitting on a bench beside her. He

removed the jacket from his head, and a paramedic checked him over and put an oxygen mask on him. She had one, too, and was trying to breathe normally, which was difficult since her heart was pounding in her chest.

"Are you okay?" she asked.

"Yeah. Now that we're out of there. How about you?"

"I'm good now that I can breathe." She wanted to say she was sorry and so many other things, but she didn't know what for. It was all tangled up with the fear inside her.

To make sure they were out of danger, they spent the next two hours in the ER as they underwent tests and X-rays. In the end, the doctor said she was okay, but he wanted her on oxygen for thirty more minutes.

She hadn't seen Carter and she wondered how he was doing. She'd ask the nurse when she came back. The curtain moved aside, but the woman who came in wasn't a nurse. It was her mother, Vita. Her brown hair was in a short bob, and the expression on her face was one of those take-charge-mother moods.

"Mom, I told you I'm okay."

Her mother hugged her and pushed back her damp hair. "Your hair's wet."

"I've had a shower to get the soot off of me."

She laid a small carryall on the bed. "I brought you some clothes, so get changed and you can come home with me. I'll take care of you."

Lila sighed. "Mom, as soon as I'm released, I'm going back to the gallery. I have tons of things to do, like deal with the insurance companies."

"It will all be there tomorrow."

Just as Lila was about to prepare her best come-back, a gray-haired man with a goatee and a big smile walked in. Her stepfather, Rick Yates, kissed her cheek. "How's my girl?"

"I'm good. I'm just trying to convince my mother of that."

"Well, she worries, you know."

"And I love her for that, but I really need my space right now. Please."

"Well, Vita, I guess we go home and do our thing and let our grown-up daughter do hers. What do you say?"

Her mother straightened the sheets as if they needed it. "You'll call first thing in the morning?"

"Promise, but I'll be out late, so don't expect it too early."

Her mother rolled her eyes. "There are always conditions with children. Let's go home, Rick. Love you, baby."

"Love you, too, Mom."

She jumped out of bed and hurriedly dressed in the jeans and stretch knit top her mother had brought. As she slipped into sneakers, the nurse came in with discharge papers and she quickly signed them. "Do you know if Mr. Finch has been discharged?"

"Yes, I believe he's already left."

No! She wanted to talk to him, but she wouldn't worry. She was sure he would come back. She'd just take a cab to the gallery and get her car. Then she realized she had no money and her purse was in the gallery, probably burned to a crisp. What could she do? She could call her mother, but she'd just made a big deal about needing her space. Her brother, Myles, was probably still working in his law firm. She could call him and wiggle cab fare out of him.

On the way to the nurses' station, she stopped short. Carter was there in scrubs and leaning on the counter, talking to a nurse. She should have known women liked him. She thought of her dad for a brief moment. He cheated on her mother constantly and had several children outside the marriage. She probably would never marry because of the scars from her childhood. How could she really trust a man?

"Hey, I was just looking for you. Do you need a ride back to the gallery?"

"Yes. Thank you."

"I called a cab. It should be here any minute."

As they walked out the door to the yellow cab, she said, "Love the outfit."

"It's better than soot-covered clothes. I'm thankful the doctor was so generous."

Carter opened the door, and she slid into the back seat and made no effort to move over. Carter sat right next to her, almost together, as one. She didn't want to move away. She needed this closeness. She needed someone. The fear was still very real, and she needed to be with someone who didn't know her well enough to know that she was about to fall apart.

They didn't speak all the way to the gallery, but he gently touched her hands, which were gripped together in her lap. "Are you okay?"

"No." She was as honest as she could be. "But I have to see what's left of the gallery and all the months of work I put into it."

"From the insurance, you'll be able to recoup and start over. You can hold my hand if you want."

She wasn't afraid to grab it quickly for support. The cab stopped in front of the gallery and they got out. All she could do was stare at the blackened rubble that once was her beautiful gallery. The roof had caved in, and the whole place was just a charred mess. Somewhere amid all the ashes were treasured pieces of art. Her eyes strayed from the building to her car parked in front. She gasped. Part of the roof had fallen through her windshield into her car and the tires had been burned off. It was totaled. She was totaled. She had to get away from here.

By the expression on Lila's face, Carter could see she had reached her limit. He had to take her home. Before he could offer, a man walked over to them and held out his hand. "Frank Richards, chief arson inspector." The man was tall and his slacks and shirt were wrinkled, as if he hadn't been out of them in a couple of days.

"Do you think it was arson?" Carter asked.

The man shrugged. "We're not sure, but we have to check everything. We'll let you know when we've finished the investigation."

"Thank you," Lila replied. "Do you think you can see what's left of my purse? My identification is in it and I'll need it if it's still usable."

The man thought about it and Carter knew he didn't want anyone to disturb the scene, as most firemen would.

"What would it hurt to let her have her identification?" he appealed to the investigator. "Just her ID."

The man sighed and hollered at one of the firemen to do as she'd asked.

"It's on a chair in my office," she said.

In a few minutes, the man came out with her wallet and handed it to her. "It's kind of warm, so be careful, but everything is intact."

"Thank you."

A Lincoln Navigator swung into the parking lot. A bald guy with a little extra around the middle got out. "What the hell happened here?"

"Somehow the gallery caught fire," Lila told him.

"I told you about all that wiring. Every month it's something about the wiring. The electrician put new lights in this week and probably overloaded the breaker, which caught fire," the man said.

The arson investigator shook his hand. "We've already checked the breaker and that wasn't it. I'm assuming you're the owner of the building."

"Yes. Lou Rossini." He pointed to Lila. "She's responsible for this and she's going to pay for everything."

"Hey, you don't know that." Carter stepped in. "You don't know what started the fire, and until they do, I'd advise you to keep your mouth shut."

The man's eyes narrowed. "And who are you?"

"Carter Finch, insurance investigator. The insurance companies are involved now and will make a decision on who pays for what."

"I'm sorry, Mr. Rossini. I don't know how the fire started."

When Lila spoke, the man seemed to calm down. "The insurance people will sort it out. I'll talk to you later."

Lila wrapped her arms around her waist and Carter realized she was trembling. He touched her arm. "Come on. I'm taking you home. Do you want to go to your mother's?"

She blinked. "How do you know my mother?"

"I heard her in the ER."

She brushed her no-doubt messy hair behind her ears.

"Oh. You know that saying about always listening to your mother because she knows what's best for you? I should've listened, but right now all I want to do is go home to my apartment and let the wounds heal. My mother would smother me with love and kindness, and I don't need that right now. I need to be strong to get through this. It's my problem, not hers."

He admired her courage, but she really shouldn't be alone. "Do you have a sister or brother who I could call for you?"

She linked her arm through his. "Wait until you hear about my convoluted family and then you'll understand when I say no. I'll do just fine by myself. I could call my sister-in-law, Faith. We've always been close, but she has her own problems right now. I could call Savon, but she's having the time of her life and I won't bother her."

He helped her into the car, which he didn't have to do, but she didn't say anything, just clutched the wallet to her chest. "Where to?" he asked as he slid into the driver's seat of his rental. She gave him her address in Lincoln Park. It was a town house and not too far away.

"Why don't you come in," she said as he stopped in the parking lot. "There's no need to go back to your hotel."

He was thirty-four years old and he was pretty good at reading women, but this one flew right over his head. He didn't know what she was thinking, but he knew what he was thinking.

"Why?" he asked. "We barely know each other."

"I feel like I've known you for a very long time and—" she rubbed the leather on the wallet "—I don't want to be alone tonight. And, yes, I'm fine," she added quickly. "Don't read more into this than there is."

"I wouldn't dream of it." He grabbed his briefcase and suitcase and followed her into the town house. It was a two-story with a living/kitchen area downstairs and the bedrooms upstairs.

With her foot on the bottom step of the stairs, she said, "There's a small bedroom to the right and a small bathroom that you can use. I have a lot of paintings and artifacts in there, but you can get to the bed and the bathroom."

"Thanks." If he had any wild notion how this night was going to go, she had just disillusioned him. She really didn't want to be alone and he understood that. He settled into the room and stared at all the paintings stacked against the wall. They were all by the same person and she was probably going to have a show for that person. There were several small sculptures and vases in a corner. On the desk were hand-drawn pictures with an old Wild West flavor. He pushed them toward the back and laid his laptop there. On the bed he opened his suitcase and put away his clothes in the chest of drawers and closet. There were also paintings in the closet, but he had enough room for his clothes. He sat on the bed and took a moment. What was he doing here?

He liked her. He liked her a lot, and if she needed someone, he was willing to be that person. Truth was, no one had ever really needed him. As a child, he'd spent more time with the lady across the hall than he had with his own parents. They were social people and went out several nights a week, and he was left to be entertained by the neighbor.

He stretched. The day had been a killer. He smelled like smoke and his muscles ached. Escaping a fire was not in his job description. He had to get all this information to Neil, but first, he needed to shower and change clothes. Then maybe he would feel better.

Nothing could change the outcome of the fire. There would be some rough days for Lila and he would stay as long as he could. His work was on the road and he would have to leave as soon as he sorted through the Tinsley debacle.

Lila felt much better after she had a shower, and she smelled better, too. She heard the water running and knew Carter had decided to take one, too. She went downstairs. Why had she asked him to stay? The answer was very simple: because she wanted him here and, yes, maybe she was a little afraid, but not of the darkness or the fire, but of being alone. She'd had that fear most of her life, and today she really couldn't shake it and she couldn't explain it.

Carter came into the kitchen in pajama bottoms and a T-shirt. Her heart accelerated at the sight of him. His wet dark hair clung to his scalp and a five-o'clock shadow enhanced his sexy masculine look. There was another reason she wanted him to stay. She was thirty years old and attracted to him, and she was old enough to act on that attraction.

"You seem better," he said, eyeing her from head

to toe in the short bathrobe. Her senses spun with an almost forgotten delight of being with a man.

She swallowed hard. "You look better, too."

He walked toward the refrigerator. "You have anything in here to eat? I'm starving."

"I ordered pizza."

"Great. Just what the doctor would suggest." The doorbell rang. He went to get the pizza, and they sat at the island in the kitchen.

"You can't stay in Chicago and not eat a deep-pan pizza."

"It's delicious, but you're not eating very much."

"Nothing seems real." She laid her pizza piece in the box. "I think I'm going up to bed. I want to be at the gallery early in the morning."

"I'll clean up down here and probably go to bed, too."

She paused on the stairway, wanting to say something to explain her strange actions. "Have you ever been afraid to be alone?"

He took a sip of wine. "Everyone has. Even big old guys, so don't beat yourself up about being afraid. It's a normal reaction."

"Nothing stays the same. Everything gets shattered and broken, and I don't know how to put my life back together without crying my eyes out."

"Then cry your eyes out. Do whatever it takes, and I promise you tomorrow everything will look better."

"You're no help." She ran up the stairs. How could she expect him to understand? He didn't even really know her or about her childhood of broken dreams and broken promises. Everything changed on a regular basis, and maybe this time it was just too much.

Chapter 3

He'd said the wrong thing, but he wasn't a kiss-and-make-better type of guy. She was hurting, so he should've done something more mature, more comforting, even though she'd said she didn't want that from her own mother. He put the rest of the pizza in the refrigerator and finished off his glass of wine. Tomorrow they would talk and he'd apologize for being so crass.

As he passed her doorway, he could see from the light in the hall that she was sitting on the floor at the foot of the bed with her knees drawn up and her face resting on them. Was she crying? He started to go in, but changed his mind. She needed this time alone.

He brushed his teeth, turned out the lights and sat on the bed. For some reason, he couldn't force himself to crawl beneath the sheets. He couldn't sleep when she was going through such a traumatic upheaval.

Her door was slightly ajar, and he tapped on it. She didn't respond and his first reaction was to go back to his room and leave her alone. Instead, he walked in and sat beside her with his back against the bed.

"I'm sorry I was so crass. I should have been more understanding of what you're going through. You lost your place of work and your car and survived the fire. That's a lot for one day."

She raised her head. "It's not about that. Those are material things that can be replaced, though I would have rather not have lost them. It's just…just… Have you heard of the Colton families in Chicago?"

"Can't say that I have."

She leaned forward, snagged a newspaper from the dresser and placed it in his lap. The lamp was on, but still he could barely read *Colton vs Colton*. She'd said something about her convoluted family, and maybe she would tell him about them.

"Are you one of these Coltons?"

"Yes. So many weird things have been happening lately that it's hard to take it all in."

"What happened?"

"I never met my grandfather Dean. He had a wife named Alice and a mistress named Carin Pederson. I'm told the marriage was a happy one until Alice couldn't conceive. There was a lot of tension in the marriage, and then Carin got pregnant and my grandfather decided to leave Alice for Carin to be with his children. Before he could break this news to Alice, she told him she was finally pregnant and he made a decision to stay with his wife and raise his proper family. This made Carin very angry and she's been that way to this day. Carin blackmailed my grandfather many times using her sons as leverage. He bought Carin a house on the outskirts of Chicago and paid her a huge monthly salary." She took a deep breath. "Carin is my grandmother."

"The mistress?"

"Yes. And to up the tension, so to speak, Alice had twin boys, Ernest and Alfred, and my grandmother gave birth to Erik and Axel. The two families lived here in Chicago never knowing about the other until Ernest and Alfred were murdered outside their office. They caught the murderers and then found out there was a codicil to Dean Colton's original will. It named my father, Axel, and Uncle Erik as heirs. Of course, this was a shock to all of us, on both sides. How could we have been duped for this long?"

"It's easy to be deceived. I deal with it every day in art and in the real world. Everybody wants their fair share and more."

"That's my grandmother. When she heard there was a codicil to the will, she hired a lawyer and forced my dad and my uncle to side with her so they could get their fair share."

"Is there a lot of money involved?"

"Have you heard of Colton Connections?"

"Sure. It's a big company."

"That's the business Alfred and Ernest created, and now my grandmother wants half of it, which comes to about thirty million. If the judge rules in my grandmother's favor, it will bankrupt the other Coltons. That's what makes me sad. It's not our money."

"But if the will says so, you're entitled to it…"

"They asked to meet us."

"The other Coltons?"

"Yes. We met at Farrah's home and talked. She's the widow of Ernest and was very gracious to have us in her lovely home. You know, you could tell they are very wealthy and yet they all hold down jobs. My father and Uncle Erik have been get-rich schemers all their lives and have accomplished nothing. They live off of my grandmother. And now she wants her sons to have what they deserve because Dean denied them all of their lives."

"And you don't feel that way?"

"It was hard to hate these people who seem to have everything. They were very nice to us and they didn't have to be. We've been trying to get along these past few months and trying to get to know each other and exactly what we want for the future. Myles—he's my brother—and I feel that the money isn't ours, and so do my cousins Aaron, Damon and Nash, Erik's sons. But we don't have a say in the matter. It's up to our fathers and they are controlled by our grandmother. I don't look for anything to change until my grandmother gets her way. She wants revenge for the way Dean treated her, and she's not going to stop until she gets it."

"It's clear you have issues with your grandmother."

"Oh, you bet I do. She manipulates my dad to the point where he is still like a little boy asking favors from her. He will never go against her."

"You weren't raised by your father?"

"No. My mom and Nicole, Erik's wife, got out as soon as they found out their husbands were cheating on them and had children by other women. I was raised by my mother, and it was hard for her that first year as we moved around a lot. There was no place to call home. And then my mom met Rick and our lives settled down. He became the father we never had. He and my mom own Yates' Yards plant nursery. It's in the suburb of Wheaton and a lovely place if you like plants of all kinds, trees, blooming flowers, shrubs and fruit trees." She flexed her arm. "That's where I got these muscles, working in the nursery."

He touched her bicep. "You don't have any muscles."

"You better watch out," she singsonged in a happy voice, "or I might show you these muscles."

He pushed her hair away from her face. "You're the most beautiful and captivating woman I've ever met."

"And you're a handsome charmer who saved my life."

"The authorities would've been there to save you."

She shook her head. "I keep thinking what if I had been in the gallery alone..."

"Shh." He gathered her close in his arms. "You weren't, so no more *what-ifs*. Now, do you think you can get some sleep?"

She blinked at him. "I don't know. I might need company..."

"Lila..."

"How long have we known each other?" She sat up to look at his face, and even though it was almost dark, she saw a lot of questions and a lot of answers there. But she couldn't decipher any of them.

"Maybe forty-eight hours."

She placed her hand over his heart and it raced like a stallion waiting at the gate. "From the first moment I saw you standing in the doorway, I thought you could be someone I could really go for. I didn't know anything else about you, but somehow our hearts connected."

"Lila, you've been through a lot today and I don't want to take advantage. I think it's best if I go back to my room and we'll talk about this tomorrow."

At his words, rejection filled her. Even though she tried to hide it, she could feel the tightness of her face scrunching into a frown. She sat back on her heels, trying to wiggle out of an embarrassing situation.

He quickly cupped her face. "Hey, hey, I didn't mean it that way. I don't want you to regret it in the morning."

"Do you know how old I am?"

"No, and I would never ask."

She patted his chest. "Good. I'm old enough to know what I want. I'm not in college, fooling around for the fun of it." She made a face. "Although, I've never been that girl, either."

"Well, then stop talking." He brought his lips to hers and the room tilted as a storm of emotions exploded in her, emotions too long denied and emotions that she needed to feel. His lips took her on a journey of pure heat as hot as the fire in the gallery. He trailed his lips to her cheeks, over her jawbone and down her long neck to her breasts. Just when she thought she couldn't get enough, he lifted her into his arms and fell backward onto the bed. They laughed like teenagers and quickly discarded their clothes. But unlike teenagers, they made love in a slow, satisfying way. It was unlike anything she'd ever experienced. His hands and lips made a thorough investigation of her body, and she could very well say he had the touch to drive her crazy. Her breasts swelled and her body ached for more. She heard moans and cries and realized it was her enjoying the pleasure of a man who knew what he was doing.

He trailed a finger down the length of her body. She shivered.

"You have such smooth skin."

"And your hands are lethal tantalizing weapons."

She pulled his head down to hers, and nothing else was said for some time as they soothed each other's aches, pains and worries in a way that satisfied both of them. The world with its gigantic headache floated away. As she drifted into sleep, she thought she could be falling in love for the first time in her life. Or making the biggest mistake of her life.

The sound of the phone woke Carter at six. He looked down at the woman beside him curled into him like a soft and warm kitten and wanted to stay there forever. His phone sounded again, and he scrambled looking for his pants and then realized they were in the other bedroom. He lightly kissed Lila and she stirred.

"I'll be right back."

"Carter…"

He found his pants and his phone. It was Neil, his boss. He'd forgotten about him. "Neil."

"I'm at the hotel and you're not here. Where are you?"

"Uh…" He looked around at the very feminine decor and the many paintings and thought he was in heaven…with an angel. "Give me a few minutes."

"Okay. I'm eating breakfast in the restaurant, so that's where I'll be."

Carter went back to Lila's bedroom and crawled in

beside her. He kissed the curve of her neck. "I have to go."

"Oh." She stretched, and his eyes strayed to her flawless white body and all his engines roared to life. "Is it morning?"

"It's after six."

She sat up straight. "Oh, heavens. I've got to go, too. I'm meeting the car insurance guy at the gallery and hopefully I can get a rental, but you'll have to drop me off on your way to wherever." She tried to crawl from the bed, but he caught her and pulled her back.

"Carter," she screeched.

"You can't just run away."

He stared into her green eyes, which were full of laughter and fun, and that was the way he always wanted to see her.

She raised an eyebrow. "What do you have in mind? You've got five minutes."

He chuckled. "I'll only be getting started."

Laughter filled the room, and once again everything faded away except their attraction for each other.

Afterward they were in a rush to get out the front door. Lila called her mother with Carter's phone to let her know she was okay. As they drove up to the gallery, Carter watched Lila's face. It was much worse in the daylight, a large pile of charred rubble, smoke still emanating from some of the destruction. The right wall and the front of the building were completely gone. All that was left was Lila's office and safe.

"Oh," erupted from Lila's throat. "It's all gone. Somewhere in that pile are the Tinsley paintings. Now you won't be able to validate them."

He reached over and took her hand. "You don't have to try to be brave. If you want to cry, cry."

She linked her fingers through his. "I've already had my cry, and thank you for being there for my meltdown."

"My pleasure." Then he reached over and engaged her in a long kiss that he would remember for the rest of the day.

A car drove up to Lila's burnt one. "That's the insurance agent. I sent him pictures yesterday, so it should be quick."

"Do you want me to wait?"

"No. The insurance guy will help me get a rental. I'll call you later."

"You don't have a phone."

She sighed. "Okay. I will get a phone after I get a rental and I will call you, but I don't remember your number."

He reached for his wallet, pulled out a business card and handed it to her. "You can usually reach me at those numbers, but my cell is the one I usually answer."

"Thank you." She tucked it into the wallet she was carrying.

She gave him a quick kiss and he drove away. He looked in his rearview mirror and saw her just standing there staring at the destruction of the fire. Was she okay? Did he need to stay?

The insurance guy walked over to her, they shook hands, and he knew she was fine. She'd gotten it all out of her system last night. She was strong and resilient, and he was lucky enough to have been there when she'd needed someone. He never had a problem leaving town, but today he was feeling a pull to stay in Chicago for a while. That had never happened to him before. He'd fly into a new city, do his job and get on a plane and go to another city. That was his life and he enjoyed it. Since the Tinsley paintings were ruined and they couldn't validate them, they'd probably be leaving as soon as tonight. How could he tell her he was leaving?

Chapter 4

Lila was in a rush mode all morning. Before she could talk to the insurance agent, Inspector Richards drove up and wanted to talk to her. She made arrangements to meet the agent later.

They stood near Richards's black Ford car with a Chicago Fire Department logo on it. Since it was August and summer in Chicago, it was a nice sixty-two degrees this morning. There was a slight chill in the air, though. She felt it all the way to her bones. If Richards was seeking her out, there had to be a reason.

"Mr. Rossini seems to think you had something to do with the fire and is being very vocal about it, so I'd like to ask you some questions."

Her nerves tingled. "Oh, sure. So it was arson?"

"It's kind of leaning that way, but we're not finished yet. Mr. Rossini said that you were in debt and had a very good reason to set the fire."

"The gallery is steadily making progress. I've only been open about six months. Why in the world would I choose to destroy what I created? I expect the profits will be more next month, but now…" She took a long breath. "I did not set the fire."

"What was the name of the electrician who put in the new wiring?" He pulled a small notebook from his pocket and began to write in it.

"Philip Boyd."

"Does Mr. Rossini know the electrician?"

"He hired him—that's all I know. When I paid my rent last month, I asked about the wiring because he had promised to get it done. He told me he would get things fixed up like I wanted. A few days later, the electrician showed up and did the work."

"Who else works in the gallery with you?"

"Savon Elam. Oh, no! I forgot to call her. May I borrow your phone?"

"Uh… I guess so, but don't be too long. That's my work phone."

"Thank you."

She told her friend everything that had happened and what she was doing now with the insurance people.

"Are you okay?" Savon asked.

"Yes. I have my own personal hero."

"You mean handsome Mr. Finch?"

"Yes. I don't know what I would have done if he hadn't been there. I'll talk to you later. The arson inspector is glaring at me because I'm using his phone. I'll let you know when I get a phone."

Lila clicked off and put on her best smile. "Inspector Richards, do you think it would be possible to get my phone back?"

"Let me check and see if they're through with it." He talked on the phone for a minute and then shoved his cell in his pocket. "You can pick it up at the station on Central."

She wanted to hug him. Instead, she said, "Thank you." Her excitement didn't last long as she realized she didn't have a way to get there. She would have to call a cab, but again, she didn't have a phone. She shouldn't have let the agent leave.

Men in red cars that had the fire department logo on them parked in the parking lot.

"That's my team," the inspector said. "We'll be working here most of the day."

"Uh…may I use your phone again?"

"What for?" His eyebrows knotted together.

"I have to call a cab."

He looked around. "How did you get here?"

"A friend dropped me off."

He reached for the phone in his pocket. "Remember…"

"Don't stay on it too long," she finished for him. "Got it."

Within minutes, she was in a cab headed for the car dealership to get a rental. It took longer than she'd expected, but she had a nice Toyota to drive. Then she went to the fire station and it was a nightmare. It took over an hour to get her phone, but it still worked. The first person she thought about calling was Carter. He said he had a meeting this morning and she didn't want to disturb him. Instead, she sent him a text to let him know she had her phone.

Last night was a moment out of time. She never dreamed she would fall for someone so quickly, but there was something about Carter that appealed to her. Maybe it was the way his eyes were so clear and honest and made her feel attractive and wanted. She never slept with guys on a first date, and for the last six months her focus had been on building the gallery into a successful business.

Carter was gentle and easy to talk to and she'd shared more of her life than she should have, but she'd needed someone. Her skin grew warm as she thought of his touch. She bit her lip and warned herself that she couldn't get too serious. Carter would be leaving soon. She had to be prepared for that, but how did she prepare herself for a broken heart? With everything she had on her plate, she would be lucky to survive the week, and she didn't want to endure it alone. She could only hope that he would stay a little while longer.

Carter slid into a chair across from Neil Dunning in the hotel restaurant. "Sorry I'm late."

Neil closed his laptop and reached for his cup of coffee. He was a man in his fifties, very suave, very sophisticated and very knowledgeable about art. He always dressed impeccably in a suit and a tie, as he was today, and always had a handkerchief handy.

"Have you had breakfast?"

"No. I didn't have time for breakfast."

Neil signaled for the waitress and Carter ordered food. As the waitress poured Carter a cup of coffee, Neil tapped his fingers on the table, a habit that Carter hated. That meant the wheels in his head were spinning and a lot of questions would follow.

"You weren't at the hotel, so where were you?"

Carter took a sip of coffee. He didn't have to tell Neil where he was. It was none of his business, but they were good friends and Carter respected him. And he knew Neil. He didn't mean anything by it.

"I met someone and I spent the night at her place."

"That quick?" One eyebrow shot up.

The waitress brought Carter's food and ended the conversation, which Carter thought was a good thing. "Have you looked at the paper this morning or the Chicago news on TV?"

"No, I haven't. I slept on the plane and arrived here about five this morning. Luckily, you put my name on the hotel room, too, and I was able to get in and take a shower. Hurry so we can get over to the gallery."

"The gallery burned down last night."

Neil's eyes opened wide. "What?"

"It burned to the ground. The large safe is left and part of the office space, but otherwise it's a total write-off."

"You're kidding."

"No."

"What about the Tinsley paintings?"

"They're in the rubble, ruined. The arson inspector wouldn't let us in yesterday, but he might today."

"Arson?" Neil tapped a finger against his chin. "That's interesting. Why would they call in the arson expert?"

"To determine the cause of the fire. I'm sure it's procedural."

"Yeah. Let's get over there and see what's left."

As Carter followed Neil out of the restaurant, his phone beeped. He looked at the caller ID. Lila. Then there was a text. I got my phone back. See you later.

Yes, he would see her later. Definitely.

Chief inspector Frank Richards and his team were

on the site when they arrived. They shook hands. "How's it going?" Carter asked.

"We're about through. I'll have my findings in a couple of days."

The fire department vehicles drove away. "Well, I guess our work here is done. There's no way to validate the paintings. They're gone, basically. That means the forger gets away with it. And he's still doing it."

"Yeah, and I didn't get to look at them really good because Ms. Colton was having a showing, but I'd stake my reputation on the fact that they are forgeries."

"Too bad we didn't get to them sooner, but don't worry—we'll catch him or her. It will just take some time. Now on to Milan."

"Milan?"

"Yes. I got a call from a man who operates a gallery there. He's being offered an Ila Chay painting, but he has a feeling it's a forgery and is willing to pay a lot of money to prove that it is. He wants to hang it in his gallery, but he's waiting until he knows for sure if it's a real work of art by Chay."

"She died many years ago and dealt mostly in abstracts. I'd be very surprised if it was real, unless a family member owns it and wants the money."

"That's what I want you to find out. Get your ticket and call me when you get there." Neil was already getting into the rental.

For the first time, Carter didn't want to leave. He had vacations, but this wasn't a vacation. He wanted to be here for Lila if she needed someone.

He slid into the driver's seat. "I'd rather not go to Milan."

"Why not?"

He told him how they were trapped in the building and how upset Lila had been and he just wanted to stay here for a while to make sure she was okay.

"So you like this girl?"

"Yes. Just give me a few days." The thought crossed his mind if he would be ready to go in a few days. Only time would tell.

"Okay. I'll see if Marla would like to go on a trip to Milan. She loves visiting her home country."

His wife had a temper that could peel the wallpaper off the walls, so Neil did all he could to please her. But she had the warmest heart of anyone he knew. She was always trying to feed him and find him a wife. Carter didn't need any help in that department.

At the hotel, they said goodbye. "Call me when you're ready to come back to work."

"Thanks, Neil. I appreciate the time off."

Neil patted him on the shoulder. "Have a good time, but not so good that you don't come back to work. Not many men enjoy being away from home that much and I don't know what I'd do without you."

Carter waved as he drove away. His tense muscles relaxed. He would get to know Lila better and explore these feelings he had for her or whatever they were. After a few days the newness would wear off and he would be ready to go. That was the way it usually went with him. Staying wasn't in his nature. That wouldn't be fair to Lila, though, if her feelings got involved. The best thing for him was to leave now while they both understood there was nothing serious between them. That was just hogwash. His nerves tensed again and he really didn't know what he was doing. He just wanted to be with Lila, and that was so telling. They were both adults and they would work it out. He pulled into a parking lot and called her.

"Where are you?"

"At home digging through some stuff Inspector Richards brought over."

"What kind of stuff?"

"Everything that was salvageable. It's not much."

"That was very nice of him."

"Yeah. I thought he was a grouch, but he's really nice, especially after almost accusing me of burning down the gallery."

"He did that?"

"Earlier this morning when I talked to him, but I think he knows I didn't do it. It still makes me nervous, though."

"I'll be there in a few minutes."

He found her sitting on a big plastic sheet in the middle of her living room. On the plastic were charred items. He sat beside her with one knee raised and his forearm resting on it. She smiled at him, and everything looked a little brighter and his fear of hurting her disappeared.

"Find anything?"

"The hard drives off the computer might still be good. They took the security cameras to the lab hoping they could get something off them. I'll check on everything tomorrow. My purse is a gooey mess." She opened it for him to look inside. He made a face. "Makeup does not stand up well to heat. The rest is trash. Inspector Richards said that tomorrow they would let me in the safe to get the items out, and my insurance agent will be there, too. I have to make a list of everything that was in the fire, and that's going to take a while." She tapped his leg with her forefinger. "But luckily, and you should know this, I'm very organized due to my mother's insistence that everything has a place, and clothes do not belong on the floor, and drawers do not need to be rattraps. My mother had rules. She would say, 'When you're on your own, you can live like you want, but while you're in my house, you will be neat and organized, just to please me.'"

"Sounds like a very smart lady."

"Yeah, my mom is the best. My dad was... Forget it. I'd rather not talk about it." She fiddled with a picture frame she was trying to wipe the soot off of.

He scooted to rest his back against the couch. He heeded her wishes because he knew her father was not a topic she liked. Another topic was on his mind and they needed to talk about it.

"About last night..."

She laid the frame beside another batch of things she was saving. "What about it?"

"I don't want you to think it was a one-night stand. It was more to me."

She turned to face him. "Me, too. I'm well aware you will only be here a few days, and like I told you, we're adults and make our own choices. I chose to sleep with you and I don't regret it. And whatever happens next is up to us. I know you're leaving and I'll be fine with that." She raised an eyebrow. "But I think we should curb the sex for now because I don't want to be clinging to you and begging you to stay. I needed you last night in ways I never imagined. It was nice and...now..."

"That sounds rehearsed," he interrupted.

"Maybe it is." She got to her feet. "Look, Carter,

I've never been in a relationship like this before, so I'd prefer to take it slow." She glanced at the mess at her feet. "I have to throw all of this stuff away."

He helped her wrap up the plastic and carry it to the garage to put in a big receptacle. The things she wanted to keep she put in a box. His mind was buzzing as they worked. Could she be that perfect? Could she be that understanding? Lila was a mystery that he was slowly unraveling, and before he left here, he might be the one begging and clinging.

Lila took a shower to get the soot off her. She never knew she was such a good liar. She gave him points for being so open. When he left, she would be strong in her hope that one day he would return. She had to let go of the most wonderful man she'd ever met. Until that time, she would enjoy every minute.

She slipped on sneakers and jogging pants and hurried into the living room. Carter was looking through an art book. "Let's go jogging and get a Chicago hot dog. You have to have one before you leave."

"Great. I'll change my clothes."

In a few minutes, they were outside her town house, jogging toward a business section of restaurants. "There used to be people on the street selling hot dogs like they do in New York, but now they've all moved indoors and have their own place."

"I've heard of the Chicago hot dog."

"You're in for a treat." She turned to look at him. "I forgot to tell you the hot dog place is almost two miles away. Do you think you can handle it?" His laughter followed her and she jogged away.

They stopped at an intersection to take a breath.

She pointed. "We're going to Portilli's. They have the best." She put her hands on her knees and took several deep breaths.

He patted her on the back. "Are you sure you're up for this?"

She made a face at him. "You work out, don't you?"

"All the time." He gave her a quick smile and linked his arm through hers, and they slowly walked down the street to the hot dog place. They ordered the original and Carter also ordered fries and a beer. She did, too. They sat at a blue gingham-covered table near windows.

"This is nice," Carter said. "Very home-style and very busy." People milled around them. Two little boys looked in the window at them. People started a line outside, eager to get in.

Carter stared at the hot dog the waitress placed in front of him. "Are you kidding? What's on here? It looks like a little bit of everything."

"It is, from the poppy seed bun, the beef hot dog, to the mustard, tomatoes, slice of dill pickle, sport pickle, green relish and onions. It's a great combination for your taste buds."

They ate in amicable silence and it was comforting to be out with a man. She'd put so much of her time and energy into the gallery that she forgot how to enjoy herself. And now she didn't know what she was going to do. First, she would enjoy this evening with him.

"How about chocolate cake?" Carter asked. He glanced at the table next to them. "They're having chocolate cake and it looks delicious."

"I'm game for anything chocolate."

Later, they caught the transit back to her town

house. They had an easy, comfortable relationship that she loved. She'd said no sex, but she was slowly changing her mind. If he was leaving…

He pulled off his T-shirt and sat on the sofa in an effortless movement of strength and muscles. Oh, yeah. He had muscles. She turned her eyes away and sat beside him, taking off her sneakers and wondering how she should handle the night.

Before words formed in her head, the doorbell rang. She jumped up to answer. A young man stood there and asked, "Miss Lila Colton?"

"Yes."

He handed her a large manila envelope. "This is for you." He then walked away.

Lila didn't get a chance to say thank you or much of anything. She stared at the envelope and saw it was from a lawyer. Her insides tightened with a foreboding. Thoughts of throwing the envelope on her desk and looking at it tomorrow crossed her mind. But she was more adult than that. She hoped. She ripped it open with more force than necessary.

Anger built in her as she quickly scanned the document. "That sorry SOB!"

"What is it?" Carter came over to her.

"Fox and the Tinsley estate have filed a claim against me for the ruined Tinsley paintings."

Chapter 5

She handed him the document. "He wants more money than the buyers paid for them. What's he trying to pull?" She sat on the sofa and curled her feet beneath her. "I don't have that kind of money."

"Fox must be desperate for money to go this far. He's not waiting for them to rule the fire arson. He's pointing the finger at you in hopes that he can get money out of you. He's hiding something and I'm almost positive he had something to do with the fire, but I'll have to prove it."

He looked up and saw her sitting there with her head on her knees, curled up, defeated and alone. He sat beside her and pulled her into his arms. "Cheer up. We're not done yet."

She tilted her head to look at him. "What do you mean?"

"I know a lot of people who are arson investigators and I'll contact a couple to see if I can get some information. People are always destroying stuff to get the insurance. It's very common and they look for that."

"And how is that going to help now?"

He kissed her forehead to ease the worry lines. "Inspector Richards said he's going to have his ruling in a couple of days. I hope by then I can get someone else to look at it."

She sat up. "Richards will never allow a stranger interfering with his team's case."

"We'll see."

A smile crossed her face. "You're devious, but brilliant."

He pulled out his phone. "I'm going to be on the phone for a while. Do you mind if I use your extra bedroom tonight?" She hesitated with her answer. What she said now she had to be able to handle. "I can go back to the hotel."

"Oh, no. You're welcome to the room." She got to her feet. "I'm going to bed. I'll see you in the morning."

He stared after her as she walked upstairs to her bedroom. What had he done now? He hated it when he got different vibes from women. Maybe that was why he was still single. He needed to adjust.

Putting his thoughts aside, he called his friend David Dreyer. He'd worked with him several times on cases and he was an expert arson investigator. "Hey, David. It's Carter. Do you have a minute to talk?"

"Sure. We just got the kids down for the night. What's up?"

"How are the kids?"

"Growing like weeds. They are three and five now

and hard to keep up with, but you didn't call about my kids. What's going on?"

He told him about the fire at the gallery and his suspicions. "I'm afraid they're going to try to pin this on the gallery owner, noting that she's the only one who had a motive."

"Is there any evidence that points to her?"

"The investigator, Frank Richards, is closemouthed and I haven't seen the file, but he keeps coming back to Ms. Colton, the renter. And Tinsley's agent is now trying to get as much money as he can. It's all a little fishy."

"Do you want me to look at the gallery? And if you do, you know what's going to happen. The lead investigator will put the skids on quickly."

"I know." Carter put the phone on speaker and laid it on the coffee table. "But between the two of us, I feel we have a good chance of convincing him. I just need a little help to point out certain things like the agent's eagerness for money and how the renter is not in debt like was told to the investigator."

"Is the owner of the building involved?"

"Well, he owns the building and would stand to gain a big sum of money from the insurance."

"How much?"

"I don't know yet, but it's in a very good location."

"I do owe you a favor."

"Yes, you do, but I would never call it in. Do what you feel is right."

"I can be there in the morning about nine. Have everybody at the table so we can discuss this or argue about it. But first, I'll have to look at the gallery fire. Has anyone touched anything?"

"Only the firefighters and the investigators."

"Okay. Can you pick me up at the airport?"

"Sure. No problem."

He finished his conversation with David, picked up his phone and went to his bedroom. Lila's bedroom door was closed. She was upset about everything that was coming down on her, and it was hitting her all at the same time. He would stay as long as he could to help her, but she had to be willing to let him. That might be a big stumbling block.

He took a quick shower and crawled into bed. The thought that she might be crying kept him tossing and turning. From the moonlight shining through his window, he could see a shape in his doorway.

It was Lila.

Lila didn't know what she was doing. She couldn't sleep alone tonight. Memories of the hot fire and the smoke filling her nostrils kept spinning in her head, keeping her awake. She just wanted to forget and get lost in something that was real.

"Lila…"

"Yes," she replied in a hoarse voice. "Are you asleep?" That was such a crazy thing to ask, but it was all she could come up with.

"No."

She walked farther into the room and sat on the bed. "I changed my mind."

"You mean…?"

"Yes."

He pulled back the comforter and she crawled in. "I'm such a ditz," she said. "But I can't get all this stuff out of my mind, and every time I try to go to sleep, I see this fire that's consuming everything…even me."

He stroked her hair and she relaxed, leaning on him. "Stop worrying. I told you I'm going to help. I called an old friend who's going to look at the gallery." He told her about David Dreyer.

"He's coming here?"

"Yes. I hope he can bring some new knowledge to the case."

"Did you get Richards's permission?"

"Not yet, but I'm hoping he'll see the good in letting another expert take a look at the case."

"Oh, Carter, thank you." She grabbed him around the neck and kissed him. The kisses continued into the night and Lila didn't even remember falling asleep. She was too excited. Too much in love and… Too much in love? The thought stopped her. She couldn't be in love. Her emotions were high, and she was just clinging to the only lifeline she had.

The next morning, they were in a rush to go their separate ways. Carter was going to the airport to pick up David, and Lila had to deal with removing the artwork from the safe.

"Remember," Carter said, going out the door, "don't schedule the truck until this afternoon. We don't want anyone stomping around in the gallery until David has a chance to look inside."

"Got it."

He gave her a quick kiss and he was gone. David was right on time and they were at Richards's office before nine o'clock in the morning. Carter had called ahead for an appointment.

"He's not going to like this," David said.

"No, he's not. No one wants to hear they might have missed something. We just have to play it by ear."

David was in his early forties and had been working arson for about fifteen years, while Richards had been working arson for about thirty. It wasn't going to play that the younger guy knew more than the older guy. But Carter was hoping that reasoning would go a long way to solving this crime. And he knew it was a crime.

They walked into a sparse office: a desk, filing cabinets and pictures of fires on walls, probably fires that Richards had solved.

They shook hands and introductions were made. Carter and David took seats in metal folding chairs. Carter was glad to see that Richards had a comfortable chair. The city didn't allow for luxuries and it showed in this small office with scuffed walls and old tile floors.

"What can I do for you guys?"

Carter took a breath, gauging his words carefully. "David has been a friend of mine for a long time and I was hoping that you would allow him to access the fire records and give his opinion."

Richards leaned back in his chair. "You don't trust my opinion?"

"Not when you're pointing the finger at Ms. Colton."

Richards shook his head as if he finally figured out something. "This has to do with Ms. Colton." He pointed a finger at David. "She's hired you, hasn't she?"

"No, sir. I've never met Ms. Colton. I only came to give my opinion because my friend Carter asked me."

"You guys all stick together, don't you?"

"I hope you included yourself in the 'guys' part because all of us are in this together. We want to catch who did this. We want to make sure that it's arson and not just a wiring problem. Don't you want the same thing, Inspector Richards?"

"All right, but I'm going with you. I don't want you planting things that weren't there before."

"I resent that," David said.

Grabbing his jacket, Richards replied, "And I resent you sticking your nose into my case. I guess we'll both have to live with it."

Inspector Richards followed David around like a little puppy while he went through everything. They had put on plastic shoes, a mask and safety covering for protection from the toxins. Carter leaned against his car and watched. Every now and then, David would squat and brush something away with a small brush and take pictures.

At the back right corner of the gallery, David squatted and motioned for Richards to come over. Richards squatted, too, and they talked for a while. Carter figured they'd found something. The two men stood and made their way out of the rubble.

Richards showed him a tiny black wire that had different-colored wires inside it. The whole thing was less than an inch long. It was burned on both ends.

"You know what that is, Finch?"

"I've seen a wire like that connected to a detonator."

"Yep. You're right. Someone set this fire and I'm opening a full investigation now. We'll catch who did this. Thanks for your expertise, Mr. Dreyer."

"You're welcome. I did it for a friend. Most of the

time, the evidence is just under the ashes, and most investigators hate digging through that."

"Well, my boys are going to get a workout and a lesson."

"You know, Richards, I've seen small detonators used before. It's like a toy. You set the time and then wait for it to explode and it explodes with a burst of fire. Teenagers are known to use them and they are sold by several companies. We tried one time to shut down the sale of these detonators, but we couldn't get it through Congress. So now the investigators have to deal with them."

"Thanks for the information. I have to go and call Ms. Colton before she gets here to remove items out of the safe. I don't want anything touched until this investigation is over, and that's going to take a while."

Carter and David shook hands. "Thanks, pal. That was one lucky break."

"You won't believe how much evidence is under the ashes. What's underneath was there before the fire started. It takes a lot of training to figure this out."

"I'm so glad you decided to come."

"It seemed important to you."

Carter shoved his hands into his pockets and thought about that for a minute. Yes, it was important to him. Lila was important to him. "How about if I buy you lunch?"

"Deal. I want to try a Chicago deep-dish pizza."

"You got it."

On the way to the nearest pizza place, Carter called Lila. Before he could say anything, her cheery voice came on. "Have you heard?"

"If you're talking about the full investigation, yes, I heard."

"Your friend must have found something."

"Yes, he did. I'll tell you about it tonight. I just want to make sure you don't move any art out of the safe."

"Oh, yes. Richards has already made it clear to me."

"There will be many eyes looking at the scene and they will find something to connect someone to that fire."

"But not me."

"But not you."

"I'm on my way to see my brother about Fox's claim and see what he can do. I'll see you later. Give David a hug for me and tell him thanks."

"I already have." It was good to hear her so happy and to be a part of it. How long could he stay here?

Lila took the elevator up to the third floor, where Myles's office was located. He had his own clients, his own space, and that wasn't enough. He wanted to make partner, to make more money, and he said it was all for his wife, Faith, and four-year-old son, Jackson. He worked all the time to impress his bosses, but he didn't impress the woman he loved. She'd taken all she could take and left him. Faith had said what good was marriage when you never saw your husband. Lila tried not to get entangled in their problems, but she loved them and it was hard to keep her mouth shut.

She opened the door that had her brother's name on it. Inside was Ellen, his secretary and receptionist, sitting at a desk wearing an unwavering smile.

"I'd like to see my brother for a minute," she said to Ellen.

She pushed her tortoiseshell glasses up the bridge of her nose. "Faith is in there now."

Oh, great. They were talking. She'd wait and come back a little later. As she turned, Myles's door opened and Faith backed out, waving to someone inside. "Mommy will be back. Bye."

Myles and Faith had been in love since high school. She was the beautiful redhead every boy wanted, but she'd wanted only Myles. How could such a good marriage go so wrong?

"Oh, Lila." Faith held a hand to her chest. "You startled me."

They hugged. "It's good to see you," Lila said. "We need to stay more in touch."

"Yeah, but that's hard when Myles is being a jerk."

"You'll work this out," Lila told her. "You love each other."

Faith looked away. "Sometimes I wonder. Myles hardly ever sees Jackson, and when he does have him, he takes him to your mother's and she takes care of him. So what's the point of Myles having days with Jackson?"

"Oh, Faith, I'm sorry."

"I have a dental appointment in fifteen minutes, and my mom has a migraine and there was nowhere else to leave Jackson, so I brought him here. Myles threw a fit, but I had no choice. I really have to go." She gave Lila another hug. "Let's do lunch sometime and you can listen to me gripe some more."

Faith rushed out the door and Lila took a deep breath. She had no qualms about just walking in on Myles. She had a few things to say to him and he was going to listen.

Myles was at his desk on his laptop and Jackson was throwing a red ball. When Jackson saw her, he ran into her. "Li." He hadn't put her name together yet and she was fine being Li.

She picked him up and kissed his cheek. "You're getting so big."

He raised his hands above his head. "Tall."

She kissed his cheek again. "Yes."

"Wanna play ball?" He still had the ball in his hand and he threw it. The ball hit Myles's desk and knocked the framed picture of Faith and Jackson to the hardwood floor. The glass broke.

"Jackson!" Myles shouted.

Jackson buried his face into Lila's neck and Lila wagged a finger at Myles. The wagging finger said more than words to stop.

Myles quickly backpedaled. "It's okay, Jackson. Daddy is just a little upset." He tried to take the boy, but he wouldn't go.

"Li," he said.

The door burst open and Faith came through it and took Jackson from her while looking directly at Myles. "If you can't keep your son with a loving heart, then you don't need to keep him at all." With those scathing words, she headed out the door.

"Faith..." Myles shouted after her.

She stopped for a moment.

"You know the office is no place for a child. He's already broken something."

"Oh, horror of horrors." She turned on her heel and left.

Lila placed her hands on her hips. "That was lovely

to witness. I sincerely hope that you two do not do this all the time in front of Jackson."

Myles ran his hands over his face. "I do not need you to come down on me today." He sat at his desk. "Did you come by for a reason?"

She pulled the document out of her purse and placed it in front of him. "I got this by courier and I thought you might be able to help me. I know you're busy. I know you have family problems, but you're the only one I know who has this kind of expertise."

"Mr. Fox, who represents Mr. Tinsley, wants his money fast, but it doesn't work that way. Have they ruled on what started the fire?"

"No. Due to new information, they're starting a full investigation and it's not going to be a right-now type thing. It's going to take some time and I don't have that kind of money to pay Mr. Fox and the estate."

"I'll draft a letter and get Ellen to send it over to—" He glanced at the top of the paper. "Look at the names on that letterhead." He paused and she could see the envy in his eyes. His dream was always to be head of a law firm, but it was coming at a cost to his family. One day he would see that.

"I'll inform them that until there's a ruling on the fire, no money will be changing hands. If not, I will take it before a judge, and no judge is going to rule on a case when there hasn't been a ruling on the cause of the fire. That should keep Mr. Fox off your back until you get your money from the insurance."

"Thank you." She threw her arms around his neck and kissed his cheek much as she had Jackson. "That gives me some breathing room. I love you, but I have to run." At the door, she stopped. "Have you heard anything on the Colton case?"

Myles shook his head. "I had lunch with Heath Colton the other day and he was wondering the same thing. The lawsuit has really put a strain on the family, and I told him as far as myself and my sister were concerned, we didn't want the money, but no one can change our grandmother's mind or our father's. Heath said he understood and I hope he does. I might try talking to Dad again. Hopefully some sort of compromise can be worked out."

"With our grandmother involved?"

"Yeah. She's not going to settle for anything less than she thinks she deserves."

"You know, it's very hard to imagine our grandfather adding Erik's and Axel's names as the heirs since he avoided them all of his life. Carter—that's the guy who was with me in the gallery when it caught fire—is an expert in forgery and I was just wondering if the will might have been forged."

"That's a good thought, but I'm sure the other Coltons have checked into that angle and have done everything possible to prove it a fake."

"I guess so. I'll talk to you later. Bye."

Myles grabbed his jacket and headed for the door, too. "I have to find Faith and get my son. I won't be able to get any work done otherwise."

He stopped long enough to tell Ellen about the broken glass in his office and to get someone to clean it up. They walked together to the elevator.

"By the way, how are you?"

"Nervous about the future. In one blow, my whole life was destroyed. I'm having a hard time dealing with that. But on the other hand, it's opening up new possibilities for me that I never expected."

"Does this have anything to do with Carter?" He pushed the elevator button.

She lifted an eyebrow. "It just might." A soft laugh erupted from her throat, but it didn't last long. Carter was leaving in a couple of days, and she would find out just how strong she really was.

Chapter 6

After dropping David at the airport, Carter went grocery shopping. He noticed there wasn't much food at Lila's house. He ate out so much that sometimes he enjoyed a meal at home or wherever home was. He got everything he needed and headed back to her town house to surprise her. She'd given him an extra key this morning, and that might mean a little more than he wanted it to. But he wasn't ready to walk away from her just yet.

Lila came charging through the door, threw her purse at the couch and grabbed him in a fierce bear hug, which ended up in a long, sweet kiss. She stepped back and glanced at the apron around his waist.

"What are you doing?"

He kissed the tip of her nose. "Fixing supper for us—spaghetti and meatballs, salad and garlic bread and a good Merlot."

"You know how to cook?"

"Sure. I eat so much in hotels and restaurants that sometimes I like to eat in."

"You should've said something. I can cook, you know."

He slanted a smile in her direction. "Your refrigerator gives a different message—yogurt, water, butter, something dried up in a bowl that's unrecognizable."

She slapped at his chest. "Don't be critical. I work long hours, and most of the time I just pick something up on the way home."

He bowed from the waist. "Tonight you're eating a home-cooked meal and all you have to do is enjoy it." He glanced toward the dining table. It was set with a linen tablecloth and napkins, and in the center was a beautiful bouquet of flowers.

"You bought flowers. You're such a sweetheart." She kissed him slowly and he eventually pushed her away.

"Hold on. Hold on. I cooked the food and we're going to eat it while it's nice and hot."

"You're hot." She chuckled, but obediently took her seat at the table.

"We're celebrating a victory today." While he put food on the table, he told her the whole story about finding the detonator wire. They conversed all through dinner and he marveled at how easy it was to talk to her. They did the dishes and took their wine to the living room.

"I have some good news, too. Myles said that I don't have to pay Fox anything until the arson investigator rules on the cause of the fire. He's making the law firm that Fox hired aware of the situation. At least, I get a breather. The last couple of days my stomach is spinning like clothes in the dryer, going round and round."

He cupped her face. "Try not to worry. That little wire gives them a very big clue the fire was set."

"That's not going to tell them who set the fire, and I'm afraid they're still going to point the finger at me."

He gathered her into his arms. "Lila, please don't torture yourself. They'll have to have evidence that you set it, like where you bought the detonator, as I'm sure Richards is checking stores right now."

"What kind of stores?"

"Stores that sell that type of device. David says it's more used by teenagers who are trying to make a statement. It's small with a timer on it and shoots out a blast of fire. David said they tried to get them off the market but failed. They're causing too many fires because they are so easy to use. And there's no way they can connect you to a detonator."

She raised her face to look at his. "You have a lot of trust in me."

"I can read people, and you, my lady, are as innocent and honest as they come."

She gave a comforting laugh and nestled into him, and it felt so good and right at that moment that he couldn't see himself ever leaving her or the comfort of her arms. He glanced around the room to get his mind on something else.

"What are you going to do with all these paintings?"

She sat up. "I don't know. At this point, I don't even know if Rossini is planning on rebuilding the gallery or if he'll rent it to me again. I have paintings and art stacked everywhere, even in the hall closet and the entry closet. I guess I could have a…" She jumped up. "Oh… Oh…"

Carter got to his feet, too. Clearly, she was excited about something. "What?"

"With everything that's going on, I forgot I had them."

"Had what?"

"You're going to be so surprised." She took their wineglasses to the kitchen and walked to the entry closet door. She pulled out several small paintings wrapped in heavy plastic and laid them on the coffee table. "Fox offered me these about a month ago, and a man shopping in the gallery said he would be interested, but it would have to wait until he got back from Europe. I promised him a private showing and stored the paintings in the closet until then."

He stared at the paintings, two on the coffee table and one on the sofa. He couldn't believe his eyes. They were all signed by Homer Tinsley or supposedly by the man.

"Do you know what this means?"

"I…I…"

"This could help us find the forger. I thought everything was lost in the fire, but now…"

"Do you think they're forgeries?"

He held up a painting to the light. "I don't know yet. They're very good if they are."

"But how can you really tell?"

"By sniffing it, for one thing. Oil changes smell over time." He sniffed one of the paintings. "The oil is probably a little over a year old. It's been painted recently. Next is to examine with the naked eye to see any imperfections. Then we check the back of the canvas, and this is painted on canvas and secured with tiny nails. If we feel it's a forgery, we take it to our lab in New York and go over it thoroughly with ultraviolet lights, X-rays and a microscopic view, and a lot of other things that will tell us the age of everything on the canvas and what colors were used to paint it. It's an involved process, but it will tell us if these Tinsleys are really Tinsleys. And hopefully give us a clue as to where these paintings are coming from." He went to his room and got his high-powered camera and the things that he needed.

Lila sat on the arm of the sofa and watched him as he got down on his knees and took close-ups of the paintings and then transferred them to his laptop. He then took his laptop to the table. Lila followed.

"Look," he said as he brought up the paintings on the screen.

"The ones on the left are true Tinsleys and the ones on the right are the ones I just took pictures of. I have to blow them up to get a better view."

Lila pulled a chair close to his and he had trouble thinking for a moment with the scent of lavender all around him. He quickly brought his thoughts back to the painting. "This guy or woman is good, but he failed on the signature. Take a look and see if you can see it."

She stared at the screen. "They look the same to me."

"Look closer. Tinsley makes a fancy loop before he makes the slant for the *H* and the end of the slant comes out slightly. On the other three paintings, the slant stops and doesn't come out. It's minor, but if you look at Tinsley's real paintings, you'll see that the slant is on every one of them."

"I would never notice that and I see a lot of paintings."

He got to his feet. "I have to call Neil and get a flight out as soon as I can. Do you mind if I take the paintings?"

"Uh… I guess not."

"Thanks, Lila. You just helped us catch a forger."

Lila sat on the sofa, staring at the paintings. And then she got up and packaged them together again, but at the back of her mind she was screeching, "He's leaving and doesn't seem to mind."

He came out of the bedroom with his carryall, briefcase and laptop and took them out to his rental. He came back in for the paintings. Standing in the doorway, he said, "I hate to leave like this, but duty calls and I will call you about the paintings."

What did she say at a moment like this? *Thank you for saving my life. Thank you for being there for me. Thank you for everything.*

She was saved from saying anything because he was already in his rental backing out, leaving her alone once again. But she'd known this would happen. She just hadn't known it would hurt this much.

She slammed the door with more force than necessary and went into the kitchen to wash the wineglasses. As she worked, she realized she knew very little about Carter Finch. She had no idea where he was going. She just assumed it would be New York, but she didn't know where the lab was or where Neil lived. All she had was Carter's phone number, and that would bring very little comfort in the days ahead.

* * *

Carter made it to New York and the flight was un-eventful. Neil was waiting for him and he climbed into the town car and headed toward Manhattan. He and his wife had a big Upper East Side apartment, which had been in Neil's family for a long time. The lab was in the building's basement, so they would be working at his home.

Marla was asleep and the kids were in college, so they went right to work. At six the next morning, Carter woke up on the sofa in the lab and wondered where he was. He reached for Lila and found nothing but a brown tweed sofa. Oh, man, what had he done? He sat up and ran his hands through his hair, trying to remember what he'd said when he left. He hadn't said much of anything. Oh, man. He buried his face in his hands.

"Go take a shower," Neil said. "And we'll go over the data."

"I need coffee first."

Neil pointed to a coffee maker on a table. "Just made a fresh pot. These paintings are forgeries and I don't have a problem validating them as such. The guy is getting sloppy. Even the elements and pigments don't match. The signature is the telling point. Tinsley would never sign his name like that. He was very meticulous."

"Yeah," Carter said, pouring a cup of coffee. "My eye caught it right away."

"Did you notice anything else?"

"Yes. I was going to talk to you about it when Marla called you upstairs, so I decided to take a thirty-minute nap instead."

"You were out for two hours."

"Really?" He glanced at his watch. "I guess I was."

"It's understandable since you'd been up all night, but let's get back to these paintings. What did you notice?"

"Some artists are left-handed and some are right-handed. We put away a guy a few years ago who was left-handed, but he could paint with any hand. He was doing so many forgeries that he forgot and used his left hand on a couple of paintings, and it showed up when we examined it. I think he got five years and is still in prison. But—" he pointed to several spots on the computer screen "—that was done left-handed and the rest of the painting is right-handed."

"Smart man. I taught you well. Now, can you remember who that guy is?"

"Tony Martell, and as far as I know, he's still in prison."

"Let's find out." Neil turned to his laptop.

"While you're doing that, I'm going to take a shower."

"Okay."

Carter quickly showered and shaved and sat on the bed he used while he was at Neil's working. Lila was getting up about now and he should call her and try to explain what had come over him. But he wanted to do that in person and he didn't know when he could get away from Neil to do that. He had to come up with a plan to see her.

He went back to the basement and Neil was getting off the phone. "Martell is out. He's been out for about a year now, and that's exactly about the time the Tinsley paintings started showing up in small galleries."

Carter reached for his phone in his pocket. "I'll call

the detective we hired to get information on Tinsley and see if he can locate Martell."

Carter sat on the sofa as he talked. "Hey, we haven't touched base in a while and I was wondering if you had any information for me."

"It's your lucky day, man."

Carter sat up straight. "What do you mean?"

"Tinsley's wife died fourteen months ago and the people in the village where he lived in France said Tinsley grieved himself to death two months later. He is buried in a small cemetery there and hardly anyone knows this. It's a best-kept secret."

"Tinsley is dead?" Carter was trying to take this in and what it meant.

"Yep. You got it. I finally located a great-nephew of Tinsley's. He's the only living relative and he inherited Tinsley's fortune. Or I should say he inherited eighty percent of Tinsley's wealth."

"And Fox, his agent, inherited the rest."

"You got it."

"This is great work, Jim. Send us an invoice."

"You bet I will. Just be sitting down when you open it." Jim always had a weird sense of humor. Carter had known him for a long time. He came from the South and was down-home country all the way, but he was one of those guys who could find a needle in a haystack and his skill was invaluable.

"Try not to be too hard on us." Neil was doing sign language at him, and Carter realized he'd forgotten to mention Martell. "Wait a minute. I have another case, if you're interested."

"Sure, but then I'm taking a vacation for two weeks."

"We need information on Tony Martell, an address,

phone number or anything you can find on him. He's an ex-con and he's probably going to be hard to find, but I have no doubt you can. I need it ASAP."

"On it." Jim chuckled and clicked off.

Carter told Neil about the new revelations.

"Damn, he's dead? That should've jumped out at us like a two-headed demon months ago. Why didn't it occur to us?"

"Because that's not our job. Our job is to determine if the paintings circulating are forgeries, and now we pretty well know that they are. There's no doubt in my mind that Fox is behind all this. That twenty percent of Tinsley's estate must've been a slap in the face. He's done everything for the old man for the past twenty years. I guess Fox found a way to continue to make money off Tinsley. Now we have to prove it."

"Marla and I are leaving for Milan tomorrow, so you're in charge of the Martell forgeries. Keep me posted."

For the first time in his career, Carter wasn't eager to leave and move on to another city. He was still stuck in Chicago. As soon as he got the phone call from Jim, he would leave for another city or wherever Martell called home. But first, he needed to see Lila one more time.

Lila woke up early the next morning eager for a new day. She wasn't going to wallow in hurt feelings and disappointments. She'd known Carter was going to leave. She just hadn't expected him to leave at the drop of a hat. But she was sure he had his reasons. She knew one of his reasons: he loved his job in tracking down criminals. She'd heard it in his voice when he talked about his work and she'd heard it when he was showing her the forgeries on his laptop. She hurriedly showered and dressed and was out the door before her mind could wander anymore.

As she slid into her car, her phone buzzed and her thoughts zoomed right back to Carter. It wasn't Carter. It was Tatum, her cousin from the other branch of the Coltons.

"Hi, Lila. It's Tatum."

"Hi, Tatum. It's nice to hear from you."

"I was hoping you would say that. I'd like to invite you for lunch today, if you have time."

"That sounds lovely." What else could she say? She liked the other Coltons, and giving them the cold shoulder wasn't in her nature.

"What time?"

"About one."

"I'll see you then." Lila slipped her phone into her purse and wondered what that was about. Tatum owned True restaurant. It was a new farm-to-table restaurant and very popular. The place was known to be packed every day. She backed out of the parking lot with a smile on her face. She would enjoy spending some time with her cousin. Tatum was getting married soon and Lila would love to hear all the details. That made her think of Carter, the man who didn't have a home and a man who didn't even want a home. In her heart, she knew he would come back, and she couldn't tell herself otherwise. She'd been told that as men aged they started thinking about home and family, and she was hoping Carter was no different. She didn't want to force him into a relationship. She just wanted them to be happy like they were supposed to be. Oh, good heavens, her mother had read her too many fairy tales.

She had a meeting with her car insurance agent to discuss her getting a car since hers was totaled. She was told that since the car was destroyed by the fire, they couldn't pay until they had a decision if it was arson or not. If it was arson, Rossini, who owned the building, would have the insurance to pay for the car. They just had to wait. The only good news he had to say was that the rental would continue to be paid with her insurance and she could use it as long as she needed. Everything in her life hinged on Richards's ruling of the fire.

Tatum's restaurant was in the updated North Center area. When they had the get-together at Farrah's house, Tatum said she'd renovated an old warehouse there for her restaurant, True. Lila had no problem finding it as she saw people sitting on benches waiting to get in. She was sure there was a waiting area inside, too. Now what did she do? She didn't want to get in front of people who had been waiting for a while.

She got out of her car and walked toward the entrance. As she was pondering her problem, the guy at the door motioned to her. "Ms. Colton?"

"Yes."

"Come this way, please."

She followed him into the restaurant, pausing a moment to look around. The inside was a rich green, and dropdown lighting reminded her of European restaurants. The windows were tall and the ceiling high, letting in lots of light and causing the crystal behind the bar to sparkle off the marble bar. Green plants were everywhere, adding a homey touch to the place. Everything was open, airy and nice.

Suddenly Tatum appeared out of nowhere and

linked her arm through Lila's. "I have a place in the dining room, just for us, where it's not so noisy."

Tatum was a blue-eyed blonde bubbling with excitement. She could imagine it would have been fun having her for a cousin when Lila was growing up. It was the same way with the other Coltons. There had been a little awkwardness at first, but once they started talking, there was a connection that couldn't be denied.

They sat in an out-of-the-way table facing huge windows offering them a view of Chicago. "This is nice," Lila said.

"And lots of work. Some days I wonder why I took on so much, but then, I can't sponge off my family. I have to have a job to support myself and to feel good about myself."

"I know how you feel."

Something must have changed on Lila's face as she reached over and touched Lila's arm. "I'm so sorry about the gallery. How are you doing?"

"Taking it a day at a time and dealing with a lot of insurance people."

A waitress in a black-and-white uniform stepped over. "Ms. Colton, would you like to order now?" Her eyes were on Tatum, and Lila assumed she was talking to Tatum.

"Give Lila a menu," she told the girl. "I really don't need one."

Lila took the menu and said, "You choose. You know what's delicious."

Tatum leaned over and whispered, "It all is."

Lila smiled. "I'd still like you to choose."

"Do you like salmon?"

"Yes, I love it."

"We got some fresh in this morning and I made a new buttery wine sauce for it, so you and I will be tasting it for the first time."

"That sounds delicious."

"It comes with couscous, chayote squash and fresh spinach salad. It's all fresh from the garden. My suppliers come in early and that means I have to be here early. Don't be surprised if I fall asleep at the table."

The waitress brought water and took their drink orders. Tatum handed her the menu and said, "I'll send Apollo our order." She sent a message over her phone.

The girl didn't move. She shifted from one foot to the other, obviously nervous. "I know you said not to bother you for anything, but Eddie didn't show up for work and the dishes are piling up."

Tatum took a long breath and then looked at the girl. "I'm sure that you, Heather, Bob or Vincent can figure out how to work a dishwasher."

"Yes, ma'am." The girl scurried back to the kitchen.

"If you need to check on something, it's okay," Lila felt she needed to say.

"No, that's fine. They'll figure it out."

They munched on appetizers and talked about any and everything until the meal was served. It was as delicious as Lila had expected. And then they were served a baked Alaska that was better than anything she'd ever eaten.

She laid her napkin on the table. "That was absolutely delicious and I can see why you're so busy. Thank you for inviting me."

"You're welcome, but I had a reason."

Lila clasped her hands in her lap, hoping it wasn't about the lawsuit. "Oh."

"I wanted to invite you to our wedding."

"Oh, Tatum, that's so nice, but with our families battling each other in court, I don't think it's a good idea."

"I think it's a great idea," Tatum said, her blue eyes bright with energy.

"There would be too much tension and it would ruin your wedding."

The waitress finished removing the rest of the plates and it gave Lila a minute to gather her thoughts. She never dreamed Tatum would invite her to her wedding. Her mother wouldn't mind, but her dad… She wasn't sure what he would say. And did she care?

"Listen to me." Tatum began her appeal again. "You and your brother and your cousins have made it known how you feel about this lawsuit, and we as a family appreciate your support and would love for all of you to attend the wedding."

"There are so many *ifs* here that I'm not sure what to say."

"Then say yes."

"And if the judge rules in my grandmother's favor, will you be able to even look at us? It would bankrupt Colton Connections and would destroy your family."

Tatum put a hand to her forehead. "Oh, Lila, you think too much. Let's just enjoy the moment that we have, and I'm getting married soon and I want you to be there to celebrate with me. Who cares what happens? We'll still survive. We all work every day and can work our way through this, build another business, because if there's one thing we are not, it's quitters. So, cheer up. I'm getting married soon and I'm dying to tell you all about it."

Lila loved her attitude. For the next thirty minutes, they talked wedding details, and Lila got caught up in Tatum's excitement. Her eyes glittered as bright as a neon light. "I kid you not, my mother calls me at least three times a day asking me questions—what to do about this or what to do about that. She's an interior designer and I trust her instincts. I told her I'm busy and just make a decision. She said, 'Young lady, you're getting married and you need to pay attention to the details.' So I'm paying attention."

They laughed and sat back and stared at each other.

"This has been fun," Lila said, losing some of her nervousness.

"Then you'll come to the wedding?"

"You're so persuasive I'll think about it."

They got up and hugged, and Tatum really did feel like a cousin. Lila hoped it stayed that way through the months ahead.

Chapter 7

Lila drove by the gallery to see if anyone was working there. Yellow tape was wrapped around it with Do Not Enter signs. For the past eight years, she'd worked steadily on building a clientele and buying more quality works, and now it was all ashes. She wanted to cry that life had been so cruel, but she was stronger than that. She'd done her crying and now she had to rebuild and look to the future. Every time the thought crossed her mind, she could see Carter's face. She wondered where he was and if he had caught the forger. She couldn't think about him anymore.

Since her talk with Tatum, she decided to pay her dad a visit. Axel Colton lived in Naperville and was nearly an hour's drive away. But she had nothing else to do and she hadn't talked to him in months. She didn't call until she was almost there because he usually would say he was busy or playing racquetball.

"I'm going out for a little while," her dad said, trying to put her off.

She'd heard that line before and she wasn't budging. "I'll be there in five minutes." And then she clicked off. He lived in a nice house, but she had never been invited there and neither had Myles. He answered the door immediately, no kiss, no hug. Like strangers who shared DNA. She went through a foyer into a large living area with stark furniture. It wasn't a place to relax, but there were nice paintings on the walls. No family pictures, though. And the paintings he didn't buy from her, which caused her temperature to rise to the danger level. She banked it down.

On the ornate coffee table were a bottle of expensive bourbon and two glasses. "Are you expecting someone?"

"Later. Don't worry about it. What's so important that you had to come all the way out here?"

"I'm your daughter and I haven't seen you in a long time."

"That never seemed to matter before." He took a seat in a Queen Anne–type chair. "Your mother made sure I never got to see you and Myles."

Lila shook her head. "No, that's not true. When it was your turn to pick us up to stay with you, you would never show up. We would sit on the front steps and wait and wait and wait. Do you know how bad that is for a child?"

"Yeah, it was all my fault." Axel Colton stood up suddenly and shoved his hands into his dress pants. At almost sixty, with gray hair dusting his dark hair at the temples, he was still a very strikingly handsome man, just like Myles. Except Myles didn't have the pouch around his middle.

"I'm not going to argue that. It's over and done with. I'm more concerned about the future."

He sat in the chair again. "What about it?"

She took a deep breath. "It's unfair what Carin, Uncle Erik and you are doing to the other Coltons. It's their business. Their life, and we had nothing to do with it."

He jumped up again. One of the things she would always remember about her father was his restlessness. He couldn't sit still for a minute. "Nothing to do with it? Our father pushed us aside while he raised his proper family. We were forgotten while they lived a life of luxury."

"He's paid for everything you've ever gotten. Your home, your clothes, your fancy cars, your schooling. Everything. The money kept coming in to Carin and she never turned it down. Now she wants revenge because she never could get Dean's attention again. She wants to flaunt that relationship in front of the other Coltons. I don't like that and I wish you could see that it's not right."

"I can't go against my mother. She would be furious."

"And the money would make it all better?"

"Do you know what it's like to be forgotten by your father?"

Lila stood to her full height and replied, "Yes, I do, every day of my life. I came to say what I had to say and now I'm going." She glanced at the bourbon. "Have a good evening."

"Lila… I've been thinking a lot about Wyatt."

The statement was like a fly ball right over her head. Wyatt was the child he had with his mistress Regina. Lila had never met the boy or his mother. It was a best-kept secret until Wyatt drowned in the swimming pool while her dad was supposed to have been watching him. He had been just a toddler and Regina wanted to bring charges against Axel, but Carin had put a stop to that with threats. Regina moved away after that and her mother divorced Axel. That was when their lives fell apart.

"Why are you thinking about him?"

Axel reached for the bourbon and poured a glass. "I don't know. Maybe because I lied. Mother told me to and I didn't feel I did anything wrong. It was Regina's job to take care of the kid. She asked me to watch him. How was I supposed to know the kid would walk into the pool?"

She swallowed something that tasted like acid. "What were you doing when he fell in the pool?"

"I was asleep on the sofa. When I heard the splash, I jumped in to get him, but it was too late."

She had no words. They were all snuffed out with his callousness and insensitivity. Years ago, he had been questioned over and over about the incident, and he'd said over and over that Regina was there and she was supposed to be watching the boy. Secret after secret, lie after lie. It seemed it never stopped in the Colton family. She headed for the front door.

"I'm not good with kids, okay?" he hollered after her. "You were lucky I was never there."

With her hand on the doorknob, she replied, "I'll look at it as a blessing. My advice is to call Regina and apologize for all the pain you caused her. My number one advice is to stop listening to Carin. She's going to take you down with her."

In the car, she rested her head against the steering wheel and took a moment. Why did she think talking to her father would make things better? It never had.

A gloomy dusk settled in as she arrived home. Raindrops peppered her head and she ran into the town house. She kicked off her shoes, sat on the sofa and called Savon. She had to talk to someone to ease the ache in her heart. They talked about the gallery and the future, and she put thoughts of her dad aside.

"Do you know if Rossini is going to rebuild?" Savon asked.

"I haven't talked to him since he accused me of burning it down on purpose, and the police are listening to him. That's what has me scared."

"Surely they don't think you did it?"

"Yes, Richards believes I had something to do with it."

"He's an idiot."

Lila laughed.

"We can open somewhere else," Savon assured her. "We don't need his building."

"There's a lot to happen before I make that decision. The first and most important thing is the ruling on the fire. It's taking forever, it seems."

"Call me when you're ready to move things out of the vault. I'll help you."

"Thank you."

She stretched out on the sofa. Tears gathered in her throat and she tried to control her emotions. Her dad had hurt so many people, yet he felt no remorse. He didn't even mention the gallery fire and neither did she. It wouldn't have made a difference. He wasn't the cry-on-your-shoulder type of father. She finally realized her father didn't have deep feelings for anyone. Carin had a sick hold over him and Erik. She brushed away an errant tear and sat up.

She reached for the TV control to see if there was any news about the fire. Just then, her doorbell rang. She wasn't expecting anyone. It could be more legal papers, like Fox demanding a quart of her blood. She made her way to the door and looked through the peephole. Her heart pounded against her ribs. Carter!

She leaned her forehead against the door. What should she do? She followed her heart and opened the door, but only halfway. "You're back," she said in a bland voice.

"I'm sorry." He was dressed in slacks and a blue pin-striped shirt, impeccable as always. "May I come in?"

She wasn't going to be one of those women who let "I'm sorry" cover a multitude of sins.

"I didn't mean to leave so quickly, but with the paintings in my hands, I wanted to get the information to Neil as soon as I could. We've been after this guy for almost a year and the excitement clouded my judgment."

She opened the door wider. Guess she was one of those women. And he apologized so nicely.

"Were you able to validate the paintings as forgeries?" she asked as she walked into her living room and took a seat on the sofa.

He sat beside her and told her what had happened since he'd left. His excitement was evident in his voice and in his eyes. She wondered if he would ever talk about her with that note of excitement, joy and deep emotions. It was clear he loved his work and he was one of those guys who would never settle down. She told herself so many times that it didn't matter and that she would enjoy her time with him. That wasn't true. Love didn't work that way, as she had learned.

She brought her thoughts back to what he was saying. "So you're supposed to be in New York?"

"Yes. We have a PI looking for Tony Martell, the forger, we believe. As soon as he calls, I'll be leaving again, but I couldn't do that without seeing you."

"Aw." She stroked his face and his gray eyes darkened. She got lost in the beauty she saw there. Nothing mattered anymore, not her hurt feelings, not his love for his job. It was just the two of them right here, right now, and what happened next was their choice. Tracing his lips, she added, "If you don't kiss me soon, my heart is going to pop out of my chest."

He cupped her face and touched his lips to hers in a long, sweet kiss that lasted all the way to the bedroom. Clothes were discarded along the way. She giggled as she fell backward onto the bed and he quickly followed, covering her with his hard body. Their lovemaking reached a crescendo equaled by the thunder. The rain pounded the roof and water dripped onto the drain outside, making a *tap-tap* soothing sound. Lila felt only the rhythm in her body and the joy in her heart.

A long time later, she lay in the comfort of his arms and told him about her day.

He rubbed her shoulder. "I'm sorry you had to go through that with your dad."

"I talk to him mostly on the phone and I rarely see

him. After having lunch with Tatum and seeing what a nice person she is, I thought I would talk to my dad and maybe get him to see reason. But reason isn't in his makeup. Carin manipulates him and Erik."

"You call your grandmother by her given name?"

"That's what we were told to call her when we were small. She hated the word *grandmother* or *grandma*."

"I guess I didn't miss anything by not having grandparents. My parents were older when they had me and my grandparents had already passed away."

"When I was smaller, I used to wish for a grandmother who baked cookies." Lila laughed. "I have no idea why I would wish that because my mom made really good cookies. It's just that other kids had grandmothers who were fabulous, and we all want what everybody else has."

"I wanted a dog." He smiled. "I can't even imagine a dog in my mother's perfectly decorated apartment. Everything was in its place and everything had a place."

She sat up. "I'm hungry. How about you?"

"We're not going to make cookies, are we?"

She chuckled as she slipped a T-shirt over her head. "Leftover spaghetti."

They sat at the bar eating spaghetti and drinking wine. Later, curled up in the bed, Lila listened to the beat of his heart mingling with the patter of the rain. It was perfect. How she wished it could stay that way.

The next morning, they were slow to get dressed. Carter was in the guest bath shaving. Lila stood in the doorway watching him, already dressed in slacks and a pullover sweater. She was beautiful in whatever she wore, tall, regal and absolutely gorgeous. Her hair was pinned up again and he just wanted to take it down. He wouldn't mind waking up with her every morning.

"When will your PI call?" she asked.

"Soon, I think."

"And you'll leave again?"

He wiped his face with a towel. "Yes. That's the way my life is and has been for years. I know you were upset…"

"I wasn't upset."

"When you opened your front door, your green eyes were flashing daggers at me."

"Okay, maybe I was. I've just never met anyone like you who doesn't have the need for a home."

He kissed the tip of her nose. "Lila, I've never really had a home, so I don't feel the need for one. I know you must have this vision in your head of a house, the picket fence, the dog and happy-ever-after."

"I've never had that vision. My vision is a man who would love me and support me and be there for me always and we could live anywhere we wanted just so we were there for each other."

"Oh, Lila—"

Her phone jangled and she reached for it in her pocket. She talked for a minute and clicked off. "That was Richards. He wants to see me in an hour in his office."

Carter grabbed his shirt. "Then let's go."

"He must've made a ruling on the fire," Lila said as they made their way out the door.

In the vehicle, she clasped her hands in her lap and he knew she was nervous. He placed a hand on her arm. "Try not to be nervous. I'll be there with you."

She tentatively smiled at him. "Thank you."

They didn't say anything else as they rushed into the building. Once they reached Richards's office, they were directed to another room and it was full of people. Rossini was there, along with several men Carter didn't know. But they were most likely fire investigators. Richards had a stack of photos and files in front of him.

He motioned for them to come in. "Have a seat."

Introductions were made, and they sat to the right of Richards's desk.

"As most of you know, the department has done an intense investigation of the fire in the Weston Gallery. We even brought in experts to confirm our findings. The fire was started with a device." He picked up a small plastic bag. "This is a wire that goes to a detonator." He pointed to more bags. "And there's more of the same wiring we found when we dug deeper." He held up a small object with the wiring attached. "This is what set the fire. Looks like a toy, but you plug it into a socket and set it and you have a fire. Simple, but deadly."

He held up pictures. "This is a photo of where the device was placed. The plate covering the wall socket was taken off and one of these—" he held up the object again "—was inserted into the electrical socket and set to go off after the showing. It was intentional. It was arson."

Silence filled the room and no one made a move.

Carter was the first to speak. "It seems really strange that no one would have noticed that. The plate was taken off and the detonator would stick out."

Richards nodded to a guy. "Greg Holder is an explosives expert. He'll explain how it was done."

The man had an electrical socket and detonator in his hand. "The plate was taken off so the device could be plugged in and pushed deep inside." He demonstrated as he talked. "When it went off, the blast would go between the walls, igniting the wiring and the insulation."

"No one would have seen it." Lila finally spoke up. "There was a sculpture in front of it. The last time I checked the gallery before the showing was at one to make sure nothing was out of place, and I checked that corner and there was no detonator there at that time."

"So someone had to come in after that," Richards replied. "Did you notice anyone, Ms. Colton?"

"No. I was busy talking to people and I didn't see anything out of the ordinary."

Richards folded his hands on the desk. "Well, it comes down to this. We have two suspects who would benefit from the fire—Ms. Colton and Mr. Rossini. We showed your pictures to stores that sell these devices and no one could identify either one of you. That's where we stand now. We're still contacting stores out of our area and contacting other fire stations who might be familiar with this MO. We'll catch this person sooner or later. Ms. Colton and Mr. Rossini, please don't leave town."

Lila stood. "May I get my artwork out of the vault?"

Richards leaned back in his chair. "Yes, I think that's possible. Our investigation now goes beyond the scene."

Lila walked out and Carter followed. She was upset, so he didn't say anything. She had to be alone with her thoughts. They spent the morning renting a van, loading the artwork and taking it to a storage facility. Savon helped. It was a busy morning and Lila said very little. When they got back to her town house, she was restless.

"I need to do something. Would you like to walk the Magnificent Mile or the Riverwalk?"

"The Magnificent Mile is shopping, isn't it?"

"Yes. Anything you can imagine."

"I'll take the Riverwalk."

She chuckled as she put on her sneakers. He grabbed his, willing to do anything she wanted. They parked his rental and walked along the Chicago River, and there were many restaurants and sites to see. The rain last night made everything seem fresh and invigorating. When they reached the Navy Pier, they were exhausted and stopped at a small pub to eat and get a beer. They caught a water taxi back to the car and Lila seemed in a better mood.

Once they reached the town house, Lila went straight to the bedroom and stripped out of her clothes. He squatted and took off her tennis shoes and handed her her T-shirt. Within seconds, she crawled beneath the comforter and he soon joined her. Lightning blasted outside and a boom of thunder followed.

"Another rainy night," she murmured into his shoulder.

"Just go to sleep."

She kissed his shoulder. "I'm glad you're here with me."

"Have you thought of calling your mother? I'll be leaving soon and you don't need to be alone."

"I'll think about it."

"I can feel your restlessness."

"I must inherit that from my father. He was always moving. I don't want to think about him."

He pushed her long hair away from her face. "Listen to me. They said you had motive—that's it. They can't arrest you on motive. They have to have evidence and they have none. If they had, you would be in a jail cell. They have nothing and they won't find anything, so please relax and kiss me."

She laughed and did as he asked. "I'm so glad you came into my life," she whispered against his lips.

"Me, too."

He held her a little tighter as he was almost certain he would be leaving tomorrow to probably some ungodly place. Tony was going to hide deep and he wasn't quite sure where that was, somewhere where he could paint in quiet.

His mind came back to the woman in his arms, and the negative thoughts of leaving surprised him. She deserved a home and family and a man who would love her deeply and be there for her always, just like she'd said. Could he give her that? Could he be a nine-to-five guy who mowed the grass on Saturdays? With her, he was beginning to believe that anything was possible.

Chapter 8

The next morning, they didn't have any plans, and she just wanted to spend time absorbing everything about Carter: his warm smile, the intensity in his eyes when he talked about something he loved and the soothing caress of his touch. After seeing her dad and dealing with Richards, Carter was her rainbow after the storm, even though the thought of him leaving made her sad. But if she was anything, she was resilient, and today she was ready to face whatever she had to.

Carter went out to get breakfast tacos and coffee while she finished dressing. It was a casual day in jeans and a T-shirt. Carter was soon back with breakfast and they sat at the bar eating and discussing what they would do today. Her phone rang and she grabbed it on the bar. It was her mother.

"How are you? You haven't called."

"I'm fine, Mom. I've just been busy dealing with everything."

"I know, but I worry. Guess who I have today?"

Lila didn't have to think hard to know that answer. "Jackson."

"Yes. He is such a sweetie. Faith had to have a root canal today and Myles is working as usual, so I'm entertaining. Faith's mother is driving her back and forth and I have Jackson. He's going to help me plant. He loves digging in the dirt."

"Have fun, Mom."

"You could come out and visit."

"Not today. I have other things to do." She glanced at Carter and realized just how important he was becoming in her life. "Bye. I love you."

"Your mother?" Carter finished off his coffee.

"Yes. She's babysitting my nephew today."

"It's nice to have family to help out."

"Sometimes." She didn't want to get into the separation of Myles and Faith. She firmly believed that one day they would get back together.

"Was that tall building we saw last night the Sears building?"

"Yes, but it is now called the Willis Tower."

"I'd like to go over there today if we have time."

She spread her arms. "We have nothing but time and, remember, it's one hundred and ten floors. You think you're up to all one hundred and ten?"

"After yesterday, probably not."

Carter's phone buzzed and he walked into the living room, talking. He turned around. "This is it. The PI has located Martell and you'll never guess where he is."

Her heart sank. "Some faraway place like Bangla-desh."

"No. Chicago. He lives in South Deering. There are rows of older two-story apartments and he lives on the end with his girlfriend and her mother. It's the girl's mother's apartment."

"Do you have an address?"

"Ninety-Seventh Street."

"There are a lot of big blocks of apartments around there."

"So you know where it is?"

"I can find it."

He went upstairs to his room and came back with a gun on his belt.

She was startled. "You carry a gun?"

"Yes, when I have to deal with criminals. Tony has never been violent, but I have to be prepared."

He slipped handcuffs into his pocket. "Tell me how to get to South Deering."

She grabbed her purse. "I'm going with you." If there was any chance of him getting hurt, she wanted to be there.

"No way. It could be dangerous and I'm not putting you in harm's way."

"If I stay here, I'll just be worried. I'll sit in the car and be very good."

She marched toward the door, hoping he wouldn't stop her. She didn't think she could sit here and wait for him to come back or not come back. That would be too hard on her nerves.

"Okay, let's get this straight," he said as he slid into the driver's seat. "You will sit in the car. It shouldn't take long. I don't want you even close to danger. Understood?"

"Understood," she said in a stern voice that surprised even her. She gave him directions and they zipped through traffic at times and others they stalled due to heavy traffic.

Once they reached Ninety-Seventh Street, Carter called the police. He explained his situation. "I will need backup." He talked for a minute more, and then he put his phone back in his pocket.

"The police will be here, so everything should go smoothly."

She pointed to where she saw the older two-story apartments. "There they are. If he lives on the end, it would be the first one."

"That's the number," Carter said. "I'm going to check and see if anyone is home, and you stay put." He parked the car on the other side of the street near more apartments.

Lila watched as he crossed the street and went up the steps to the front door. The car was parked three apartments down and she had to twist her head to see. A wooden railing enclosed the small porch, plus a metal fence circled the apartments. Most of them had screen doors, but this one didn't, just a white entry door peeling from age. Carter stood to the side and knocked on the door. The person inside wouldn't be able to see Carter because he wasn't standing in front of the peephole. Smart.

She put down her window so she could hear. She worried about Carter's safety. A short man with a graying ponytail opened the door. His jeans and T-shirt were covered in blotches of paint. The moment he saw

Carter, he tried to slam the door shut. Carter put his foot in the door and pushed it open. He reached for the man's T-shirt and pulled him onto the porch.

"We meet again, Tony," Carter said.

"Come on, Finch. I did my time. Why are you always picking on me?"

"Because you're back to your old ways painting forgeries."

"I need to make a living and it's not hurting anyone."

"You can think about that statement while you spend a few more years in prison."

"I'm not going back to prison."

"That's exactly…"

The man shoved Carter, who stumbled back against the railing as the man leaped over it to the yard and sailed over the metal fence. Carter quickly followed, but the man had a head start. Before a sane thought could enter her head, she jumped from the car and collided with the man. They both went flying into the neighbor's yard. Carter was there and he jerked the guy's arms behind his back and cuffed him.

"That was a big mistake, Tony. Resisting arrest is just going to make it worse."

Carter helped Lila to her feet with a frown. "Are you okay?"

She let out a long breath. "Yes."

"You don't look okay." He glanced to the front of her shirt and jeans, which were stained with grass and dirt. Her right hand throbbed where she'd tried to catch herself, but she kept it at her side, not wanting Carter to see. It was just a little thing.

A police car drove up. Carter talked to the officer

exiting the vehicle and they put Tony in the back seat. "I'd really like to look inside the house," Carter said.

"You have to get a search warrant for that and it takes time," the officer replied. "Or the owner's approval. All of these apartments are rentals owned by Sapp Realty, and the main man would be Donald Sapp. I'll see if I can get a number for you."

Carter turned to Lila, took her by the elbow and led her across the street to the car. "Can I trust you to stay put?"

"Yeah." Her body ached in places and her hand was on fire. She didn't plan on going anywhere or doing any more heroics.

"What were you thinking?"

She brushed grass and dirt from her clothes and slid into the car. "That's the point—I wasn't. I just didn't want him to get away. And—" she held up a finger on her left hand "—I do not need a lecture."

He reached in the car and kissed her lips. "We'll talk about it later. The officer is motioning for me. I'll be back."

She leaned her head against the back of the car seat. She'd landed on her shoulder and right hand as she'd tried to keep from sliding into the fence, and they both ached. Taking a deep breath, she forced herself to open her hand. *Oh, no!* Dirt and grass were embedded in the meaty part of her palm, and it was red, throbbing and bleeding in spots.

Carter ran back to the car and jumped into the driver's seat. "I'm taking you to the town house and then I'm coming back. Mr. Sapp is on the way, and you don't need to sit in the car all the time."

She smiled at him. He always did the right thing.

He was such a nice man and she just wanted to hold him and never let him go. Her thoughts were zigzagging all over the place, but she wanted to go home and deal with her hand.

"Thank you. I appreciate that."

He started the car. "No argument?"

"No. I plan to be a very good girl for the rest of the day."

He touched her face with the back of his hand and her tummy fluttered with excitement. "That was very brave what you did today, but don't ever do it again. My heart wouldn't survive it."

"Mine, either." She held her hand where he couldn't see it until she had a better look at it. In the few days she'd known him, she knew he was going to be upset if she was hurt. So she would be as quiet as a mouse until she cleaned the dirt and grass from her hand. Carter was eager to get back and didn't notice her awkward movements. She kissed him goodbye and ran into the town house before he could notice anything. She went straight to the bathroom to look under her makeup lights so she could get a better view.

She found tweezers and tried to remove the grass, but found it impossible without a lot of pain. She ran cool water over her hand and jumped. It stung.

The doorbell rang. She dabbed at her hand with a towel and went to the front door. Who could it be? It wasn't Carter because he wanted to be there when the owner arrived so he could find incriminating evidence against Tony whatever-his-name-was. She glanced through the peephole. Savon. Oh, no. She'd forgotten their lunch date. She had intended to cancel since Carter was here, but she'd forgotten that, too.

She yanked open the door. "I'm sorry. I forgot."

Savon walked in. "The hunk is back, huh?" She looked around. "No big deal. I'll talk to you later."

"Come with me."

"What?"

Lila dragged her into the bathroom and opened her palm. Handing her the tweezers, she said, "Can you pick the grass out?"

A look of horror crossed Savon's face. "Are you kidding me? I faint at the sight of blood. What happened to you?"

Lila told her the whole story.

"You tackled the guy? Are you insane?"

"I'm beginning to wonder that myself."

"Come on. I'm taking you to the emergency room."

"Savon, no. I don't want Carter to know."

"Why?"

"He didn't want me to go, and I promised to sit in the car and be good and... Well, the guy was coming right toward me and I couldn't let him get away. I wasn't even thinking."

"You got that right."

"Savon—"

Her friend handed her the tweezers. "If you can pluck the grass from your palm, we won't go."

"You're evil."

Savon laughed as they headed out the door and over to the hospital. As they sat in the waiting room, she tried not to look at her hand, but it was swelling and hurting more. When she was called back, things happened quickly. The doctor asked what had happened and she told him. She thought he would ask more questions, but he didn't. He was more concerned about her hand.

"I'll have to clean and remove debris from your palm. There's grass and dirt under the skin, and I'll have to remove it or your hand will get infected. It will be painful, but I'll deaden it first. It should take about an hour. Is someone with you?"

"She's in the waiting room and she's kind of squeamish."

The doctor looked at the nurse. "Tell her friend that Ms. Colton is going to be a while and get her a gown and into the bed. We'll need the attachment for an arm."

The nurse handed her a hospital gown with a slit up the back. Oh, yes, it was fashionable. She crawled beneath the cool sheets and wondered how things were going with Carter. She had no choice now but to tell him. It was silly to keep it a secret anyway, but she didn't want him to feel guilty.

The nurse came in with a long, padded board and attached it to the right side of the bed. The doctor stood behind her with a needle. She turned her head away. Maybe she was squeamish, too.

"Ms. Colton, stretch your right arm out on the board and I'm going to deaden it. Just be very still."

She closed her eyes and gritted her teeth. The sting made her grit her teeth a little harder, and then she couldn't feel anything. The nurse gave her an injection in her left arm. "That should help you to relax."

She dozed off a couple of times while the doctor worked. He was meticulous with a small scalpel and tweezers, and the nurse flushed it with a sterile saline solution several times. When they finished, the nurse rubbed antibiotic ointment on it and wrapped it. She brought Lila a sling to go over her shoulder so she could rest her arm in it. Then she was ready to go home.

In the town house, she rested her head on the back of the sofa and laid her arm across her stomach. It wasn't painful, but the doctor said it would be later. He'd given her a prescription for some pain pills and they'd stopped and picked them up. She had thought that Carter would be here, but he must still be at the apartments or at the police station. Maybe by the time he came she would feel better. At the moment she felt queasy.

Savon made herbal tea for Lila's nausea and ordered soup and sandwiches for dinner. Lila could eat very little. The vegetable soup tasted bland and she went back to lie on the sofa. Where was Carter? If Carter was here, she'd feel better. He was her rock and… She had to stop depending on him.

When Donald Sapp finally showed up, Carter was relieved. He was worried about Lila. She was acting very strange after her tumble with Martell. He wanted to make sure she was okay, but things here were holding them up.

Sapp allowed him to look inside the house and he signed a piece of paper that the officer had brought in case he changed his mind later. Inside was a messy apartment. Clothes and empty cartons of takeout seemed to be everywhere, even dishes in the sink and food on the stove. Sapp started cursing at the conditions inside. They didn't find any paints or painting materials in the downstairs or upstairs. That surprised Carter. If Tony lived here, he was painting here.

"Is there an attic?" he asked Sapp.

"It's very tiny and I don't allow my renters to keep stuff up there. It's just a fire hazard."

"I guess that's it, Mr. Finch," the officer said.

No, he wouldn't believe that. He kept searching. He walked out the back door to a small porch, but there was nothing out there, either. In the kitchen was a small door he'd taken to be a broom closet earlier.

"Where does this door go?"

"To the basement."

Basement! Why hadn't Sapp mentioned that? Carter opened the door, and the scent of turpentine and oils hit them in the face.

"What the hell?" Sapp yelled. They went down the narrow stairs and Sapp continued his tirade. "What's all this stuff? It stinks."

Across the room were easels with paintings half-finished on them and they were all Homer Tinsleys. Old wood was stacked in a corner from which Tony was making frames. Boxes of tubes of paint were stacked everywhere with gallons of turpentine.

"What does he do with all this stuff?" Sapp asked.

"He paints, Mr. Sapp." Carter waved his hand toward the paintings on easels. "And then he sells them, but they're not really his creation." He pointed to the first painting, which was complete and ready to go. "See the signature? Your tenant is a forger."

Carter took pictures of everything, and he went through the small desk against the wall and didn't find anything. No name. No address. Nothing to incriminate anyone else. But he had Martell against the wall and he was going down for a long time.

They walked out of the house and onto the porch for fresh air. Sapp was on the phone, talking to the lady who rented the apartment. "I should just kick her out," Sapp said as he clicked off. "She's rented from me for many years and I know this is not her doing. I told her she's got to get rid of that stuff in the basement, and if I find anybody else in the apartment, I will kick them out."

"It's very nice of you," Carter said. Sapp was a hell-and-brimstone kind of guy and Carter felt sure he would bring his full wrath upon the old lady, but he seemed to have a fondness for the woman. That just proved there was a little good in everyone.

At the police station, he hit a waiting wall. Tony was still being processed and he couldn't interview him until that was over. He sat in one of the interview rooms when an assistant district attorney walked in. She introduced herself and asked about Tony. He told her everything he knew.

"I'd need your file and everything you have on him." She pushed her card across the table and she had written in hand her private number.

"I'll get everything to you."

"It sounds like an open-and-shut case. Maybe we can make a deal."

"A deal? He's been out of prison a little over a year and almost immediately he's back doing what he did before, making money off the talents of others."

"He's not a violent guy. We have a jail full of violent characters who we have to prosecute. If we can get this one off the table, I'm going to do it."

Carter stood. "It's your choice, but I'll be in there fighting all the way. I've been tracking the forger for almost a year, and for him to get a light sentence because your docket is full is unacceptable to me."

The lady picked up her briefcase and walked out the door. Carter fiddled with the business card she'd given him. He would send her a boatload of information on Tony Martell, and then they would talk deal again.

The man himself walked into the room in handcuffs and jail clothes. The officer behind him unlocked the handcuffs and Tony took a seat across from him.

"Sorry I hit you, man, but you don't know what it's like in prison."

"Did you lose your memory when you got out?"

"No." He shuffled around in the chair.

"Then why go back to doing the same thing?"

"People won't leave me alone. They keep telling me how much money I can make and how I won't get caught this time. I guess I'm weak."

Something in Carter eased in his feelings toward Tony. He wasn't a violent guy, like the ADA had said. He was just weak and criminals often preyed on the weak. Money was always the bait. In that moment, Carter knew he would agree with the ADA and try to make a deal in hopes that Tony could be rehabilitated. First, Carter wanted something from him, and until he got it, Tony wasn't getting anything.

He placed his forearms on the table. "We have tons of evidence against you this time. There's no question you've been painting fakes and someone is paying you to do it. If you want a lighter sentence, you're going to have to talk to me. I want the name of the man who's paying you."

"Ah, Finch, I can't do that. He'll have me killed."

"Why do you think that?"

"I don't know. Just get the feeling that nobody crosses him."

Carter leaned back in his chair and stared at him. "Well, it comes down to this. If you don't give up his name, you're probably going to get five more years tacked onto your original sentence, and this time you won't be getting out for good behavior. It's your decision."

"It's not much of a decision."

Carter leaned forward. "I already know the man's name." He pushed the tablet that was on the table toward Tony. "Write down his name. That's all you have to do and I'll take it from there."

"Ah, man, you're killing me."

"The name, Tony."

Tony picked up the pen and scribbled a name and then shoved it toward Carter. Walter Fox was on the tablet. Carter pushed it back to him. "Sign it. Tell me how he got you involved in this."

"He came to the house."

"Where you're living with your girlfriend?"

"Yeah."

"How did he know you were here? Did he call you? How did he find you so quickly?"

"I don't know, man. He showed up one day at our door and says I have a talent he wanted to utilize and he was willing to pay for it."

"Like an angel from heaven, huh?"

"I told him I wasn't into that anymore. I was going to stay clean. Three days later he came back and offered me more money. I turned him down again. But he came back again and offered me more money and I couldn't turn it down. The rent was overdue and bills needed to be paid and I had to help my girlfriend out."

The story was a little far-fetched and Carter had a hard time believing it. There had to be a connection between Fox and Tony, or how else would Fox know where to find him?

"If you're lying to me, I'll make sure you get more years than you ever dreamed about."

"Come on, man."

Carter pointed to the tablet. "Write down everything you just told me and then sign it."

As he wrote, Carter kept thinking about a connection. There had to be one. It usually involved someone who knew both parties. "Where does your girlfriend work?"

"At a bar on Weston Avenue. Her mother works there, too."

Her mother works at the bar, too. That didn't make sense.

"Is the mother the cleaning lady?"

"Man, look, I don't know what she does in there and I don't ask."

The bar was on the same street as the gallery. What were the odds? Could Tony be involved in setting the fire? He immediately shook that from his head. Tony was too weak for that kind of work. Carter stood and gathered the papers on the table. Putting them in his briefcase, he said, "Either the ADA or I will be in touch with you."

"Thanks, man."

Carter stretched his shoulders and was ready to go home to Lila. *Home.* Did he just think that? He'd said he didn't need a home. He was happy traveling around the world, but something about Lila was making him think about home.

Chapter 9

Carter entered the front door and yelled, "I'll put my gun up and be right down. I have so much to tell you." He removed his jacket and his gun and then stored the gun away in his bag. Lila hadn't answered him. The TV was on. Maybe she didn't hear him. He ran down the stairs and stopped short in the living room. She lay on the sofa with her right arm in a sling and resting on her stomach. Her hand was bandaged. Why was her hand bandaged?

He picked up the remote control and clicked off the TV. Lila stirred and sat up, her dark hair all around her. She pushed it away with her left hand. "Oh, you're back. Did everything go okay?"

He eased down beside her. "What happened to your hand?"

"Oh, well...now don't freak out."

"I'm not freaking out. What happened?"

She told him a story that had him close to freaking out. "Why didn't you tell me?"

"I didn't know it was that bad. Not until I tried to remove the grass with tweezers. That didn't work. It hurt. Savon came by and made me go to the ER. The doctor deadened my arm and I don't feel much pain right now, but he gave me a prescription, which I had filled for later. In a few days I'll be as good as new. So it's nothing to worry about and no reason to give me a lecture."

He rested his head against hers. "I'm just glad you're okay."

"Yes, I am, but right now I need to go to bed. The nurse gave me something to relax and I'm feeling very relaxed."

He helped her up the stairs and into bed. "Do you need anything?"

"No, just for you to get that guilty look off your face." She held up her hand. "This is my fault, not yours." She snuggled beneath the comforter. "There's a sandwich in the fridge if you want it."

"Thanks." He looked closely at her pale face. "Are you sure you're okay?"

She didn't respond. He pushed her hair away from her cheeks and saw she was sound asleep. "Sleep tight." He kissed her cheek and cursed himself all the way to the bathroom. Even though she'd said it wasn't his fault, it was. He should have never taken her with him.

He took a quick shower and put on pajama bottoms and a T-shirt. When he'd seen her open the car door and run into Tony, he'd screamed, "Lila, no!" She just kept running and his heart jolted like it never had before. He feared Tony might hurt her. And the last thing he wanted was for her to get hurt, and she had. Tonight and tomorrow she'd probably be in a lot of pain because of him. He would be right here to help her with whatever she needed.

He grabbed his laptop and checked on her one more time. She was out and he hoped she would be for the rest of the night. Taking the stairs two at a time, he went to the living room to work on the file for the ADA. At least he would have that ready to send in the morning. Then he realized he was hungry and went to the kitchen to find the sandwich and something to drink. All the while, his ears were tuned to the upstairs in case Lila needed him. An hour later, he made his way back up the stairs to find Lila still sleeping.

He flipped off all the lights and crawled into bed. Just as he got comfortable, Lila crawled out of bed. "Where are you going?"

"My hand is throbbing and I'm going to get a pain pill."

"No, no, no!" He jumped out of bed. "I'll get it. I saw them on the counter in the kitchen. Go back to bed."

Once again he ran downstairs, grabbed the pills and a glass of water and went back up. She was sitting on the side of the bed. He gave her a pill and a glass of water. Dutifully she swallowed it and he helped her back in bed.

"Anything else you need?"

"Maybe another pillow."

"And that would be where?"

"In the closet."

He found the pillow and stuffed it behind her head. "How's that?"

"Better." Her voice was groggy and he quickly turned off the light and crawled in beside her, hoping she would go back to sleep. He was almost asleep when she stirred.

"What's wrong?"

"I don't feel good."

"What do you—" Before the last word could leave his mouth, she leaped out of bed and ran to the bathroom. A moment later, he heard her vomiting. Oh, man! He got out of bed and walked toward the bathroom, not knowing what to do. He'd never been in this situation before, but he couldn't lie there while she was sick.

He peeked around the corner and saw her sitting on the floor with her head over the toilet, making gut-wrenching sounds. Finally, she flushed it and leaned back against the wall, noticing him.

"Go away, Carter. I don't want you to see me like this."

"That's not going to happen." He stepped into the bathroom and opened the cabinet for a washcloth. Putting it under the water faucet, he got it wet and squatted on the floor beside her. He held her hair and wiped her face.

"Carter—" she protested.

"Shh."

"I stink. It's on my hair, my clothes and the floor. Just go back to bed, and when I feel strong enough, I'll get cleaned up."

"No way." He scooted closer. "Now let's get your

clothes off and get you in the shower. That's the only way to get it off of you so you can sleep and rest."

She held up her right hand to indicate she couldn't get in the shower.

"I'll fix that." He ran downstairs again looking for a plastic bag and a rubber band. When he had the goodies, he went back upstairs and she was still sitting there looking disgusted with herself.

"Get that look off your face," he said. "I've seen you naked before, so what's the big deal?"

"I didn't have vomit all over me," she shot back.

"Doesn't make a difference," he told her as he removed her T-shirt. At the sight of her breasts, his thoughts went in a completely different direction and he curbed them quickly. He adjusted the shower's water temperature while she removed her panties with her left hand and stepped into the shower.

"Hold your right hand up so water can't get in it."

"I'm not a bronc rider." She laughed under her breath. "Do I get eight seconds?"

"You're getting giddy." He poured shampoo into her wet left palm.

"Smells like lavender," he said.

She made a face at him as she attempted to lather her hair. She wasn't doing a very good job, so he helped her. Standing under the spray, she tried to get rid of the soap and the smell. He grabbed a couple of towels out of the cabinet and reached in and turned off the water. One towel he wrapped around her head and the other he wrapped around her body.

"Better?"

"Yes. Thank you."

She got out and sat in the chair at her makeup table,

drawing her fingers through the thick wet strands. "I'll have to dry it some before I go back to bed." She opened the bottom drawer and he helped her to get the dryer out and plugged it in.

"While you're doing that, I'll get cleaning supplies. Utility room, right?"

"Right." She stood up.

"Where are you going?"

"To get a clean T-shirt."

"I'll get it."

"Second drawer of my dresser." He helped her get it through one arm and over her head. She stiffened. Obviously, the hand hurt.

"I'll take these clothes down and put them in the washing machine and bring back cleaning supplies."

The smell gagged him a few times, but he powered through until the bathroom smelled like bleach.

"Thank you," she said in a sleepy voice as she crawled into bed.

"You're welcome. Now I'm going to get out of these wet clothes and join you." When he came back, she was asleep. He slipped in beside her and tried not to move the mattress too much. Time and rest would help her. He lay there looking into the darkness and saw a new side to himself. He never thought of himself as a loving, nurturing person. He felt sure the young Carter would have run from the bedroom until she had everything under control. But with Lila it was different. He cared about her and you didn't run from people you cared about.

He looked at her beautiful sleeping face. *What have you done to me?*

* * *

Lila woke up to pain. Wincing, she slid out of bed as quietly as possible. She didn't want to wake Carter. She grabbed the pill bottle, picked up her bathrobe from the floor and made her way to the kitchen. Taking the pill was her top priority. Once that was done, she made coffee, and it wasn't easy with her left hand, but she was sure Carter would want a cup when he woke up. After what he did last night, she would do anything for him.

She sat on the sofa wrapped in the bathrobe, waiting for the pill to do its thing. Last night she was so embarrassed and just wanted him to go away. The fact that he'd stayed shocked her since he didn't have a sense of family values. Mr. Finch had a lot of family values he didn't know about. Most men would have left, but he'd stayed right with her. She wondered how he felt this morning.

"There you are." Carter stood there in his pajamas and T-shirt, looking as handsome as ever. "When I woke up and you weren't there, I got worried."

"I woke up to pain and needed a pill, so I came down very quietly so as not to wake you."

"Is the pain better?"

"Yes, it is."

Carter looked around. "I smell coffee."

"I made it."

"With your left hand?"

"Yes, just for you."

He leaned his face against hers and her left hand stroked his stubble, and new, deeper emotions surged through her. She loved him and she knew he would leave one day and that would be sooner than later, probably as soon as tonight. Every second she had with him, she was preparing herself for the inevitable. She wouldn't beg. She wouldn't cry. She would be grateful for the man who'd held her hair while she puked.

"I'll get us a cup of coffee." In a minute, he was back with a mug of coffee for her. "Can you handle it?"

"Yes."

He headed for the stairs with a mug in his hand. "I'm going to shower and shave while you're resting, and then I have to go get groceries and food for us to eat."

"Okay."

"What would you like to eat today?"

"My mom's chicken noodle soup," she mumbled, realizing she was falling off to sleep. She sat up straighter. "And if you call her, I would have to kill you. Understand?"

He laughed. "I understand." He went to her desk and got a piece of paper and a pen. "What would I need to make chicken noodle soup?"

"A chicken, of course, but that's too much for the two of us. Just get a split breast and a couple of thighs with the skin on and the bone in. Celery, onions, carrots, chicken broth and those little squares that Mom drops in."

He smiled at her. "You're going to have to be more specific."

"It's little squares of flavor. Bouillon. That's what it's called. They're wrapped individually in a small jar and it just gives the soup a little more flavor. That's what my mom says."

"I will find them." He finished his way up the stairs and Lila tried to get comfortable, but the pain was bad. She went to the kitchen for another cup of coffee and just walked around the living room trying to ease the pain.

Carter came back all dressed, and he looked so nice and handsome with his dark hair combed neatly. She just wanted to hug him. He handed her her laptop. "I thought you might need these." He put a pillow on the couch.

"Did you see my phone in your car? I can't find it."

He went outside and came back with her phone in his hand. "It fell between the seats."

"Thank you."

"I'm going to the groccry store and you rest."

"I want to take a shower and wash my hair. I think it still has shampoo in it."

"No." He shook his head. "You'll have to wait until I get back."

"I'm not helpless." For some reason, he ignited her temper. She didn't want to feel helpless. She wanted to go out with him and enjoy their time together instead of being stuck at home with a throbbing hand.

He lifted a sharp eyebrow.

"Okay, go, go."

He walked to her. "You're not helpless. You hurt your hand and it will take a couple of days for you to feel better. Just rest, please. Can I trust you to do that?"

She took a long breath. "Yes. Being stupid once is enough."

He gently kissed her. "I'll be back as soon as I can."

Lila put her coffee cup in the sink and went to the sofa to call Savon, but then realized Savon wasn't up yet. Instead, she called her mother. Sooner or later she would find out about Lila's injured hand and would be upset that Lila hadn't told her.

"Hey, Mom, how's everything?"

"Where have you been?" There was a lot of worry and concern mixed in her mother's voice.

"I'm at home."

"Myles has been calling and calling you. He's on his way over. We worry when we can't get you. Are you okay?"

She bit her lip. "Actually, I'm not."

"What happened?"

She hesitated, but only for a second. "I fell and hurt my hand."

"How bad?"

"I tried to catch myself with my right hand as I slid through some dirt and grass. I scraped my palm and got some dirt and grass in it. I had to go to the ER and the doctor cleaned it up very nicely. Just a little accident and I'll be okay tomorrow, but I'm resting today."

"Are you in pain?"

She bit her lip a little harder and gauged her words. "A little, but the doctor gave me some pain pills. I'm okay, Mom. Really."

"I'm coming to get you. You can stay here until your hand heals."

"Absolutely not. I'm thirty years old and you don't have to baby me. I can really take care of myself."

"Then why aren't you answering your phone?"

"I lost it and found it this morning." That was about as good a lie as she had ever told. But it was to protect her mother, she told herself. She changed the subject quickly. "Why is Myles calling me?"

"Carin has been calling him and your cousins."

"Why?"

"She's upset that her grandchildren are interfering in the lawsuit. She's been calling you, too, but since you lost your phone, she hasn't been able to get you. So be prepared."

Her doorbell rang. "Mom, Myles is here." Or she hoped it was Myles. "I'll talk to you later."

She let Myles in and he stopped short. "What happened to you?"

"I fell."

Myles burst out laughing. "I believe that. You've always been a little clumsy."

"I have not."

"Remember that time you fell into the big cactus Mom had? She picked stickers out of your butt for a whole afternoon."

"That's because you, Aaron, Damon and Nash were ganging up on me and I lost my footing."

"You were always interfering in what we were doing."

"I had no one to play with and you guys were mean."

He took a seat on the sofa. "We were not. Sometimes we let you play."

She stuck her tongue out at him.

He pointed a finger at her. "That's what you were doing that day. You were sticking your tongue out at us and we tried to make you stop and you fell into the cactus."

She laughed and sat beside him.

"We let you play, remember?"

"Yeah. I'm so grateful." And then she laughed again. They did have good times as kids and most of the time they let her play. But as she got older, things changed.

They wanted to meet her friends and she would stick her tongue out and prance away. She found ways to get even.

"Does the hand hurt?" Myles asked.

"Yes."

He put an arm around her shoulders. "I'm sorry, sis. I'm happy to say my clumsy sister has turned into a beautiful young woman."

"Aw. That's so sweet."

"That's me." He grinned.

"Why aren't you at work? Isn't it crucial that you spend almost every moment there?"

"Carin is a pain in my backside. Since I'm a lawyer, she wants me to talk to the judge to see if I can get the case moved up. I told her I have no authority to get the case moved up and the judge wouldn't listen to me anyway. I told her, too, that I didn't want anything to do with the case. She got angry and hung up. Then she started calling our cousins and I'm sure she called you, too. I'm not interested in getting the case moved up."

Lila picked up her phone. "Neither am I. I have seven calls from her."

"That should be a nice conversation when she does get you," Myles said tongue in cheek.

"Yeah, but I'm not having anything to do with the lawsuit."

Myles got to his feet. "Since you're okay, I've got to go to the office. Good luck with Carin."

"She's maniacal about this."

"Unrequited love, I think it's called."

"She can't hurt Dean, but she's putting a big old hurt on his grandchildren and she will be one happy woman if she brings down the other Coltons."

As soon as she closed the door on Myles, her phone rang. She picked it up from the coffee table and stared at the caller ID: Carin Pederson. Showtime. She clicked on.

"Lila, is that you?" Carin asked.

"Yes, it's me."

"Why haven't you answered your phone?"

"I lost it."

"Lost it! You're a grown woman and you should have enough sense to take care of your phone."

Lila took a long breath. "Did you call for a reason?"

"Yes. I want you to stop filling your dad's head with nonsense about the lawsuit."

"I only told him the truth."

"Truth? You don't have a clue about the truth."

"I know that Alfred and Ernest created the patents that are still making money for the family and Heath has taken up the legacy. We have no right to anything they have earned."

"You silly girl. Your grandfather ditched me and my sons for his proper family. He should pay for that. We were discarded like trash."

"But he made sure you lived in luxury, and Dad and Erik never had to work. This is all about revenge and I don't want any part of it."

"I'll remember that when I'm awarded a large sum of money."

Lila laughed. She couldn't help herself. "When have you ever given Myles or me anything?"

"You don't teach children by handing them money every day."

"It wasn't just the money. When Mom finally got

the courage to leave Dad, she needed help for the rent and other things for us. But you refused to help."

"She should have stayed where she was and she wouldn't have had any worries. Men cheat. That's a fact."

"Is that what you did? Stayed where you were so Dean could fund your lavish lifestyle? Blackmail was a good way to keep Dean in line. It worked and…"

The phone went dead in her hand.

She carefully laid her phone on the coffee table. Her nerves were stretched to the max and her hand was throbbing again. Carin had the power to raise her blood pressure and made her view the world a little differently. Through all the bitterness and resentment they'd endured because of their grandmother, Lila, Myles, Aaron, Damon and Nash turned out to be good human beings. And they all believed in love, home and family. Myles, Aaron and Damon had found their special person to spend the rest of their lives with. Lila had, too, but it was only temporary.

Chapter 10

Carter saw an SUV drive away from Lila's town house. He didn't recognize the man. Maybe it was someone from her family. He hadn't met anyone in her family, and she hadn't met anyone in his. Of course, he had only his mother and father. He had no idea why he was thinking that, but it had been nice the last couple of days spending time with Lila and being in one place. He'd never really thought about it before because he liked being on the road. Now the idea was waning.

He carried grocery bags into the house and saw Lila sitting on the sofa, her face creased into a frown.

She quickly stood. "Now that you're back, I'm going upstairs to take a shower and get dressed."

He followed her upstairs to see if she needed anything. She shrugged out of her bathrobe and he hurried to help. The plastic bag lay on the vanity and he reached for it, securing it to her right hand with a rubber band. "How's that?"

"Should I raise my right hand?" she asked with a twinkle in her eye.

"Yes." He tried not to smile and failed. "You're not going to let me forget that, are you?"

"No, because you blush so nicely."

He changed the subject. "I saw someone leaving when I drove up and you looked a little upset."

"It was Myles, but he didn't upset me. My grandmother called and told me to stop talking to my dad and to stop interfering in the lawsuit. She knows how to push my buttons."

"I can see." Her left hand was gripped into a tight fist and the beautiful lines of her face were clenched into a one-size-fits-all frown. He took her into his arms. "Have a nice shower and I'm going down to start lunch. Do you need anything?"

"For you to stop worrying and hovering over me. That's my mother's job."

He held up his hands and backed away. He hurried downstairs to start lunch. Lila was in a cantankerous mood. Most people were when they didn't feel good. When Neil had prostate cancer, no one could get along with him, not even Marla. He seemed to take his bad moods out on her. Once he found out he was going to be okay, his moods changed drastically. He was back to being his old self. It was mind changing when you were perfectly healthy one day and the next you needed help.

Since the two Colton families were at odds, he knew Lila was worried about that, too. She was probably still worried about the arson charge and how to replace everything that had been destroyed. He hadn't even had a chance to talk to her about Walter Fox. That would cheer her up, and he intended to talk to her just as soon as he could.

He went to the internet to see if he could find a chicken noodle soup recipe. Wow! There were so many places to get recipes. He chose a simple one and washed and dried the chicken and then found a big pot to put it in. It surprised him that she would have a big pot. He put in the designated amount of water and then washed the vegetables and cut them up. As he dumped everything into the pot, he heard her coming downstairs. He wiped his hands on a towel and just stared. She was completely different from earlier. Her hand was still bandaged, but the bad mood was gone and her eyes lit up with a happy-to-be-alive gleam.

"What a transformation."

Her hair was up and held in place with colorful combs. In skinny jeans and a white long-sleeved knit top, she looked fresh and happy.

"I feel better, too. I had to put all the gloom and doom behind me."

He frowned.

"What?"

"You put up your hair."

"It keeps it out of my face and it's been annoying me." She walked into the kitchen to see what was in the pot. "You put it all together."

"Yeah. Is that wrong?"

"The chicken is supposed to cook longer."

"No problem." He scooped the veggies into a bowl. "When do I put these in?" He held up the jar of tiny squares of bouillon.

"Not yet."

He put the lid on the chicken. "Good. I need to talk to you."

"About what?"

He took her arm and led her to the sofa. "It's nothing bad. With everything that was going on, I forgot to tell you what happened with Tony yesterday."

She got comfortable and laid the lower part of her arm on a pillow. He told her everything that had transpired with Tony. "The ADA is going to make a deal with him."

"A deal?"

"By the tone of your voice, I can see you don't like that. I didn't at first, either, but the ADA pointed out that he's only been arrested once and he's not a violent man. So I talked to Tony and we made a deal. He gave me the name of the man who was paying him to paint the forgeries. And I'll work with the ADA to get him a lower sentence."

Her eyes grew big. "He gave you the name?"

Carter nodded. "It wasn't a big surprise."

Her eyebrows drew together. "You knew?"

"I didn't really know, but I had a feeling Walter Fox was involved."

"Walter Fox is paying Tony to paint the forgeries?" She shook her head. "That doesn't make sense. Why would he destroy the Tinsley paintings?"

"I don't have an answer for that. All I can think of is that he got wind that he was being investigated and he wanted to destroy everything that my company could get their hands on. I don't have anything else, but I intend to. I will talk to Richards after lunch while you're resting."

She shook her finger at him. "Oh, no! I'm going with you."

"Lila—"

"He destroyed more than the Tinsley paintings. He destroyed my whole gallery and I have a right to face him."

"You're going to be stubborn about this, aren't you?"

She leaned over and whispered, "Yes, and I want to know why he did it."

"Money," Carter told her. "Everything is about money. Getting the short end of the stick on the Tinsley estate meant he had to cut back on his lifestyle. I'm going to do some more checking into his background. There has to be a connection between Fox and Rossini. I'm only guessing here. That's why I want to talk to Richards. He may have more background information."

"But will he give it to you? Richards is not my number one fan."

"Well, he hasn't come up with anything and he might be looking for a little help. I'm sure the insurance companies are pushing for answers, too."

A bubbling sound came from the kitchen and Carter got out. "I better check on the chicken."

"I have to change the bandage on my hand this morning. Are you willing to help?"

"I have to do it if we're going to catch criminals together," he said with a big grin. "Do you have the supplies or do I need to go get them?"

"A white pharmacy bag is on the counter."

"Got it. Where are the scissors?"

"First drawer near the pantry."

"Got it." He gathered all the goodies and went back into the living room. "Do you need a pain pill for this?"

"Probably." She looked at the clock on the wall. "It's not even nine yet."

"No. We got up early. Does that make a difference?"

"Yes. I took the pill at six and I have to wait four hours."

"Okay, we'll wait until ten."

In the meantime, they talked about Fox and his involvement with Tinsley and maybe the fire. Her eyes lit up with hope that they might connect Fox to the fire as well as the forgery.

"Tony seems scared of Fox and that got me to thinking. What has Fox done that Tony knows about that scares him? There has to be some answers out there and we're going to find them."

"How much time do you have? I mean, you usually leave after an investigation."

He reached over and kissed her cheek. "I'm not quite through investigating yet." Leaving was constantly on his mind and it wasn't like before. He wasn't anxious to see the next city. He wanted to stay in Chicago with Lila. It would work out in time, he told himself. Right now, finding answers was the main goal.

He got to his feet. "I'll check the soup and then we'll get started on your hand. It's almost ten." He gave her a pill and sat beside her, removing the gauze. When he got down to the palm, he didn't want to jerk it off, so he left a piece. "I'm afraid that might be stuck and really hurt when I pull it off."

"There's a lot of stuff in the bag. Check and see if he gave us anything for that."

He pulled out the contents. "Numbing cream, a box of gloves, sterile water, gauze, tape, antibiotic cream and instructions. We have to pour about a cup of ster-

ile water over your hand to clean it and then add antibiotic cream and numbing cream."

He looked into her eyes. "Ready?"

She nodded and they walked to the sink and did
as the instructions had said. She gritted her teeth and
leaned on him until it was finished.

"Oh, the numbing cream is wonderful. The doctor
said to leave the bandage off for about thirty minutes
and to flex my fingers and to move my shoulder."

While she walked around flexing her fingers and
moving her arm, he finished working on the soup.
The chicken was almost done. He held up the bouillon cubes.

"Ready?"

She gave a thumbs-up and he dropped the cubes in
and stirred. "Taste test."

"Oh, that's good." She licked the spoon. "Noodle
time."

It wasn't long before he had it on the table. Lila had
a hard time eating with her left hand, but it didn't take
her long to get the hang of it. Afterward, she sat on the
sofa and he cleaned up the kitchen. They had plenty of
soup left for later. He turned around and saw she was
asleep. It gave him time to call Richards.

"What can I do for you, Mr. Finch?"

"I'd like to talk to you for a few minutes."

"I'm very busy at this time. Unless this is urgent,
I'd prefer to do it later."

"It's urgent. I have new information that you could
use."

There was a pause. "I can see you in about thirty
minutes. That's all the time I can spare."

"I'll be there."

"Where?" Lila stood behind him, pinning up her hair that had come down. Elegant movements with her left hand and arm drew his attention. Everything about her was elegant.

He cleared his throat. "Richards's office." He didn't even try to stop her. That would just bring on another argument, and he was learning that arguing with Lila wasn't something he enjoyed.

"Oh. I'll grab my purse, freshen up and be right with you."

He removed the towel he had tucked into his jeans while he'd cooked. The interview could prove vital to the investigation. Richards had to be ready to listen and Carter wasn't sure he was ready yet. It was Richards's investigation and Carter had stuck his nose in once. Would he be willing to listen a second time?

"Thanks for not making a fuss." Lila had intended to come whether he did or not, but it was nice not to have to fight the battle beforehand.

"Could you let me do the talking?"

She rested her hand on his shoulder. "If you're a good boy."

He laughed and it filled the car with a happy mood, and that was what she wanted to feel right now. A little happiness. A little calm. And a whole lot of love.

Her arm was tucked neatly into the sling and her hand wasn't throbbing as much. She was ready to talk to Inspector Richards. Or at least let Carter do most of the talking. He knew more about the situation than she did. It was nice to lean on someone.

He took her hand as they walked up to the big door

that housed the arson experts and held it open for her. They walked to Richards's office and he got to his feet.

"Ms. Colton, I didn't know you were coming." The sarcastic tone triggered her anger. She wanted to slap that sly grin off his face, but she maintained her composure. "Have a seat."

"I tend to show up every now and then." She responded with a wisecrack, but he didn't seem to notice.

But he noticed her arm. "Were you in an accident?"

"That's part of what we wanted to talk about." Carter pulled up a chair.

A frown stretched all the way to his eyes. "If you got hurt moving stuff out of the gallery, there's nothing the fire department can do money-wise and little else."

"She's not saying that." Carter jumped in. "You asked and she told you, and she's not asking for anything."

Richards leaned back in his chair. "Then why are you here with Ms. Colton?"

"You know that I was here checking the Tinsley paintings to see if they were forgeries."

"Yes. I know all of that."

"Well, they are. Tony Martell was arrested for the forgeries and he's in a jail cell here in Chicago. He had some interesting things to say."

"Like what?"

"He wanted a deal, but before he could get one, he had to tell me who had paid him to paint the forgeries. He wasn't eager to do that. I had to apply pressure. In the end, he gave it up, and I thought you might be interested in who it was."

"What has this got to do with the gallery fire?"

"That's what I'm trying to figure out and I thought you might be able to help."

Richards leaned forward. "You want information, don't you?"

Carter stood, his back ramrod straight. "I don't need to put up with your attitude, Richards. I can go over your head and give someone else the credit for solving the arson. That's what I believe this information will do." He turned to leave the room and Lila was immediately on her feet.

"No, wait a minute." Richards was on his feet, too. "I didn't know you had a hair-trigger temper. I didn't say I wouldn't help you."

"Then lose the attitude, and you were disrespectful to Ms. Colton. She doesn't deserve that."

"My apologies, Ms. Colton."

Lila eased back into her chair. "Thank you." She didn't say what was rolling around in her head because her mother had raised her to be polite.

Taking his seat, Carter told him about the arrest of Martell. "That's how Lila hurt her hand. I'm going to visit him later today and try to get more information out of him. I asked about the fire and he said he didn't know anything about it. He's not into that and I believed him."

"But you believe he knows who is?"

"I'm hoping he can point me in the right direction."

"So what do you need from me?" Richards resumed his seat.

"Information on Rossini. Is he in debt? And a little about his background, like where he spends his time. His hobbies."

Richards picked up a pencil and scribbled something on a pad. "But first, you tell me who was paying the forger."

"Walter Fox."

Richards threw the pencil on the desk. "Come on—Fox? Tinsley's agent? Why would he set fire to paintings that he would profit from?"

"Think, Richards."

"They were forgeries?"

"Yes. And he must have found out that my company was investigating him and that he could go to prison. He'd do anything to stop that, and destroying the paintings was a way no one would ever know."

"And you think Rossini is in on this?"

"Yes. I just have to connect them in some way."

Richards scooted back in his chair, leaning on one arm as he thought things over. "Good luck with that. I don't have anything that ties Rossini to Fox. Rossini is a rich man. He took the real-estate business over from his father-in-law. He owns several strip malls, hotels, apartments and houses all over Chicago. If he gets in trouble financially, he just sells something and he's back doing business again. He knows how the system works and I don't think you'll be able to get anything on him. He also knows how to cover his tracks. The only thing we had on him was that he liked to party and gamble and has a mistress living in one of his hotel suites, but we got nowhere with that."

"Gamble? Poker?"

"Yes. There's a group of rich gentlemen in Chicago who have a high-stakes get-together about twice a month, and Vice has been trying to catch them for years. I'm sure Rossini is one of those gentlemen."

Carter leaned over and pushed the tablet closer to

Richards. "Write down any others who might be a member of that group and I'll take it from there."

Richards picked up the pencil. "This is just a guess. You won't be able to use it in court."

"I'm just fishing right now. Something has to connect Rossini with Fox."

Richards began to write. "As I told you, good luck. I've been on this case since the fire happened, and I've come up with nothing and neither has my team. We're all trained professionals."

"The problem is, Richards, you keep looking at the same old thing and this arson goes beyond that. It has to do with money. I know, you said Rossini is loaded, but everyone has a weakness. And somehow that gallery was a weak spot for Rossini." Carter stood and ripped the page off the pad. "I'll be in touch." At the door, Carter turned back. "Would it be possible to get a listing of all the properties Rossini owns in Chicago?"

"You're asking for a lot, Mr. Finch, and something better pop from all of this or your name will be mud in Chicago."

"I'm well aware I'm putting my name on the line here, but…"

"Where do you want me to send the file?"

Carter wrote his email address on the pad. "Thank you, Richards."

"Now I have a question for you."

"Shoot."

"What's the deal with Fox? Has he been arrested?"

"I have a tail on him right now, waiting to see what he does. If he tries to leave Chicago, he'll be arrested."

"It's probably best to get more than Martell's word."

"That's what I was thinking. Talk to you later."

"Hope your hand gets better," Richards called to Lila.

Lila didn't respond as they walked out of the office and through the big doors. All the while, Carter was reading the gamblers' list.

"Anything interesting?"

"Yeah. I figured out how Fox found Tony."

She looked over his arm at the list. "How?"

"Donald Sapp's name is on here and I'm guessing that he told Fox at a poker game about his tenant in the basement. That was all it took. Of course, I have no way to prove it. I think I'll just have to talk to Mr. Sapp to see what he has to say. But first, I have to get over to the jail." He folded the list and stuffed it in his pocket.

"Wait. I didn't get to read all the names. I'm from Chicago, so I should know most of them."

"There's no need for you to look at the list. I got this."

She grabbed it out of his pocket. "What are you hiding from me?"

"Lila, I'm just trying to protect you."

"Well, don't. I can do that all by myself." Her eyes quickly scanned the names and froze on one near the bottom. Axel Colton. She stopped walking and just stared at the name. Where would her father get money for high-stakes poker games? Carin, of course. If he begged enough, she would give in.

She crammed the list into his pocket. "Stop keeping secrets from me, even when it includes my family."

"I wasn't going to keep it a secret. I was just trying to figure out how to tell you."

"Don't treat me as if I'm fragile." She opened the passenger door and got in, slamming the door so hard it jarred her arm.

Carter crawled in beside her, trying to straighten out the list she'd managed to wrinkle. With the list on his thigh, he painstakingly stroked out the wrinkles. As she watched, laughter bubbled up inside her. She was feeling anything but humor. It was his calm demeanor. Nothing ever seemed to shake him.

"Do you ever get angry?"

"I try not to." He placed the list on the console. "I learned that as a kid. If I got angry about something, I was always punished by having to stay in my room. And I hated that. Learning to control your emotions is not an easy thing."

"You'll have to teach me. I can be wide-eyed and crazy sometimes, and I'm almost positive I get that from my grandmother's side."

He smiled. "I like you wild-eyed and crazy. It makes me realize what I'm missing in life."

"What? Someone to light your fire?"

"Exactly." He glanced at her. "Do you want to talk about your father?"

"I don't know what to say. I had no idea he had money to gamble. I know he did when I was younger, but Carin pulled the money strings on him and he had to cut back. Now he's playing in the high-stakes games. You know, I'm wondering why Richards didn't mention his name. Surely he knows Axel is my father."

"I was thinking that, too."

"Do you think Richards is playing us?"

"I doubt it, but anything is possible."

He pulled into a parking garage of a stark-looking building. The sign read Cook County Jail. "Sorry, you can't go in, but I'll only be a few minutes. Keep the doors locked."

Lila watched as he walked away to a door farther down. She hadn't been inside a jail cell before and she didn't want to start now. She leaned her head back against the car seat and thought about everything that was happening, especially with her father. She was tired of agonizing over their father-daughter relationship. The truth was, they didn't have one. To get the answers she needed, she had to talk to him. She pulled her phone out of her purse.

"Lila, you again? This is very unusual."

"I have a few questions I hope you'll answer."

"I'm not talking about the lawsuit. Mom had a hissy fit when I told her what you'd said. I'm going along with what she wants and that's it."

"It's not about the lawsuit. Do you know Walter Fox or Lou Rossini?"

"Where did that question come from?"

"Are you gambling again? Does Carin know?"

"This is none of your business."

"Do you know them? I already know that you do, so don't try to lie."

"All right, I know them and have attended a few games when Mom supplies the money. Fox even got some original artwork for Mom and she was happy about that."

"Carin bought artwork from Fox?"

"Yeah. That's what he does. Mom liked him, so she didn't complain about giving me money to gamble."

"Does she know that Fox sells forgeries?"

"No, he doesn't. Why are you making up all this stuff?"

Lila closed her eyes and wondered just how insane her family was.

"You do know the fire is being investigated and they've called it arson. Are you aware of that? Are you aware the police and the arson teams are involved? Someone is going to get arrested for the crime. If you know anything, please tell me."

"My life is none of your business. Stay out of it, just like Mom told you."

Her father clicked off before she could say another word, and she sat there with the phone in her hand, not knowing what to do.

Could her father be involved in the arson?

Would he set fire to her place of business for money?

Chapter 11

Carter signed in after they checked his credentials. An officer showed him to an interview room. The place had the bare essentials: a table, two chairs and a legal pad on the table. The floor was bare concrete. No frills here.

Tony was brought in dressed in jail attire and handcuffed. "Mr. Finch, have you gotten me a deal?" He slid into a chair.

Tony had a one-track mind. "The ADA will be contacting your lawyer appointed by the court, and then you'll meet and she will lay out the deal for you. You will agree to it or not, but I'd advise you to take it."

"I intend to. Why are you here?"

"I have more questions."

His shoulders sank. "Oh, man. I don't know anything else."

Tony wasn't in a cooperative mood, so Carter had to give him a little incentive. "I know how Fox found you."

"How?" Tony sat up straight in his chair. Carter had his attention.

"Did Sapp know you had a record and was convicted of forgery?"

Tony hung his head. "Wendy told him and talked him into letting me stay at the apartment until I could find a job."

"Who's Wendy?"

"She's my girlfriend's mother."

"Is she the elderly lady who rents the apartment?"

Tony laughed. "Hell, no. She's not even fifty. She had my girlfriend when she was seventeen."

That was interesting. Why would Sapp lie about something like that? Why was he afraid of the truth? And what was the truth?

"So Sapp and Wendy are seeing each other?"

"If you want to call it that. She works in a bar, serving drinks. That's how she and Sapp met. She was looking for a place to stay and Sapp had one. I'm not sure she even pays rent, but I'm not asking as long as she lets me stay there."

This had nothing to do with the information Carter was looking for. It just proved that everyone had dirty little secrets.

"Sapp was one of Fox's gambling buddies. That's how they know each other. And when Fox was looking for a forger, Sapp found him one."

"That son of a…"

"I have another question."

"Man, you're full of questions and I don't even know what kind of deal I'm getting."

"I don't know what it is, either, but trust me, it will be better than going to trial. As soon as I find out, I'll let you know. Just be patient."

"Yeah." Tony was anything but patient. With the ADA's caseload, Carter figured she'd get it off her plate real soon, so Tony had to hang in there.

"When I first talked to you about a deal, you were afraid of Fox. Is he violent?"

"I don't guess it matters now."

"No. You're both going to jail." Carter waited for a second and then asked, "Did he ever threaten you?"

"He always comes to pick up a painting when no one is at home. One day he asked if I would carry the painting to the rental. I noticed there was a fresh scar on his neck, which I could barely see 'cause he's always dressed in a three-piece suit with a bow tie and a fedora. I casually asked if he hurt himself and he replied that a guy owed him money and thought he could convince Fox otherwise. He then gave a funny laugh and said that man is now in the Chicago River, and if I ever went to the cops, I would join him. He had this evil look in his eyes and I knew he meant it."

Carter doubted if Fox had ever killed anyone. It was just a way to keep Tony in line. He got to his feet. "If you think of anything else, have someone call me."

The clanging of metal doors followed him out of the building. He slid into the driver's seat and placed his briefcase in the back. With a look at Lila's face, he knew she was upset about something.

"What's up?"

"I talked to my father."

"Why do you put yourself through that?"

"I had to know about his part in the gambling."

"Did you find out anything?"

"Not really. He admitted to the gambling and told me it was none of my business. He also said that my grandmother supplies him the money to gamble. And, get this, Fox has sold my grandmother paintings for her home."

"Let's see if we can put this puzzle together. It's getting very muddled every time we check something. And yet no one has a clear motive. Sapp's involvement is only that he found Tony for Fox. Other than that, I don't think he has anything to do with the fire."

"Does my father?"

Her eyes begged for an honest answer and he didn't have one, so he went with his gut feeling. "From what you've told me about him, I don't think he has the guts for something like this. And what would he gain? If Rossini offered to pay him, I still think he couldn't do it. He just doesn't have the guts to face much of anything in his life, especially his own children."

It was after five when they walked through the front door of the town house. "I'll put the soup on the burner while you check your laptop for Richards's files. We'll look at them after dinner."

"Okay. They're here." Carter loved the way they worked together so well. It wasn't long before they had the soup on the table. Lila made coffee and it was a peaceful time before they started sorting through all the information Richards had sent. At least he was cooperating.

Lila took a pain pill and he didn't say anything. Since they had a lot of work to do, he wanted her to be as pain-free as possible. He really wanted her to rest for a while, but he knew without asking that wasn't going to fly.

Carter brought his laptop to the table and sent all the files to Lila's computer. They started to go through them. "Richards was right. Rossini owns a lot of real estate."

"My gallery was just a drop in his pocket."

They were deep in when the doorbell rang. Lila jumped up to get it. "Faith," she exclaimed, and Carter got up and made his way to the door. He knew Faith was her sister-in-law.

A beautiful redhead stood in the doorway with a dark-haired little boy standing in front of her. "I'm sorry. I didn't know you had company."

"Don't be silly," Lila told her. "This is Carter and we're sorting through some papers about the fire."

"It's nice to meet you," she said, and he shook her hand. She bent down to her son. "And this is Jackson. We heard Lila hurt her hand and we came by to bring her some goodies to make her feel better."

The little boy held up a bag in one hand; a toy truck was in the other. He handed the bag to Lila. "For you. You got a boo-boo."

Lila leaned down and kissed his cheek. "Thank you, Jackson."

"They're chocolate chip just like you like and I do, too."

Lila took the bag. "Come in and have a cup of coffee."

"No, we better go."

"I want a cookie," Jackson muttered.

Carter knew the hesitation was about him. "Please,

come in and have a cup of coffee. I'll get it while you visit." He took the bag from Lila.

He didn't realize the little boy had followed him until he almost tripped over him.

"What's your name?" Jackson asked.

"Carter." He found a decorative plate for the cookies.

"My name is Jackson and I'm four years old."

Carter had never been around children and he had no idea what to say to the boy. Luckily, he didn't have to. The little boy kept talking.

"Can you throw a ball? My daddy can, but he's not home too much."

Carter handed him the plate of cookies. "Can you carry this into the living room?"

"Sure. I'm a big boy."

"Yes, you are." Carter followed with the coffee.

"Thank you," Lila said with a smile. It was clear she liked Faith and enjoyed talking to her.

He handed both women a cup. "Lila was just telling me what you do for a living," Faith said. "That sounds interesting and fun to be able to travel the world."

"Can I please have something to drink?" Jackson asked.

"How about milk or a soda?"

"Milk," Faith answered for him.

"Mommy—"

"Soda has caffeine and it will keep you up all night, so the answer is still no."

Jackson followed him into the kitchen to get the milk. He drank about half of the glass and set it on the counter. "Want to play with my truck? It's real neat."

"Uh…" He really didn't want to play with the truck,

but he couldn't tell the little boy that. From the few minutes he had talked to him, he could see his father's absence was hard on the boy. At least Carter's parents had always gotten along. His parents argued like all parents, but he'd never feared that one day they might get a divorce and he might have to go live with one of them. That had to be hard for a four-year-old.

"Carter, where are you?"

He looked around and saw the boy was at the top of the stairs. "Let's play. The truck's coming to you. Don't let it have an accident."

Carter was totally confused, but he was sure Jackson would show him the way. The boy gave the truck a push and it came flying down the stairs and landed in about eight pieces at Carter's feet.

Jackson hurried down the stairs and sat on the bottom step. "Oh, no, we had an accident. Now we have to fix the truck."

Carter sat beside him on the step and started putting the wheels back on the truck, then a hood, then a tailgate, then a motor...

"Jackson, let's go," Faith said.

"We're working on the truck."

"We have to go. Lila has to rest."

Carter handed Jackson the truck all back together. "That is a really neat truck."

"Yeah. Can I come play sometimes?"

"Jackson! Do not invite yourself."

"Mom—"

"Jackson."

"Okay. Okay." He ran into the kitchen and finished drinking his milk. Then he ran into the living room for another cookie and met his mother and Lila at the door.

Jackson probably knew his way around his mother, and that last "Jackson" must have been it. The kid was fun to be around. Since he'd never been around kids, he didn't see them in his future. Nor did he see a wife or a home. That was just the way he'd thought since graduating high school. He would be the bachelor who had gotten away and that suited him fine. Back then.

Lila squatted and hugged Jackson. "Thank you for the cookies. That was so sweet of you."

Jackson then ran to him, stuffing the cookie in his mouth before Faith could notice. "Bye, Carter," he mumbled around a mouthful of cookie.

Did he shake his hand or just say bye? Good heavens! It couldn't be that hard.

He reached down and picked up Jackson. "It was nice to meet you and your mother, and I hope you can come by again."

"See, Mommy?" Jackson glanced at his mother and then he kissed Carter's cheek. "Bye."

Carter cleared his throat. "B-ye," he managed.

Lila closed the door after them and patted Carter's chest. "You look a little shell-shocked."

"I've never been around children and it was nice."

"Didn't you say Neil had two daughters?"

He picked up coffee cups from the table and Lila took cookies to the kitchen. "Yes, but the only time I really spent with them was on holidays. And they're in college now." As Carter put cups in the dishwasher, the doorbell rang again.

"Jackson must've forgotten something." Lila headed for the door.

"Mom!"

Carter almost dropped a cup. He juggled it for a second and then caught it in time. Her mother and step-father were here. He wasn't usually a nervous person, but today his nerves were taking a hit for stability. Lila was grown and so was he. What was the nervousness about?

A woman of medium height with graying brown hair and a big smile walked into the kitchen carrying a big pot. "Oh, Lila, why didn't you tell me you had company?"

"Mom and Rick, this is Carter, the man who was in the fire with me. We're working on some information that might help catch the arsonist."

Her mom set the pot on the stove. "Nice to meet you, Carter. When my baby is sick, all she wants to eat is chicken noodle soup, so I made her some." She turned to Lila. "How are you, baby?"

"I'm fine." She held up her hand. "It's not throbbing as bad as it was before."

Rick walked up to Carter and shook his hand. "Are they close to solving this thing?"

"Lila and I are searching for something that might help the arson investigators. It just takes one little thing to point us in the right direction."

"Well, hon, let's go and let these two get back to work."

Lila hugged her parents at the door and Rick shook his hand again. Lila's mother hugged him until he thought he was going to pass out from lack of air. Her mother was a hugger.

"Call if you need anything," Rick shouted as Lila closed the door.

"You didn't tell them."

"I didn't want to hurt their feelings. Besides, I love

chicken noodle soup and I'll be eating it for about a week."

They laughed and sat at the table, getting back to work. Before Carter could open a folder, the doorbell rang again.

"How many family members do you have?"

"Too many right now," she called over her shoulder. "Nash. Come in."

"No, no. I just saw your parents leaving and I was out this way and wanted to stop and see how you were doing. I told the brothers I would check in. Oh…" He noticed Carter in the kitchen doorway.

"This is Carter, the guy who saved our butts from the fire. And this is my cousin Nash, the architect."

They shook hands. The guy was well over six feet tall with dark blond hair and hazel eyes. He and Lila looked about the same age and they must have played together as kids. It had to be nice to have those kinds of memories.

"I really can't stay. I'm looking at an old house out this way to see if it can be restored, and I told Aaron and Damon that I would look in to see if you were okay or needed cheering up."

"I just fell and I'm fine, but thanks for thinking of me."

"It's hard to imagine sometimes that someone who is so beautiful and graceful can be a klutz."

"Don't start…"

He put an arm around her waist and kissed her forehead. "Love you. Gotta run. I'll spread the news that you're okay. Nice to meet you, Carter." In a flash, he was out the door.

Carter stared at her serene face. She loved her family and she loved that they thought of her. That was what life was about, he'd heard. Love, family and home. He could see in her eyes why it meant so much to have someone there for you. If he got sick, he would be on his own with no one to make him chicken soup. Part of him had always known that and he was comfortable in that skin. Why was he now having doubts and second thoughts and insecurities? That wasn't him.

"Want to chance it?" She walked toward the table. "I think that's the last of my loving family."

Before Carter could sit, his phone buzzed. "My turn." He pulled his cell out of his pocket. "Neil," he mouthed and walked into the living room to talk.

"The painting in Milan was a forgery," Neil said. "The police were waiting for the man when he came in to get his money. Marla wants to spend a little more time here, so I won't be coming home for about a week. I got a call about a painting in London that is suspected to be a forgery. I haven't had time to go over all the details, but when I do, you'll be going to London."

"Oh, London, okay."

"Did everything go smoothly with Martell?" Neil asked.

"Yes. They're working out the details and he'll go straight to prison."

"Have the authorities arrested Fox?"

"No, but the police are keeping a tail on him in case he's involved with the fire. We thought that since Tony was in jail, Fox would bolt. So far he's staying quiet. He may not even know Tony has been arrested."

"Carter, the fire doesn't concern us. Arrest Fox and get it over with."

"It concerns me." His voice grew rigid.

"How are things with the Colton woman?"

This was what Carter hated: the questioning. Neil was an expert at it. "Listen, Neil, I have to go. Just let me know when you're coming home or when you get details about the London painting."

He turned to see Lila's eyes on him. "Are you leaving?"

"Not just yet." He tried to take the hurt from her eyes but failed. They both knew his time was almost up.

"You're going to London?"

"In about a week." He didn't lie, but honesty came with the price of hurting her. He tapped his laptop on the table, wanting to think about something else. "There's so much information here that it will take forever to get through it. I think our best bet would be to talk to the main players."

"Like?"

"Fox, Rossini, Sapp or any name that is on a file. I have this gut feeling that something was missed."

Lila went through the titles of files on her screen. "Looks like Richards sent us everything he has."

Carter had the same thing on his laptop. "Yeah, everything. Even Savon is on here."

"She said they interviewed her and that they even checked out her story with the boyfriend. They even confirmed it with security cameras at the restaurant. Richards and his team did a thorough job. I just don't know what they could have missed." She got up and went to the counter for a pain pill.

What was he thinking, keeping her up this late? He gently put his arm around her waist. "Bedtime. We're not going to argue about this. You need some rest and we'll start over tomorrow."

She leaned against him. "I'm not going to argue. I am feeling a little tired."

They went up the stairs and Lila was more than ready to go to bed. He tucked her in. "Need anything?"

She shook her head and went to sleep.

Carter wasn't ready for bed, so he went back downstairs to go through the files again, hoping something would catch his eye. He kept coming back to the same file. Tanya Wilcox, Rossini's mistress. She lived in a suite at a hotel that Rossini owned near downtown. She'd been there for about two years, and what stood out to him was Tanya and Wendy worked at the same bar. If they had millionaire boyfriends, why did they have to work?

He ran his hands up his face and stretched. Every time he kept digging, he found information that didn't make sense. Like the Wendy/Tanya situation. He scrolled down the information, looking for the owner of the club. And there it was in black and white. Lou Rossini. Once again, the thought visited his mind: Rossini had no motive to burn down the gallery for money. The bar was very profitable.

He went to bed to give his eyes a rest, hoping something would come together in his head. But all he was accomplishing was pointing the finger more and more at Lila.

Chapter 12

When Lila woke up, the room was dark and quiet. He wouldn't leave without telling her. Then she heard running water and felt a moment of relief. She sat up and saw it: a glass of water and a pain pill. He was the sweetest guy. She quickly took the pill and headed for the shower.

As she was drying herself, she noticed she had a message on her phone. Darn! She had a doctor's appointment this morning with her primary care doctor. She told Carter that as she poured a cup of coffee.

"Okay." He gave her a once-over. "You're looking perky this morning."

"I am perky." She gave him a long, lingering kiss. "But I'm mad, too, because you didn't wake me up last night when you came to bed."

"You needed the rest."

She glanced at the bar. "Eggs? Where did we get eggs?"

"I bought them yesterday when I went grocery shopping. Eggs, toast and coffee." He pulled out a bar stool. "Have a seat."

"I don't have long. My appointment's at nine. I didn't notice it until this morning, and Savon wants me to meet her for lunch to view new locations for my business."

"I'll go with you."

"No. You'll be bored sitting in a doctor's office, and viewing vacant buildings."

"Lila…"

"I'm fine, Carter."

"Okay. I have some things I want to do this morning." He told her about Rossini's and Sapp's mistresses.

"That's odd. It could be very simple, though. If Rossini owns the club, he probably gets to choose the girls who work in there and probably shared some comments with Sapp."

"It's probably not that simple."

She carried her plate and cup to the sink. "I've got to go and I'll call you when I'm free."

"Okay. Go ahead. I've got the dishes."

She wanted to shout "I love you" but refrained from doing so. There was so much she wanted to say to him, but she had to choose her words wisely. Within the week, he would be leaving, and as she'd said so many times to herself, she had to be prepared and she had to be ready to handle the gallery fire. Carter was working very hard to solve it and she had faith in him.

At exactly nine o'clock, she walked into the doctor's office and then waited forty-five minutes for him to see her. He cleaned her palm again and said everything looked great. He put very little gauze back on and mostly for protection. In a couple of days, she could take it off completely. She hurried to meet Savon. A Realtor showed them three places. The first two were lacking in size and the third one was very expensive. It once had been a jewelry store that had gone bankrupt. It had a big safe, which was on the plus side, and it would need very little renovation. It was in the updated North Center and Lila liked it, but she couldn't afford it, especially since the insurance people were dragging their feet.

"What do you think?" Savon asked.

"It's nice, but unaffordable for us."

"I knew you would say that. I was hoping Carter could find the arsonist and put us back in business."

"Keep dreaming. He's working on it, but there doesn't seem to be any luck coming our way. Carter says there's something that will connect everything. We just have to find it. I keep waiting and hoping. The insurance money will make a difference in what I decide."

Savon hugged her. "How about margaritas for lunch?"

"Oh, do you mind if Carter joins us?"

She shook her head. "I don't do well as a third party, especially when I'm number three. Have a good time. I'll keep going over the numbers and the Realtor will call if anything else comes up."

"Thank you."

In the car, she called Carter, but there was no answer. She left a quick text. I'm going home. Call me.

Home was such a nice word, big, inclusive and

happy. It filled every part of her, and she had only a few days to enjoy that feeling of home.

Carter made it to Wendy Olson's apartment by nine. Sapp's Cadillac was parked outside at the curb. As if by magic, Sapp and Wendy came out. She had long blond hair, and a satin robe was wrapped around her curvy body. She definitely was not elderly. They kissed at the car and Sapp drove away. Carter followed him to a large real-estate office in northeast Chicago. The two-story brick structure looked more like a house than an office.

He watched the clock on the dashboard, and after a few minutes, he went inside and asked to see Mr. Sapp. His assistant said he needed an appointment.

"Thank you," he replied and walked straight into Sapp's office.

"Hey, you can't…" The assistant's high heels made *tap-tap* sounds on the hardwood floors as she followed him. They were met by Sapp.

"I've got it," he said to the woman and closed the door.

Carter sat in a leather chair across from Sapp's desk. "I don't like it when people lie to me."

"Lie? I haven't lied to you. You got Tony, didn't you?"

"Wendy Olson was harboring a criminal and you knew about it and you encouraged him to continue his criminal activity after his release from prison. The ADA will have a few more charges to tack onto the indictment, which would include you and Ms. Olson. You know, the elderly woman who rents from you."

"Okay. I upped her age because my wife takes care of the books. If she suspected Wendy was pretty and younger, she'd be on my case. We've been through that before." Sapp got to his feet in a nervous gesture. "I had nothing to do with the fire. I allowed Tony to stay at the apartment because he was dating Wendy's daughter. How was I to know about his past?"

Carter stood. "Walter Fox. Does the name sound familiar?" He held up a hand. "And before you lie, I already know the truth."

"Listen—"

"I'd advise you to get a lawyer. You pointed Walter Fox in the right direction when he was looking for a forger. You didn't care that it was illegal. You just wanted him to start making money so he and his girlfriend could move out."

"You're just making this up. You can't prove that I know Walter Fox."

"Poker games." Carter swung toward the door. "Get a lawyer, Sapp. You're going to need one."

From there he went to the hotel where Rossini's mistress, Tanya Wilcox, lived. The place wasn't far from downtown and had a lively business. He found a parking space in the garage and made his way to the entrance. A valet tried to take his briefcase, but he declined.

The foyer was huge with glass and stainless steel and lighting that made visitors stop and stare. It was a swanky place. There were people at the checkout and the check-in counter. He chose the check-in one because the guy was young and he might be a little more agreeable.

"Good morning." He gave him his best smile.

"What can I do for you?"

"I'm looking for Tanya Wilcox. She said she lived here."

The guy looked to the other employees who were busy working. "I'm sorry. I can't give you any information. You have to contact her yourself."

Damn! He got a smart one. Carter leaned in closer. "Can you at least tell me what floor she's on? I would like to surprise her."

"I'm sorry. I can't help you." He typed something into the computer and whispered, "All our suites are on the top floor."

Carter took the unexpected gift and headed for the elevators. A cleaning crew was at the end of a long hallway. They were starting their day by arguing across their cleaning cars. Their angry tones carried to him and he quickly made his way there.

"Good morning, ladies."

"How can we help you?" one woman asked.

"I'm looking for a friend."

"Well, unless you've got a key, we can't let you in." The other woman made to push the cart away.

He ignored the snide comments. "Tanya Wilcox. Do you know her?"

The two women looked at each other, and now Carter became their number one enemy. They weren't talking about Tanya Wilcox.

A third woman with long dark hair and a bathrobe stepped into the hallway behind the cleanup crew. "What's going on out here?"

"Nothing, ma'am," one of the cleaning ladies replied. "This gentleman is looking for someone and we told him we don't know her."

"Go," the woman in the robe said. "You're not paid to gossip in the hallways."

As the cleaning crew got on the elevator, the woman asked, "What's your deal?" She folded her arms across her ample breasts and leaned against the doorjamb.

"I'm afraid I was being rather sneaky. I'd heard there were poker games here and I wanted to get in on one."

She laughed. "Mister, you're looking in the wrong place."

"I don't think so. Someone told me the games were here and the payout was big."

She moved a little closer to him and he got a strong whiff of delicate perfume. "Take it from me. There's no game here. Go home and play cards with your neighbor or something."

"My money is as good as anyone else's."

"Who did you hear this from?"

"A guy in a bar."

"Oh, sweetie, every guy in a bar is tipsy, so I wouldn't take everything at face value. There is no poker game going on here."

"If you're sure, Tanya Wilcox…" He threw out her name to shake her up, and it did.

She threw back her long hair. "How did you get my name? Did those insipid maids tell you?"

"No. They weren't willing to give out any information."

"You sound like a cop."

"You never know." He saluted, turned his back on her and headed for the elevators. He didn't have to sneak a glance to know that Tanya was back in the suite, calling Rossini. His visit should shake things up, and that was what he wanted. Someone had to get nervous and offer up information. He hoped that day was soon.

Lila stopped at a bakery to get éclairs for dessert. They would need something to make the chicken soup more appetizing. Newspapers were outside the door and Lila noticed the headline: Colton Fighting Back.

She bought a newspaper and went inside to purchase the éclairs. She didn't open the newspaper until she was back in her car. Her grandmother was up to her old tricks. She'd hired a new lawyer to get the lawsuit moved to an earlier date. The attorney obviously had had a press conference this morning and had said that Erik and Axel had been ignored for so many years by their father and it was time to recognize them and their rights. And he would make sure that the other Coltons paid.

Lila threw the newspaper on the passenger side of the car and went home. She hated that everywhere she went she would see the Colton name again, strewn all over the newspapers. People whispering behind her back, pointing fingers. Carin craved all the attention and Lila did her best to avoid it and her grandmother. If she could survive the fire, she could survive this. But could she survive Carter's leaving?

Carter's car was at the town house and it meant he was here, too. Her spirits lifted. She opened the door and smelled soup.

"Mmm." She kissed him. "Just what I wanted for lunch—you and soup." She held up the newspaper. "And reading material. A judge is going to rule on it by the end of the week."

"Your grandmother doesn't miss a beat."

"No. Now everyone will be talking about it again."

"That bothers you?" He put his arms around her and held her close against his chest, and that was what she needed. His comfort.

"A little. I wish it didn't, but my family is involved."

"Let's not talk about it."

She drew back. "Why not?"

"Because it upsets you."

"So? I'm not a weak woman who's going to crumble at your feet when something goes wrong."

"I didn't say that."

"And in five days you'll be leaving and won't have to deal with it at all."

Silence filled the room. "Yes, I'll be leaving in five days," he replied in a low voice. "We talked about this."

At that point she realized she was making a fool of herself. "I'm just overwhelmed by everything and taking it out on you. I'm fine, though. Really."

"Lila—" his voice softened "—a judge will have the final say in the Colton case, and there's nothing you can do to change that."

"I know," she mumbled.

"How did the doctor's appointment go? And why aren't you eating lunch with Savon?"

"I wanted to call and ask you for lunch, but Savon would rather not be a threesome. Besides, she had some other things to do." She wiggled her right hand. "It's great. He said I can take the bandage off tomorrow if it feels okay. I didn't put the sling on this morning. How did your morning go?" She reached for bowls in the cabinet as he told her about the mistresses.

"You certainly got their attention. I'm sure Rossini and Sapp do not want their mistresses involved."

"Probably the last thing they wanted. It's frustrating that nothing is popping up like a target ready for us to hit the bull's-eye."

"Wouldn't that be lovely?"

Carter put the soup on the table. "What's in the white box you brought in?"

"Éclairs. I thought we needed something decadent."

"You're decadent. You're my éclair."

He grabbed her around the waist and swung her round and round until her laughter filled the room and her heart. She was happy in his arms and she wouldn't think beyond that. After all, she had five days. That was a lifetime to her.

After they finished eating, Inspector Richards called and wanted to know if Carter had come up with anything. He put it on speakerphone so Lila could hear.

"Why aren't you finding anything?"

"There are a lot of files to go through."

"Then go through them instead of antagonizing Rossini and Sapp. They both are filing restraining orders against you."

"They'll have to come up with a good reason to get one, and I only visited Sapp's office and a hotel that Rossini owns. They can't prove that I was there for any other reason than real estate and poker."

"You asked about the poker games?"

"Yes, I did. And that's what has everyone in a frenzy. The poker game is supposed to be a secret in law enforcement. Why is that, Richards?"

"I don't know. Just find something so we can close this case."

"Did you tell Rossini I talked to you?" Carter asked.

"Of course not. I'm on the side of justice, Finch, whether you believe that or not."

Carter turned off the phone and looked at Lila. "Ready to work all afternoon?"

As long as he was beside her, she could get through this. She'd never needed anyone before. She wasn't a needy person, but she needed him in ways she couldn't even explain to herself. "I'm ready."

They spent the next few hours going through the files, looking for something that was out of place, something that would grab their attention, but there wasn't anything. In fact, there was too much stuff, too much information on Rossini and the others. No one had a motive except Rossini and Lila, and that was beginning to make her nervous.

At six o'clock they warmed up the soup and laughed until they couldn't breathe. "We can order in, you know."

Carter grabbed his chest. "And let this good food go to waste? Never!"

"I'm ordering a pizza."

"You're weak."

"So I'll order just for one."

"You better not." His eyes gleamed with a lot of feelings, and the one she wanted to recognize the most was love. It was there, but would he ever recognize it? Or admit it? They were so good together. Why couldn't he see that? Yet he was set on leaving and breaking her heart.

Soon they went to their laptops, searching and hoping for answers, but the happy-in-between moments kept her going.

"I keep coming back to Tanya Wilcox. I saw another

Tanya somewhere. Could they be the same person?" Carter scrolled through the file doing a search-and-find on his laptop.

"Wait. I have her page up on the screen. As a teenager she married Ken Wilcox. The marriage lasted about a year and they divorced. She then started working at the club and got involved with Rossini. She's twenty-four years old and Rossini has to be over fifty. What an age difference!"

"She has olive-toned skin, brown eyes, brown hair. What's her maiden name?"

"Boyd."

"Wait, wait. That name is familiar. Who else do we have named Boyd?"

Lila shook her head. "I don't remember any, but again, there are so many names."

"Think, because I've heard that name before."

"Wait a minute. Wait a minute." Lila jumped out of her chair as the name fully hit her. "I can't believe it. I can't believe I didn't remember it."

"What?"

"Philip Boyd was the electrician who put in the new lights at the gallery."

"What? This is the connection we've been looking for." Carter leaned back in his chair. "And how is Tanya Wilcox related to Philip Boyd? Husband? Brother? Cousin? There has to be a connection."

Lila went back to her laptop. "She doesn't have another marriage license on record, but that doesn't mean anything. Let's see what else we can find."

"I'm already on it. I have three Philip Boyds in the Chicago area. And one of them lives in South Deering on the same street as Wendy Olson. What are the odds of that happening? Continue looking," Carter said. "Let's make sure it's him."

Lila went back to Philip Boyd's file. "He works for Sapp Electric and has been for about two years. He's lived in the apartment a little over a year. This doesn't tell us much."

Carter didn't respond and she looked up. "Carter…"

"Sorry, I got involved in this report."

"From where?"

"Police report. Boyd was arrested four years ago on a drug charge and spent one year in prison. When he was released, he went to electrical school and got the job with Sapp. We won't get anything beyond this until we question Sapp and Boyd." Carter closed his laptop. "Someone had to pay for him to go to school and my guess is Rossini. Tanya is at the center of all of this, pulling Rossini's strings the way she wants."

"I don't even know them. Why would they burn down my gallery?"

"We'll be closer to an answer tomorrow. I'm just wondering why the police report wasn't in the file."

"This makes the second misstep," Lila said. "Richards didn't mention my father's gambling, either."

Carter put an arm around her waist. "You need to go upstairs and go to bed. Tomorrow is going to be a long day and you'll need your rest."

She raised her hand. "It's fine. And I'm not going to bed unless you go, too. I don't like sleeping by myself when I can have a strong, broad-shouldered guy beside me."

Arm in arm, they went upstairs and took a shower… together. It had to have been one of the most sensual experiences of her life. He didn't touch a place on her body that didn't beg for more. They managed to push the Colton lawsuit and the fire out of their minds and enjoy each other's company.

Time with him was too valuable to miss and his touch gave her strength to face tomorrow. He didn't seem to realize that these special moments were coming to an end. But she was very aware of each day passing and her time with Carter.

Chapter 13

They were up and out of the apartment early. Electricians were on the job early to avoid the heat of the afternoon, but in Chicago the heat would probably reach eighty-two degrees. It was a nice fifty-seven degrees this morning and rain was in the forecast.

"We have to go into this with our eyes wide open," Carter said. "Since Boyd is working for Sapp, we have to assume Sapp and Rossini are connected, too."

"This isn't getting us any closer to solving the fire."

"It will. It just takes time."

"You're a very patient man."

He winked at her and he was in that kind of mood. Something had to pop today because he didn't have a lot of time left. Sapp had inherited a lot of property and businesses when his father had died. Sapp Electric was one of them. The business was near West Town with a storefront and a warehouse in back. It was in an older area. Carter figured the electrical business was the best place to find Sapp this early in the morning. They went inside a little after seven and the receptionist wasn't in yet. Everything was quiet, but someone must've opened the door.

"Anyone here?"

A man from the back shouted, "I'll be right with you. It's early."

"No hurry."

"Oh, Finch," Sapp mumbled as he saw Carter. "Would you like a cup of coffee?" He was startled at first but recovered nicely.

Carter glanced at Lila and she shook her head. "No, we're good."

"What can I help you with?"

"I'd like to talk to Philip Boyd."

"It's about the fire, isn't it?"

"Yes, it is. Philip is the electrician who put in the new wiring and lights."

Sapp glanced around Carter to Lila. "That's the lady whose gallery burned down."

Lila took a step forward. "Yes, I'm Lila Colton. We'd like to talk to Philip just for a minute."

"Why? The police cleared him and the only suspect they have for the fire is you, Ms. Colton. I see no reason for you to talk to Philip."

A young man with dark hair and eyes walked in. "The truck's ready to go…" Philip looked from his boss to Carter and Lila. "What's going on?"

"He's an insurance investigator and he's investigating the fire and wants to talk to you."

Even though Philip's demeanor was calm, his complexion changed a shade. "I don't mind talking to them again. I've done nothing wrong."

"I'm calling a lawyer," Sapp said and walked into his office.

"I don't need a lawyer," Philip shouted after him and pointed to some chairs in the lobby. "Have a seat. Nice seeing you again, Ms. Colton."

"Thank you."

Philip continued to stand. "The arson investigator didn't find anything wrong with my work. Did you find something?"

Carter decided to go honest on this all the way. "One little tidbit jumped out at us when we were going over the files."

"What was it?"

"That Tanya Wilcox is your sister."

He shoved his hands into the pockets of his jeans, the second sign of nervousness. "Yes, she is."

"Did she get you this job?"

Philip thought it over for a second. "Yeah. Mr. Sapp is a friend of Lou's."

"Rossini?"

"Yeah."

"Did Mr. Rossini get you an apartment?"

"I'm not going to lie because I know you already have the answers. Tanya found it for me and asked Lou to rent it from Mr. Sapp. The man owed Lou money and it was a way to get his money back. I would pay Lou until the debt was paid off."

"That's why you didn't rent from Rossini?"

"Yeah. And he didn't want to get involved with Tanya's family. Because of my record, I wasn't able to rent anything, so Tanya helped me out. You see, I have a girlfriend and she was pregnant and I wanted a home for us."

"You're being very honest, Philip," Lila told him.

"That's about all I have left. I didn't set the fire. I had no reason to do anything like that. Everything was going good in my life and I wouldn't do anything to change that."

"Not even if you were paid a lot of money?" Carter watched the emotions as they flickered across the man's face. He was actually thinking about it—if someone approached him, would he take it? At that moment he knew Philip had nothing to do with the fire. He was trying to make a life, not destroy it.

"No. I wouldn't take the money. My girlfriend would leave me and we have a three-month-old baby girl that I would never see again. No, I wouldn't do it."

"Would you testify to everything you've just told us?"

"Aw, man." He sank into his chair. "This is never going to go away, is it?"

"Not until we get to the reason why someone wanted the gallery gone."

Philip twisted his hands in his lap and didn't speak.

"You know something about the fire, don't you? If you do, it's time to tell us and get it off your shoulders."

"I know. I just wish I didn't have to say anything."

"Saying it now would be best for you."

"Or it could be worse."

Carter frowned. "What do you mean?"

"When I went over to do the wiring for Ms. Colton, I noticed it was outdated and it needed to be replaced. Some of it was just bare wires. All the brittle insulation needed to be replaced, as does the plumbing. I told

Lou the whole place could go up any day with that kind of wiring. He told me to forget it. The place was built in the 1930s and is a fire hazard. I guess Lou and his father-in-law must have been able to pay people off and do nothing about it. I did not set the fire, but it wasn't a surprise when I heard about it. Now I'll probably lose my job and my apartment."

Carter got to his feet. "I believe you. You just got caught up in a terrible mess. Just don't tell anyone what you and I talked about, not even your boss. Don't do anything until I do more investigating."

"What?" Clearly, Philip was confused.

"Just keep quiet for now. If you do tell your boss, Rossini will find out within minutes and your job and your apartment will be gone. Trust me on this one."

"Sure."

"Not even your sister. I know she helped you, but her number one loyalty is to Rossini, and the man is up to his neck in this. When your boss asks you what we talked about, just tell him I had a few more questions about the fire. And be sure to mention to your sister that I was here asking questions. That way it won't be a secret."

"What kind of questions?"

"Like the type of wiring Ms. Colton requested. Did she ask for any changes? Was she satisfied with your work or did she complain? Did she say anything about Mr. Rossini? Things like that."

"Okay. I hope you catch the person who did it."

Carter shook Philip's hand, as did Lila. "I'm sorry you lost your business, Ms. Colton. I didn't have anything to do with it."

"Thank you, Philip."

The man nodded and walked back into the building.

"What do you think?" Lila asked as they got into the car.

"I think Philip just gave us a real good motive."

"What motive?" Lila turned in the seat to face him.

"I'm guessing that pulling out all that insulation, putting in new wiring and plumbing would amount to a lot of money. Money Rossini is not willing to pay. But burning down the place would've been a big profit for him."

"I love the way your mind works."

"Devious, huh?"

"You got it. Now let's go visit Richards and yank his chain for a while. I'd just like to know why he didn't mention my father."

"I love the way your mind works," Carter said back to her.

They smiled at each other with remembered kisses and last night's passion.

They got out of the car and went through the double doors of Richards's office building. In the foyer were newspaper stands and vending machines. Lila walked over to the newspaper stands. She reached in her purse for money and bought a paper.

"You need the torture, huh?"

"I guess. Just don't bug me about the craziness of my family."

Carter held up his hands. "Never! I would never do that."

They were smiling as they went down the hall to Richards's office. There must've been a meeting, because men were coming out. They walked in and took seats.

"Since you're here, I'm guessing you have something." Richards leaned back in his chair and waited.

Lila glanced at Carter and he nodded for her to go ahead. She had something on her mind and he let her go with it.

"Why didn't you mention my father's name was on the list?"

Richards raised his hands in a defensive gesture. "Finch asked for wealthy gamblers in Chicago and I gave them to him."

"My father is not a wealthy gambler," Lila said.

"I beg to differ on that. You have to have at least ten thousand dollars to get in the game, and Mr. Colton has gotten in the game several times."

"How would you know this?"

"The police do manage to raid these poker games every now and then, and of course, being the people who they are, like city council members, elected officials and big-time businessmen, they are given a warning and let go. A big fine comes with that. Your grandmother has gotten your father out three times. That's how I know."

"I think you enjoyed writing his name on that piece of paper. And I also think you're hoping I'm the one who set the fire. You're wrong, Inspector Richards. And there's nothing you can tell me about my father that would shock me."

"You think I enjoyed that?" He slapped his hand on the arm of the chair. "I wrote it on the list to spare you any embarrassment with Mr. Finch. I didn't know if he knew. That way you could tell him about it in private. I thought you would appreciate that, not be insulted by it."

"I'm sorry if I misjudged you." She was awesome in battle and defeat, and if Carter wasn't wrong, he thought Richards might have a crush on her. He was trying to impress her and that had misfired.

"You may be unaware of it, Ms. Colton, but your grandmother is a very wealthy woman, and your father has access to that money. Not to mention the lawsuit with the other family of Coltons. If your grandmother gets her wish, she will be much wealthier, as will you and your father."

"If you believe that, you have not investigated thoroughly. My grandmother hasn't given my brother or me anything, and we are not expecting, nor do we want, anything from the lawsuit."

"That's very big of you, but talking to your father, I got the feeling that he feels differently."

"Yes, he does, as does my grandmother. But I don't believe my father had anything to do with the fire. Someone pointed out to me that he doesn't have the guts and I believed them. My father is after money, Inspector Richards, and he would receive nothing from the fire. And getting money out of me would not be an easy task for him. Thank you for being honest about it, though."

Inspector Richards leaned forward, his eyes totally on Lila. "I'm sorry if your father's name on the list insulted you. I did not mean it that way."

"Could we please get back to the fire?" Carter asked in a voice he didn't recognize. That jealous voice was his and he had no right to be jealous. Lila could talk to anyone she wanted. He didn't have any hold over her.

"Tanya Wilcox," Carter said slowly and waited for Richards to take his eyes off Lila.

Richards turned to Carter. "She's Rossini's mistress and lives a very high-dollar lifestyle. We double-checked her and couldn't find anything that connected her to the fire. We had tons on her and Rossini, but not the fire."

"Philip Boyd."

"He's the electrician who did the work in the gallery for Ms. Colton?"

"Yes."

"What about him?"

Carter was getting to Richards. He pulled out his laptop from his bag and clicked it on.

"He's Tanya Wilcox's brother."

Richards shook his head. "I'm sure we would have caught that."

"You didn't, and you didn't catch that he has a record."

"No, that can't be correct." Richards tapped a few keys on his computer. "There's nothing on Philip Boyd."

"Try Daniel Philip Boyd."

"Dammit!" Richards hit the table with his fist. "How did this slip by us? Are you sure these names are correct?"

"You can continue to investigate if you want to make sure, but I talked to him a little while ago and I believe we have the correct man. Although everything is pointing to him right now, I don't believe he's our guy. He's trying to turn his life around and I don't think Tanya Wilcox would allow Rossini to put the screws to her brother. The first thing would be to check his banking account to see if any money was deposited besides his weekly check."

"We did that. Nothing else showed up. We couldn't find motive on Boyd unless he was paid in cash and has it hidden somewhere."

"It's not Boyd," Carter said. "I was told this in confidence, and you might check it out. It's part of my conversation with Philip. I made some notes and I'm sending them to you."

Carter glanced at Lila and she was reading the headlines of the newspaper. How agonizing it must be to have her family's affairs splashed all over the newspaper for the public to read.

"Damn! Now we have motive."

"What do you think it would cost Rossini to replace the wiring, the insulation and the plumbing in the building?" Carter asked. "And why wasn't the defunct wiring noticed by building inspectors and electricians?"

"The gallery is in a good location and it would cost Rossini a bundle to put in all those repairs. Money is the answer to the second part of that question. I think you mentioned that a time or two."

Carter packed up his laptop and got to his feet. "We have work to do."

"And I hope by the end of this week we'll know who set fire to the gallery. First, I'm going to talk to Rossini about Philip Boyd and get his response. I know he's not going to come out and admit to hiring Boyd to set the fire. I just want to make him nervous. And then I'm going to talk to Boyd, and don't worry—I'm not arresting anybody."

"You might interview Sapp. When Philip told him

about the defunct wiring, he was told to forget it, that it was a Rossini building. And today he was real defensive on Philip's behalf for some reason. Instead of telling him to cooperate, he told him to do just the opposite. I thought that was odd for a man not to step up and guide this young man to keep him out of trouble."

"I asked him some questions before and he bragged about Boyd. Said he was one of the best workers he'd ever had. Call if anything pops up."

"See you later," Carter said, and Lila tucked the newspaper under her arm.

Richards noticed the paper. "Sorry about that, Ms. Colton. Your grandmother is determined to bring the other Colton family to their knees to pay for what has been done to her and her sons. Everyone is interested in the outcome."

"Yeah," she replied as they walked toward the door.

"Maybe when this is all over, you and I could go out for a drink. It would be my way of apologizing for my big gaffe."

"Uh…maybe."

"Hope your arm is better."

"Yes, it is. Thank you."

Carter watched her as they walked to the car. Was she serious? She would actually go out for a drink with the man? Had he misjudged her?

"You seem a little down."

"Why wouldn't I be down? I have to read that crap almost every day, and Carin is… Oh, she makes me so angry in how she thinks we should all march in line to her step."

"You have a new fan. That should cheer you up."

"You mean Richards?"

"Yes. I think he's interested in you."

"Carter, you're giving me a headache," she said with a frown as she slid into the passenger side of the car. "Isn't he married?"

"I don't know. The people I've talked to since I've been here have said that his work is his life."

"He's a lot older than me."

"What? You're thinking about him?"

"You brought him up."

"I did, and I don't have any right to judge you or make comments about the men you date. I'll be leaving in a few days anyway."

His stomach clenched as he said the words and he wanted to yank them back. How could she be interested in Richards? How could she think of anyone else? That was when the lightning rod of reality struck him. She would be dating other guys, and the thought made him feel ill. Could he be falling in love?

Lila got a call from Savon, and Carter dropped her at the town house to get her car. Her friend had three more listings for Lila to look at and the Realtor had given her the keys. Savon wanted them desperately to rent something, but they were all too expensive. And she hated to make big decisions when she didn't have any idea of what her future would be. Her whole life hung in the balance. They had made progress, thanks to Carter, but they still didn't have a suspect in jail.

They stopped at Colectivo Coffee Shop on Clark Street, not far from where she lived, and went over their options. The patio under the brown awning was fresh and inviting, so they sat there and ordered their favorite coffee.

"You're not even trying, Lila. You've vetoed everything before we've even had a chance to really look at the property."

"I know and that's not fair to you, but my future is very insecure."

"You were very positive about what Carter was doing and you felt sure the arsonist would be caught soon."

"Yes. It was all positive, but the deeper Carter dug, more suspects kept popping up. It's very frustrating."

"This is about something else. You're not usually like this. It has to be Carter. Did you have an argument?"

"He thinks he has the right to tell me who I can date." The words came spewing out before she could stop them.

Savon's eyes grew big. "What? Aren't you dating Carter?"

"He's leaving on Friday and I don't know if I'll ever see him again." She might never see him again. Tears stung the backs of her eyes.

"You knew that before, though."

"I knew he would be leaving, but I had no idea he would have an opinion on who I can date."

"This sounds too complicated for me. One guy at a time is all I can handle." When Savon realized how that sounded, she burst out laughing, and Lila joined in. They ordered a specialty beer and Lila got into a better mood. They talked on and on and then ordered nachos. She'd known all along that Carter was leaving. She didn't understand why he was jealous. That was what it all boiled down to—his jealousy. He had no right to be jealous if he was leaving.

"Is there ever a perfect relationship?" she asked, sipping the beer.

"No. Remember that jerk you dated in college?"

"Don't go there." Lila popped a nacho in her mouth and thought how different Carter was from the other men she'd dated, not that there were a lot. But he'd touched a part of her that had been waiting for someone to love. She loved him. There was no way to explain the obsession of her heart. She had to let go.

The neon sign blinked the time. It had to be wrong. "Is it really six o'clock?"

"Yes, it is, and I have a date at nine."

"I had no idea it was this late and that we had been talking this long. I have to go." Carter was probably worried about her, but he didn't call. That bugged her even more.

Savon leaned in close and whispered, "I don't know if you've noticed, but we're a little tipsy."

"I'll call a cab."

They ordered coffee to go. During her cab ride home, she wanted to think reasonably instead of getting clogged up with happy-ever-after. When she entered the town house, the lights were on and Carter was at the kitchen table on his laptop.

"Sorry, I'm a little late."

"You don't owe me an explanation."

The tension was so thick that she'd need a snowplow to get through it. She carefully placed her purse on the sofa. He wasn't going to do this and make her feel guilty. She walked to the table.

"Are you upset that Richards asked me out for a drink?"

"Of course not. That's your decision, not mine."

"Even though we've only known each other a small period of time, I feel like we could talk about anything. And that we can be honest. I'm aware your plans are to leave on Friday, and that will hurt. I've gotten used to you being here and it's been nice. But I also understand your reasons and I hope you would understand mine and realize I have no desire to go out with Richards. We've gotten to know each other so well. This jealousy is out of place."

"I'm sorry." He closed the laptop. "You're right. It's totally out of place, but I never expected to feel this way and I'm not good at dealing with it or saying goodbye to someone I care about."

"Then why get mad at me?"

"Because I just want to smash my fist into Richards's face at the way he looked at you."

"And that makes you mad at me?"

"Lila," he sighed. "I don't know what to say."

"How about 'I love you' or 'I want to spend forever with you'? Anything like that would work."

He ran a hand through his hair. "It's not that simple."

"To me, it is." She waited for more, but it seemed there wasn't anything he had left to say. "I think you better sleep in your room tonight and until you leave."

Chapter 14

The next morning, Carter had breakfast ready when Lila came into the kitchen. She held a hand to her head. "I don't usually drink that much. I need coffee."

"Are you still upset with me?" he asked as he handed her a cup. "I was out of line."

"Yes, you were. Your jealousy threw me."

He carried their plates to the table. "I don't have a response for that. It threw me, too."

"Let's forget about it and enjoy the time we have left together." She stared at the plate in front of her. "I'm going to miss this. It was nice having you around, but I've finally accepted that you'll be leaving on Friday." That sounded natural and not like her heart was breaking.

"I talked to Neil last night and I definitely will be leaving. I have an eleven o'clock flight out of O'Hare. I don't want our relationship to end on a sour note."

She took a sip of coffee. "I hope one day you take an honest look at what it really meant."

"Lila—"

"It's okay, Carter. I won't press you for anything, but I will say I have enjoyed this time with you, and I don't regret a minute. If you say it's over, it's over. I'm not the clinging kind."

"I don't regret a minute, either, just that I might have hurt you."

Lila thought it best to skip the topic. It wasn't getting them anywhere. "Do you have any more information on the fire?"

"I'm totally committed to that until my plane leaves. I'm waiting on a call from Richards to see how his interviews turned out yesterday."

"And I'm going to get dressed and meet Savon. She's really pushing me to rent a new place."

"Then do it. Go forward. I believe it's clear to everyone that you're not the arsonist and you can make plans for the future."

Lila went upstairs and Carter sat for a long time thinking about their relationship. They had a perfect relationship. How long did perfect last? She was easy to talk to and to share his life with. And again, how long did that last? Why was he so afraid it would end? That was his problem. He couldn't put a finger on what scared him so much. People got divorced every day and moved on. He had nothing to move on from except...

He picked up his phone and called his parents for the first time in three months.

"Hi, Mom. It's Carter."

"Oh, my goodness, George," she shouted to his father. "It's our son. Come talk to him."

"How are you guys doing?"

"It's so lovely here. I wish you could see it. We spent the whole day on the yacht yesterday and everybody says I look so much younger and tanned. I think it's getting away from the crowds and the noise, and out here we have time to just be quiet and enjoy the sunshine in an easygoing lifestyle. It was certainly the right decision for us. We're not so edgy all the time."

"Let me talk," his father said.

"I'm talking. You can talk when I'm through."

"Then why did you call me?"

"Okay. Here he is."

"Hey, son. How you doing?"

Carter smiled. It was reminiscent of so many days of his childhood, the two of them trying to talk over each other.

"I'm doing good. I caught a forger in Chicago and I'm getting ready to move on to London."

"You lead an exciting life. I'm proud of you, son," his father said.

"Yeah, but sometimes it gets frustrating. I met this girl…"

"Dorian, he's met a girl."

"A real live girl, not a criminal or anyone like that?" his mother asked.

Carter closed his eyes and groaned. Why had he thought he could have a normal conversation with his parents? Their thoughts always went off in a different direction and it wasn't his direction.

"Yes, she's a live girl. What did you think she was?"

"Someone who can have babies?" His mom was back on the phone.

"Babies? You never mentioned babies before."

"Our friends here just had a new grandbaby and she's so sweet. I told your father we'd probably never have one because Carter is never settling down."

"Is this Dorian Finch?" His mother had thrown him for a loop, because she never talked about having grandchildren. At times, she didn't even seem to want the son she had. Had he been looking back and seeing a fake life?

"Don't be silly. I like babies, just like everyone else. When you were small, I had to work so we could make a living. It's expensive to live in New York, but it was close to my job and your father's, and it was near the school we wanted you to go to."

"Then why leave me so much with Mrs. Kinkoski? I loved her, but I would've liked to spend more time with my parents."

"Now, Carter, don't bring all that up. We were in a social circle and we had to keep up and we were young and enjoyed it. You were well taken care of and Mrs. Kinkoski taught you to play chess. Remember all the walks you took her on because she was afraid to walk alone?"

"She was like my grandmother."

"Exactly. Now tell me about this girl."

"It's nothing, really. I was going to tell Dad she owns a gallery and we worked together to catch the forger. She's a very nice lady."

"But nothing serious?"

"No, Mom, nothing serious."

A long sigh filled his ear. "Talk to him, George."

"You had to bring up babies and scare him away."

"I'm here, Dad." He had to get his dad's attention, and the only way to do that was to shout into the phone as his parents argued with each other.

"Hey, son, how about coming home for Thanksgiving?"

Now he knew he had the wrong number. His mother did not cook or celebrate holidays with food. What was up?

"Mom's cooking?"

"She has been taking cooking lessons and plans on making a big Thanksgiving dinner, and it would be nice to have you home. It would be even better to see you."

He swallowed. "It will be great to see you, too. I'll plan to be there. Who else have you invited?" As he'd gotten older, strange women tended to show up at his parents' and it didn't take long to figure it out. His parents were playing matchmakers.

"Just our neighbors. Your mother doesn't want to invite too many people in her first attempt at Thanksgiving dinner. She wants them to meet our handsome son."

"Dad, I met them when I came for Christmas two years ago."

"Yeah, but don't tell your mother," he whispered into the phone. "They're bringing their niece."

"How does that concern me?"

"Never mind. Here's your mother."

They talked a few minutes longer and Carter was left holding the phone and wondering if he would ever understand his parents. That was probably true for all kids. There was no doubt his parents loved him, but he never felt their love because his parents had been so busy, and he'd wanted their full attention. As an only child, he'd wanted it even more. Wow! The mist on his rearview mirror cleared.

Lila came back in skinny jeans and a colorful blouse tucked in at the waist and wearing low ankle boots. Her hair, as usual, was twisted at her nape and she looked as beautiful as he'd ever seen her. It was no wonder Richards couldn't take his eyes off her.

"That was my parents," he said, slipping the phone into his pocket.

"You were talking to your parents?" She didn't disguise the shock in her voice.

"Yes. They want me to come home for Thanksgiving."

"That's nice and I hope you go."

"I told them I would."

"If I can manage a relationship with my father, you can manage one with your parents. It just takes a lot of gritting your teeth," Lila said.

He smiled at her and dreaded the days ahead. He would miss her.

"Do you have time to drop me at the coffee shop to get my car?"

"Sure, no problem. Just let me put these dishes in the dishwasher."

"You know, you can leave dishes in the sink sometimes. I do it when I'm in a rush, but I think you have a 'perfect' problem. Everything has to be perfect. And no one is and no one will ever be."

"It's just… You let me stay here and I appreciate it and want to keep things tidy," Carter said.

"You can sing that song to someone else, Mr. Perfect. Let's go. It's going to take most of the day to wake up Savon. She has appointments for us to see more buildings."

Carter dropped her off in the parking lot and there were only two cars there. She waved as she ran to her car and he watched her fluid movements. *Perfect.* She had said he was perfect. Maybe he tried to be just a little too much. He always wanted his parents' apartment in New York to be neat when his parents came home so they wouldn't yell at him. Not that they yelled that much, but he always wanted their approval, their attention. *Oh, man, you might need a therapist.* The woman walking away might be the only person who saw him as he was, a man with faults and dreams and a heart that may never be the same again.

She asked him to be honest. Why was he jealous of Richards? Carter didn't want her to be with anyone else. There it was. Honesty. It burned like Tennessee bourbon going down strong.

He entered the offices of the arson investigators of the fire department and noticed by the big clock on the wall that it wasn't even nine o'clock. Richards was hard at work, his head bent over a laptop, his tie hanging loose and his grayish hair tousled as if it hadn't been combed in a while.

"Do you ever go home?" He had nothing against Richards. He just wanted to see this case through to the end for Lila. Carter's problems were within and he was the only one who could fix them.

"Now, that's a good question." Richards stood for another cup of coffee and handed Carter one. "When I was with my wife, I thought I had a home, but my wife informed me that since I was never there, I could move out. I moved in with my mom so I could pay for my kid's college. So to answer your question, I don't know where home is anymore."

Home was a place Carter shouldn't have brought up. It weighed heavily upon him. "Have you found out anything?"

Richards touched a big file on his left. "Enough to put Rossini away for a long time."

"Who was the arsonist?"

"I haven't tied that one down yet. I'm trying to tie up all the loose ends and there are a lot of loose ends. Rossini packed an attitude at the interview and Philip wouldn't say much about his sister's boyfriend except to say that the wiring needed attention. I can't arrest a man for that. I have Sapp coming in at nine thirty. Thanks for that tip. It's proving very lucrative. My guess is that it's someone who works for Rossini. I don't believe Sapp would personally place the device for Rossini. But then again, I don't know how much money was involved. I'm waiting on Sapp's financial records and I should have them sometime this morning."

"So Rossini wanted the gallery torched? Why? Have you answered that yet?"

Richards flipped through the folder. "The insurance payout on that building would be one-point-two million, a little over what it's worth. I'm leaning heavily on that answer."

A knock at the door interrupted him and a woman poked her head around. "Sorry, sir, but Sapp is in the interview room."

"Thanks." Richards got to his feet. "Let's shake some answers loose. Look at your laptop. I just sent you some information on Sapp."

While Carter went over the information, Richards took a moment to go to the bathroom to freshen up. As they walked into the interview room, Sapp got to his feet. "What's this bull about? I had nothing to do with the fire."

"Sit down, Mr. Sapp, and take a deep breath," Richards told him as they took seats around a metal table. "Mr. Finch and I would just like to ask you some questions." He glanced from Finch to Sapp. "You do know Mr. Finch?"

"Yes, I know him. I don't understand what's his involvement in this case. He works in a different field. And, yes, I looked him up."

"Not that I owe you an answer, but Mr. Finch has worked very closely with the fire department since the fire happened. We have now caught the forger and Mr. Finch is staying on the case until we catch the arsonist. But we can end this meeting quickly if you'll answer one question."

"What?"

"Tell me and Mr. Finch who set the fire at the Weston Street Gallery."

"How am I supposed to know that?"

Carter glanced at his laptop. "You do a lot of work for Mr. Rossini?"

"Yes. He's a good customer."

"You've actually been working for him for over twenty years."

"I guess. I haven't added it up."

"Mr. Rossini has been paying invoices from Sapp Electric for twenty-one years. Is that correct?"

"I guess it is."

"In all the years Rossini has owned the building and

your company has done work at that site, which had previously been a bank, an investment company and a gallery, no one who works for you has written up a report for the defunct wiring? Or the bad insulation?"

"It wasn't reported to my office?"

A tap sounded at the door and Richards bellowed, "Come in."

An assistant came in and handed Richards some papers. Richards studied them for a second and glanced at Sapp. "Do you want to do this the easy way or the hard way, as they say?"

Richards laid one of the papers on the table and turned it around so Sapp could see it. "Does that look familiar?"

Sapp glanced at it and turned away. "No."

Carter could see clearly what it was: burned parts of a device, probably from a very tiny pipe bomb.

"Pieces of this device were found in your work area in your electrical business. Someone bought it and put it together in your building. Do you want to tell me anything?"

"I want a lawyer."

"Stand up, Mr. Sapp. You're under arrest for arson. You have the right to remain silent. Anything you say can and will be held against you…"

As Richards continued to read Sapp his Miranda rights, an officer came in and put cuffs on him.

"I didn't do this," Sapp said, his face red and deviant. "You won't find my fingerprints anywhere on the device. I didn't do it."

"Think about it, Sapp. Rossini's going to let you take the fall." Carter pointed out the obvious, but Sapp didn't take the bait.

As they walked back to Richards's office, Carter said, "It was too easy. I expected a lot more indignation from Sapp. What's his motive?"

Richards ran his hands through his hair. "That one has me and I'm going to need a good one to take this to court. Sapp stood to gain nothing from the fire. Rossini is the only one who profits." He handed Carter the rest of the papers in his hand.

"Interesting. Ten thousand cash was deposited into Sapp's account the day before the fire and no way to trace it. This kind of sets him up."

Richards reached for his jacket behind him. "I got a lot more legwork on this one. Just when you think all the answers arc clear, they're not. If you have any suggestions, just let me know. I won't be going home tonight, either."

Shuffling into the jacket, Richards asked, "Where's Ms. Colton today?"

Carter kept his emotions in check. "She's looking for a new place of business."

"That's probably a wise idea."

"It might be an even wiser idea to let the insurance company know Ms. Colton is not involved in any way in starting the fire."

Richards nodded.

At least when Carter left he would know that Lila would not be prosecuted. But he was hoping before that time came that the suspect would be arrested and in jail.

When Lila made it to Savon's apartment, she was surprised to find her up and drinking coffee.

Savon winced. "Who had the idea to try the beer?"

"You."

"And I also made appointments at ten and eleven, so we better hurry," Savon said.

For the next two hours, they looked around properties that were priced out of their range and would need a lot of renovations. She tried not to get too down, but depression was one big wave washing over her.

This time they went to a coffee shop to get a sandwich for lunch and go over their options once more. She hesitated in telling Savon that she wasn't all that crazy about spending so much money and not having anything to back it up. First, they would have to be able to pay the rent. Second, they would need to renovate as quickly as possible. Construction workers were known to be late, late, late.

"Our best option is still the jewelry store," Savon pointed out.

"Yeah, but first, please try to understand where I'm coming from. Carter feels that the arsonist will soon be caught, and I'd like to get that behind me before I jump into something else."

"When is Carter leaving?"

"On Friday. His plane leaves at eleven."

"That's going to be a rough day for you. We'll have a margarita night. No more beer."

"It's going to take more than a few margaritas."

"I'm sorry, Lila." Savon reached across the table and touched Lila's hand. They'd always been good friends and Lila hoped that would never change, but she couldn't just come out and tell her that her interest wasn't in the gallery anymore. She would soon, though.

Savon fiddled with her napkin, folding it over and over. "Do you mind if I continue looking for work?"

"No, no. Go ahead. You have to find a way to make a living."

"You're talking like it's over."

Lila tried not to fidget. "I'm just not into it right now. Maybe I need a little more time. I don't know." That was what best friends were: they made life easier. And that was what Savon had just done.

"It's a heartache, that's what it is, and it will take more than time," Savon pointed out.

"Please don't say that. I told myself going into this relationship that I could just walk away. Be tough like a man. That's laughable. Women can't just turn off their feelings. It's all or nothing. Why didn't I realize that sooner?"

"You aren't the only one involved in the relationship. It's not going to be easy for him, either."

"I don't want him to be forced to stay here because of me."

"Why not? Grab him while you can."

Lila chuckled. How she wished it was that easy.

Savon leaned over. "There's a man staring at you."

Lila lifted an eyebrow. "Is he handsome?"

"Very. Tall. Dark blond hair that curls into his collar."

She turned to look and saw it was Heath Colton, the oldest son of Ernest Colton and president of Colton Connections. "I'll be back." She placed her napkin on the table and walked over to him. "It's nice to see you." They shook hands.

"Our offices are not far from here and I stopped in for coffee. I'll be working late tonight." He grimaced.

"Is that a regular thing?"

"No, but your grandmother is putting pressure on

us now. She's got the media's attention and they won't leave us alone. She's hoping we'll cave and give in to an earlier court date."

"Don't do that." The words came out before she could stop them, but then, she didn't know why she would want to. Maybe family loyalty should mean something. The family had never meant anything to her grandmother.

"That's nice of you to say. We don't plan on giving up anytime soon."

"Should I be indignant?" she asked with a laugh in her voice, and it must've gotten to him.

He smiled. "I wish we had the time to get to know each other as a family."

"We are family, just a little different from most."

"Thank you, Lila. I needed to hear that today. Take care."

All the way home, she thought about the other Coltons, and it took her mind off Carter. At least for a moment. She saw his car was back at the town house and her heart leaped at the thought that she had a little more time with him.

Carter was on his laptop at the table, engrossed in whatever was on the screen. Probably studying the painting he was asked to authenticate in London. In a polo shirt and jeans, he looked right at home. In her home. Would he never want a family and a home?

"Hey, you're home. Did you find anything?"

She dropped her purse into a chair. "No, and I finally had to admit that my heart's not in it right now. I need capital before I can do anything else. I'm trying to be wise." She kicked off her shoes and found a comfy spot on the sofa.

"You're deep in thought."

"I was thinking about the other Coltons. Savon and I had lunch at a small coffee shop and Heath Colton walked in to get coffee. He's the head of the family and I could see the role is taking a toll on him, but they are a close-knit family. I just wish my grandmother..." She got up and paced. "There is something about that will. Why hasn't it shown up before? If my grandmother knew about it, what took her so long to confront the other Coltons? There's no one greedier than her. She would have no problem taking the money and using it for her own purpose. I just don't understand how this will was somewhere and no one knew about it."

"Are you thinking forgery?"

"Forgery! That's it."

"Who has a copy of the will?"

"It was in the safe at Ernest and Alfred's offices, and now I guess it's in Heath's."

"Would he have the original?"

Lila looked at him and a light bulb finally went off in her head. Could Carter tell them if it was a fake? She could ask him. He was getting ready to leave. It,...

"I'm not in the signature field, but I know a couple of experts who might be able to help you or, more specifically, the other Coltons. Probably the most important thing they could do would be to test the ink. It would have to be the same age as Dean Colton's signature. Everyone puts different pressure on the pen when they write, and that can be tested, too. An expert will run several tests to validate that it is the original will of Dean Colton. Of course, after looking at it, sometimes, if you know what you're looking for, it's obvious to the eye."

"I'm probably stepping out of my bounds, but would you recommend someone to Heath?"

"Sure, if he's interested." He looked directly at her. "Are you sure about this? It will go against your family."

"Yeah, that." She paced again, that thought going around in her head. "If it's a fake, everyone on both sides of the Colton family needs to know."

"Sounds reasonable."

"Then you'll do it?"

"For you, I will talk to Heath and offer my advice."

"You would do that?"

"For you, I would do just about anything." Except stay. Their eyes collided as if they were thinking the same thing; she held on to him with all her strength and he kept pulling away. They couldn't continue the push and pull. Their relationship wasn't about that. It was about their hearts. Carter had to decide what he wanted and he couldn't do that while she was hanging on. She had to let go, and she'd known that for some time. And she had to do it with a smile, which might prove the hardest thing she would ever have to do.

Chapter 15

Before doing anything, Lila called her brother and cousins to tell them what she had in mind. They thought it was a great idea. Everyone needed to know if it was a forgery. She then called Heath. He was startled at first but listened to what she had to say. He then talked to Carter and Carter gave him a name and a phone number and told him to use his name, if needed.

The next morning, Carter went over to Heath's office because he had asked him to. Carter looked at the original will and spoke to his expert friend on Zoom. Heath was afraid he wouldn't be able to give the expert enough detail to takc thc case. The expert said parts of the document looked doctored and agreed to delve further into it and ask some of his colleagues to participate. It was a win-win all around. It would give everyone time, except her grandmother. Lila expected a call at any minute.

She and Carter were worlds apart and acted more like friends than lovers. Last night they'd talked and talked about Sapp's involvement with the fire. It didn't make sense and they couldn't figure it out. Like always, it was nice to have someone to share her life with. They shied away from a personal level. He slept in the guest room and she slept in hers, just as if their nights together had never happened. In two days he would be gone and she wondered if she would ever get used to that.

That morning, Lila had an appointment with the insurance agent about her car. It wouldn't take long. Her cell rang as she reached for another cup of coffee. Rossini Realty? Why would they be calling her? The only way to find out was to answer.

"Hello, Ms. Colton. I'm Mona Tibbs, Mr. Rossini's secretary, and I would like to go over some things with you."

"Like what?"

"We have a list of the items that were taken out of the safe and we need your signature to say that everything is correct so Mr. Rossini couldn't be held liable if items come up missing."

"You need me to sign a piece of paper?"

"Yes. They are tearing down the big safe tomorrow and I'm trying to get all these papers in order."

It sounded strange to Lila, but she agreed to meet in Rossini's office in thirty minutes. She should call Carter, but she knew he was busy with Heath. He was meeting her later at Richards's office to see if they could get a confession out of Sapp. He had no reason to burn down her gallery. He profited nothing.

As she was going out the door, her phone rang again. "Hey, you okay?" Savon asked.

"Yes, I'm fine. You don't have to worry about me."

"I have two job interviews today."

"Good for you."

"But if you change your mind, please let me know."

"Rossini's secretary called and I'm headed there to sign some papers."

"For what?"

"About the inventory in the safe. He wants to make sure that I can't come back and sue him for a missing item."

"He's covering his butt."

"I'll talk to you later and it's great about the job interviews. Let me know how they go."

Rossini Realty was in a large two-story sparkling and bright building with many office spaces. The glass and steel made it stand out. Rossini occupied the upstairs, which she'd heard through the grapevine, but she wasn't sure where to go. He'd always come to the gallery for the rent, and when she'd signed the lease, they'd done it at the gallery.

A huge chandelier hung over her head. In front of her was a desk with pamphlets on it. She glanced at a few, then noticed a map on the wall of all the offices. She studied it and found Rossini's office was right above her head.

She went up the stairs to double doors leading to his office. It said so in gold letters. Opening the door, she found a big foyer and a receptionist's desk, but no receptionist. She looked around and took a seat in a plush chair, hoping the receptionist would return.

At the sound of heels tapping against the wood

flooring, Lila got to her feet. A blonde with long hair and dark eyes came into the room and offered her hand. The woman was the opposite of what Lila had been expecting.

"Mona Tibbs. Come this way."

She led her into a large office, and Lila noticed some of the artwork had been bought from her gallery. Maybe he wasn't such a scumbag.

"Have a seat," Ms. Tibbs said and handed her a document. "Mr. Rossini just needs to know if this is correct."

Lila sat and pulled a file out of her purse. She compared the two documents and noted they were the same.

"If they're the same and you're satisfied with it, please sign at the bottom."

She scribbled her name and said, "I would like a copy."

"Yes, of course. My printer is broken. I'll go down the hall to make a copy."

The woman disappeared out the door and Lila had an uneasy feeling. She got up and looked at the paintings she'd bought in France. It had been a good deal. What was taking so long? She walked into the receptionist's office. No one was there, either.

She opened the door to the landing and saw Walter Fox coming through the big double-door entrance below. There was no mistaking him. He always walked with quick steps as if he was in a hurry. His vests on his suits were an eye catcher, the fabric interwoven with different colors of threads and ribbons. It was topped off with a bow tie and a fedora. He was a colorful character.

She quickly jumped back so he couldn't see her. Mona had a private bathroom and Lila hurried there. After several minutes, she went back to the secretary's office to get her copy. Pulling out her phone, she started to call Carter, but then she heard voices and clicked off.

"What the hell are you doing here?" That was Rossini's voice.

The door was slightly ajar, and Lila took a peek to see if she could see them.

"I want my money." Fox's beady eyes narrowed in anger.

"Haven't you heard Sapp's been arrested?"

"Everything is clear now for you to get the insurance money, just like we planned, and I want my share. I need to get out of town."

"I'm not giving you anything until the police are off my back."

"You can pay me ten thousand now and pay me the rest later. No one knows what really happened that night and it will stay that way if I get my money. Do you know what I'm talking about, Lou?"

"You sorry—" Lou stopped and then started talking again. "They're going to arrest you anyway. The forger gave you up, Walter. Money is not going to save you now."

"It was a stupid idea. I don't know why I let you talk me into it."

"You kept selling those fakes and were afraid of getting caught. Finch was on your trail and it was just a matter of time. When you get greedy, bad things happen. Now get out of my office."

"I'm not going anywhere until you give me the

money." Walter pulled out a small gun from his jacket pocket.

Lila gasped before she knew it. She covered her mouth, but it was too late. Rossini yanked open the door. "Walter, we have company, the lovely Ms. Colton." He grabbed her arm and almost flung her into the room. Catching Walter off guard, Rossini swiftly took the gun from him.

"What are you doing?"

"Shut up, Walter. The better question is, why is Ms. Colton eavesdropping?"

Lila tried to swallow and then she tried to speak, but fear had a death grip on her throat. She managed to sputter out, "You…set…the fire. You burned down your own building and everything I own for no reason but money. You are scum, Rossini!"

"Shut up." The gun wavered in Rossini's hand. "What are you doing in my secretary's office?"

"She…called me."

"Why?"

"You told her to."

"What?"

"To sign a document that stated I took all of my belongings out of the safe. She went to make a copy and I heard you and Mr. Fox talking." She glanced at Mr. Fox. "How could you take profit from an old man who had such talent? You are more than scum."

"Ms. Colton, my secretary was supposed to call you this afternoon. Why are you here now? Who sent you? Finch? Richards?"

"I told you it was your secretary…"

"Where's the paper?"

"Your secretary has it. She went to make a copy."

"Shut up." A dark shade of red colored his face. "Get the duct tape out of the bottom drawer of my desk."

Duct tape? She'd seen all kinds of movies and TV shows where victims were duct-taped and then their bodies were disposed of, dead or alive. Chills popped out on her skin. She would not make this easy. She bolted for the front door. Rossini caught her and tumbled to the area rug in front of his desk. She saw stars for a second.

"Get the tape, Walter."

She recovered quickly, kicking out with her feet, trying to dislodge Rossini from her back. Her hand hit the gun and it went flying.

"Walter!"

She scooted toward the gun and Rossini put a knee in her back. She screamed in pain just as duct tape went around her wrists and then her ankles. She still didn't give up. She raised both arms to hit Rossini as Fox slapped duct tape across her mouth. Fear held her motionless and a scream died in her throat. What were they going to do to her?

"Now what?" Mr. Fox asked.

"Open the closet door," Rossini ordered.

No, no, no! She couldn't breathe. She would suffocate.

Carter left Heath's office and called Lila. She didn't answer and that puzzled him. She had a meeting with the insurance guy and then she would wait for his call. Five minutes later, he called again and still didn't get a response. Where could she be? The meeting could have lasted longer than she'd expected, but she would still answer her phone.

He tried Savon. "Have you heard from Lila?"

"Earlier this morning."

"Did she say where she was going?"

"She had to meet with the insurance agent, but Rossini's secretary called and needed her signature."

"On what?"

"Basically it was a document that said everything that was in the safe is now in her custody."

"Okay, thanks."

"Is anything wrong?"

"I don't know, but I'll call you later."

He called Richards and told him the story. "You think something's up?"

"Yes, I do. I'm going over there and I would like backup."

"I'll meet you there. Don't go in without me."

It didn't take Carter long to reach Rossini Realty. He drove into a parking spot, and Richards drove in right beside him, followed by a police car. The man had covered his bases. Carter hurried in and Richards and two police officers were behind him. People stared and stretched their necks to see what was going on.

A young girl about eighteen greeted them at the receptionist's desk. She was on her phone. They walked straight through to the secretary's office. A woman with brown hair and tortoiseshell glasses got to her feet. "May I help you?"

"We're looking for Lila Colton," Richards informed her.

"I haven't seen her."

"Are you sure? Are you Rossini's secretary?"

"Yes."

"What's your name?"

"Mona Tibbs."

"Is Rossini in?"

"No. He was supposed to be, but when I got back from my beauty shop appointment, he wasn't."

This was taking too long. Carter stepped closer. "Ms. Colton came here to sign a document. Do you know anything about it?"

"Yes. Mr. Rossini told me to call her later in the afternoon to get her signature. I left the document here on my desk and when I got back it was gone. I just assumed Mr. Rossini took it."

"Where is Rossini's office?" Carter asked.

She pointed to the door on the left. Richards opened it and they went inside. They looked around at the lavish office with mahogany furniture, hardwood floors and windows from ceiling to the floor that looked out onto Chicago. "Look at that view," Richards said.

"Concentrate, Richards. Where's Lila?"

Richards scratched his head. "She came here to meet with the secretary, but Ms. Tibbs hasn't seen her. Do you think she's lying?"

"No. She seemed more confused than lying."

Richards picked up a gold paperweight from the desk. "Twenty-four-karat gold. Nice gift." Richards cleared his throat. "If she didn't meet Ms. Tibbs, who did she meet?"

"Whoever was in the office, and that's a chilling thought. Rossini was supposed to be here, so I can only conclude that it was Rossini. Now, where did he take her? Let's check the security cameras. I noticed them on the way in." Carter hurried back to the secretary. "We'd like to look at the security cameras footage."

"You'll need a warrant for that."

Carter leaned over and said, "If you don't tell me where the security cameras footage is, I'm going to make sure your name is on the indictment. Ms. Colton told a friend she was going to a meeting with you and that's the last we've heard from her. Where do I find the footage?"

"I'm not involved in this. I'm just Rossini's secretary." She ran her hand up her arm in a nervous gesture.

"Do you know what jail is like?" Carter asked.

Her face turned a pearly white. "Down the hall, last door. Tell Steve I sent you."

"Call him."

Carter ran down the hall and into the room. A young man got to his feet. "What's this about?"

They showed him their credentials. "We need to see the footage from nine o'clock this morning."

"Sure. I guess you talked to Mr. Rossini. He gets very upset if we don't follow the rules and the rule is you need a warrant." A smug expression told its own story. He had them.

Just when Carter thought all hope was lost, the door opened and an officer came in with a piece of paper in his hand. He handed it to Richards.

He waved the warrant in front of the young man. "Is this what you need, you little piece of crap?"

"I have to follow the rules or I'll get fired."

"Sit down and start showing us pictures."

"Let's start with the camera that faces Rossini's office," Carter said. "That should take less time.

"How did you get that so fast?" Carter whispered to Richards.

"It helps when you've been around for twenty years."

The young man tapped on the keyboard, no smug expression. Carter and Richards stood, one over each shoulder of the guy, and watched as a few people entered the office. Two businessmen who the young man said had offices at Rossini Realty. A janitor and cleaning crew flashed across the screen and then...

"Stop it," Carter asked. "Back it up." The young man did as asked and Carter pointed to the screen. "That's Tanya Wilcox. I'm almost positive, but she's wearing a blond wig. What the...? Keep going."

Soon after, Ms. Tibbs came out. A minute or two later, Carter asked him to stop again. Lila was on screen. She opened the door of the office and went in. "That's it. We don't have cameras inside the offices. That would violate a person's privacy." The film kept rolling.

"Wait. There's Tanya Wilcox again in the wig, leaving alone."

After a minute, Carter said, "Stop it." He looked at Richards. "Did you see him?"

"Yeah. Fox went into the office."

"Does Mr. Rossini have a private entrance?" he asked the man.

"Of course. He has a private parking space in back and can go straight into his office."

"So we won't find him on these tapes?"

The man shook his head. "Not likely."

"Do security cameras cover the back?"

"Yes." He sighed.

"Bring them up from about nine this morning."

"I'm sure to lose my job," the young man mumbled under his breath.

It didn't take long for the photos to come up. Rossini and Fox came out of the office, hurried down the stairs and got into Rossini's car.

"Now, isn't that something?" Richards said.

"But Lila's not with them." A tremor of fear ran through him. "Where is she? She went in, but she didn't come out. She still has to be in there."

"I'll call in more officers and search every inch of this place." Richards looked at Carter. "Do you have a photo of Ms. Colton?"

"No, but I know somebody who would." He called Savon and she sent him a photo. She wanted to talk, but he told her he didn't know anything. He had to get back to searching for Lila and he couldn't let himself get involved in endless conversations.

He showed the young man the photo from his phone. "Transfer it and keep looking for this woman."

"Wow. Now I know why you're anxious to see her. She's gorgeous."

"Shut up," Carter told him with a spark of anger.

"Run off some copies for us," Richards said.

"I don't run a photography shop," the young man replied.

Richards glanced at an officer. "Arrest him for obstruction of justice."

"Wait, wait. Man, you guys have hair-trigger tempers."

"No more lip. We don't have time for it."

Carter and Richards stepped outside the room. "What's your take?" Richards asked Carter.

"She's still in there somewhere. I don't want to think

about her being hurt or anything else, but I can't be naive. I have to be realistic. She was a thorn in their side and…" He had to take a breath. Thoughts of Lila made his heart ache and his nerves stretch near the breaking point. His feelings for her had happened so suddenly. The moment he saw her standing in the gallery, looking at him with those beautiful green eyes, he was lost. He was supposed to be thinking about the Tinsley paintings, but his concentration was totally on her. If he had been doing his job, he would've seized the paintings and kept them until he could prove they were fakes. Instead, he let her keep them for the showing. That should have told him something. Now he might have lost her.

"As soon as the guy gives us the photos, I'll get officers to start searching. I'm going to shut the building down until we find her. And I've got an APB out on Rossini's car. We should catch them shortly and we'll learn more about what happened in that office."

"I'm checking Rossini's office. We must've missed something."

"Sure. Just hang on, man. We'll find her."

That was his fervent prayer.

He went back into the secretary's office with a fierce determination. "We're going to go over this again, Ms. Tibbs. Who else came into this office?"

"I don't know. I get my hair done every week on the same day at the same time and I wasn't here."

"Who was?"

"The receptionist is supposed to be here answering phones, but she's in the bathroom a lot talking to her boyfriend. Mr. Rossini was going to fire her."

"So she wasn't here earlier?"

"She was supposed to be, but when I got back, she was gone, and then later she told me she went to lunch early."

"Did she say anything about what happened while you were gone?"

"No. The less I talk to her the better."

"Someone else was here, Ms. Tibbs. Who was it?"

"I don't know what you're getting at."

"We just looked at the film and another person came into these offices. Do you still want to keep on saying you don't know?"

She frowned. "You mean Tanya?"

"Yeah, Tanya with the blond hair."

"She was here in that ridiculous wig."

Carter moved in closer, anger chewing at his insides. "Ms. Tibbs, when I said another person, that's exactly what I meant—another human being like Tanya Wilcox. Did I not make myself clear?"

"I just didn't think she was of any interest."

"Let me decide that."

"She wore a god-awful tight dress and ostentatious wig. She said she was going to surprise Mr. Rossini. A minute later, she was back in my office, complaining that he was on the phone and ignored her. She asked what I was doing and I told her I was preparing a document for Ms. Colton to sign later on this afternoon. She said she could do that and I told her no thank you. Mr. Rossini has told me several times not to let her do anything in the office. She wants to work here but he keeps refusing. His wife and his kids come in occasionally and he doesn't want her here." She let out a long breath, having used every ounce of breath she had saying what she had to.

"Wait a minute." He thought about everything she'd said and something stood out. "What time did you go to your beauty shop appointment? And remember I can check it."

"I left about ten minutes to ten. My beauty shop is just around the corner."

"Was Tanya still here?"

"Oh, yes."

"And Mr. Rossini?"

"He was in his office."

"And Ms. Colton?"

"She was never here while I was."

"Thanks." He hurried down the hall to the computer guy. "I need to know something."

"I don't work for you, Mr. Finch."

He calmly picked up the warrant on the desk. "This says you do, and if you don't comply with what I want, you'll be spending some time behind bars. Have you ever spent a night in jail?"

That line always worked and didn't take long to work this time, either.

"All right. All right. What do you want?"

He reached for a pen and paper. "I need to know the time Tanya Wilcox entered the office and the time she left. The same with Ms. Colton, Walter Fox, Ms. Tibbs and Mr. Rossini." He laid the names in front of the guy.

"You want me to do it now?"

"Like an hour ago."

"You guys don't ask for much."

Carter waited patiently until the guy handed him back the paper. "Thanks," he said and walked out. He went back into the office and studied the times. Everyone who entered the office from nine o'clock that

morning until almost eleven had come out. Lila was
the only one who hadn't. What stood out the most was
that Lila and Tanya were in there together alone for at
least fifteen minutes. What was Tanya's part in this?

"They caught Rossini and Fox, both at the airport,"
Richards announced as he entered the room. "They're
being transported to the jail. We should be able to interview them in about an hour. Rossini had a gun on
him and… It had been fired."

What?

"Now, man, don't freak out. We'll get the whole
story soon enough."

Soon enough.

He clenched both hands into fists and wanted to lash
out, wanted to hurt somebody. Lila didn't deserve this.
He sucked air into his tight chest and tried to breathe
without feeling the pain.

Chapter 16

The duct tape cut into her skin and Lila could barely breathe. The darkness closed in on her and she tried to stay calm. With the tape on her mouth, a feeling of claustrophobia washed over her. She started counting and taking slow, deep breaths to ease the feeling. Carter would find her. She kept her eyes closed to avoid the real darkness. Dust and tobacco filled her stomach with a sick feeling. She couldn't throw up. She would choke to death.

Her whole weight was on her left side and she moved around to ease the pressure on her shoulder. Depression hung on her like a dead weight, but she refused to give in to it. She moved around, making noises to try to get someone's attention. There was nothing but complete silence.

She raised her head. She heard voices. Had Rossini come back? She listened closely.

"Did you hear something?" That was Carter. Her heart almost pounded out of her chest.

"No, I didn't hear a thing." That was Richards. "Let's go to the station. They'll keep searching here."

No, no, no! They couldn't leave her here. She had to do something to get their attention.

She still had her ankle boots on and scooted until she could get her feet against the door. The first kick didn't do anything but jar her body. She drew a deep breath, raised her knees toward her chest and kicked with all her strength. The door broke away from the hinges.

"What the...? It's Lila!" Carter shouted. With his hands on the door, he yanked it away and then fell down beside her. She tried to talk but couldn't.

"Shh. Shh." He kissed her forehead. "Don't try to talk. You're the best sight I've seen in a long time."

"Is she okay?" Richards asked, leaning into the closet.

"Call an ambulance. She has duct tape on her wrists, feet and mouth. They can take it off without injuring her skin. Do you have a pocketknife? And get some water."

Richards handed him a small one and he cut the tape on her ankles and wrists so she could move freely. She wanted it off her mouth and she pointed to it.

He shook his head. "The paramedics will be here any second. You've been brave so far. Just a little more time."

How long had she been in the closet? It felt like forever, but it was probably more like an hour or so. She did her best to fight claustrophobia, but she could feel it coming on again. She had to move. She had to get out of here, and there was no way to explain that to Carter.

"Mona, do you have any lotion?" he shouted.

The woman was there instantly, and Carter massaged the lotion onto the tape and around it. Bless him. He could read her mind.

"Just stay calm and I'll try to get it off."

She nodded and raised her hands to do it herself. He caught them. "No. Give the lotion a chance to soak in. Where's the damn ambulance?"

"I can hear it in the distance," Richards replied.

Carter started at the top of her lip, the narrowest part. She pushed with her tongue as he began to peel it away. She exhaled a long breath as her top lip came away from the tape. "Carter," came out hoarsely.

He picked up the knife to cut away the loose tape. "The paramedics can do the rest."

Richards handed him a bottle of water with a straw in it. He held it to her mouth and she sucked greedily on it.

"Take it easy."

"Carter."

"Shh. The ambulance will be here soon."

"Does my family know?"

"It's all over the news."

She winced. "Did you call my mom?"

"I haven't had time and I don't know her number."

Lila quickly gave it to him. Her mother must be worried sick. How could Lila let this happen?

The paramedics rushed in, pushing a gurney. Carter helped them load her onto it. "Carter..."

"Take a deep breath." He wrapped his arms around

her and held her for a second. "I'll be right behind the ambulance after I call your mother."

"Thanks." That was all she needed. She didn't want her mother to worry more than she already had. She closed her eyes, trying to forget this nightmare.

Carter followed the gurney down the stairs and called Lila's mother. It was answered the moment it rang. "This is Carter Finch."

"Did you find Lila? Please tell me you found my daughter."

"We have. She's in an ambulance on the way to the hospital."

"Oh, my heavens. Thank you! Is she okay?"

"She looks fine, just a little shook up."

"We're on our way."

Richards shouted at Carter as he reached his car. "Where are you going?"

"Hospital. I won't be able to interview Rossini tonight. I'm staying with Lila until I know she's okay."

"I just got a call from the police station and we're not going to be able to interview anyone tonight. Rossini's lawyer is out of town and we have to wait until he arrives at about nine in the morning. Will that work for you?"

"Depends on Lila. When I looked at her scared face, I just wanted to hurt Rossini real bad, and I still do."

"That'll wear off by morning."

Carter didn't know how he would feel in the morning. So much was going on inside his head, but uppermost was his concern for Lila. She had to be okay or he would never be able to leave Chicago. That thought buzzed around in his head for a while and made him realize just how much she had come to mean to him.

He tried to join Lila in the exam room, but a nurse stopped him. Lila must have heard it. "Please let him in," she called.

She leaped into his arms and held on tight. "Did you catch Rossini and Fox?"

"Yes, we did. They're both in jail. Now we'll see how they like being locked up in a room."

She sat back and put her hands over her face, which had a little red around her mouth. "It was terrifying. The smell was sickening. There had to be boxes of cigars in there."

He stroked her hair away from her face and sat by her on the bed. She rested her face in his neck. There were red marks around her wrists and around her bare ankles, but it didn't seem to bother her. The hospital gown fit her loosely. He gathered it together at the back.

She smiled at him. "You don't want anyone to see my backside?"

"No." He kissed her forehead. "What made them lock you in the closet?"

"The secretary had called and said she needed my signature. I signed the document and wanted a copy. She said she had to go to another office to do that. I waited and waited, but she never came back. I went to look out into the hallway, and I saw Fox coming. I hurried back inside and went into the bathroom. When I came out, I could hear voices in Rossini's office. I eavesdropped at the door, which was open a crack. Fox wanted his money and Rossini told him he wasn't getting any money and he needed to get out of town as quick as possible. Fox pulled a gun. I was so shocked I gasped and they knew I was there. Rossini yanked me into the room and demanded to know who'd sent me. That's when I lost it and told them what scumbags they were. Rossini took the gun from Fox and then Rossini and I got into a tussle. I tried to take the gun, but that didn't work because he was much stronger. Fox helped to hold me down while they put duct tape on my hands and wrists and mouth. Now they were genuinely afraid and didn't know what to do with me. Rossini said to shove me in the closet. I was terrified." She rubbed her face against him.

"It's over and tomorrow we'll have a long talk with Mr. Rossini."

"What do you mean I can't see my daughter?" came from the hallway.

Carter got up and went to talk to the nurse. "Lila wants to see her mother and family."

"Okay, but the doctor's getting ready to see her."

"I'm sure they'll get out of his way."

The next two hours Carter sat with the family and waited while Lila underwent tests. The doctor appeared in the doorway of the waiting room. "Family of Lila Colton."

Mrs. Yates got to her feet. "I'm her mother and this is her family."

The doctor walked up to Mrs. Yates. "Your daughter is going to be fine. She has some bruises that will heal. We were most concerned about the knot on her head. She said she hit the floor, but everything looks good. I would suggest resting for the next couple of days, but Ms. Colton didn't seem to like that idea."

"I'll take care of her," Mrs. Yates said with determination. Lila had that same determination.

Mrs. Yates and her husband went back to talk to Lila. Her brother and cousins went in to say goodbye. The cousins' mother was there, too, and she hugged Lila and left. It surprised Carter that Lila was already dressed and her hair was pulled back and tied with a rubber band.

"You're going home with me and Rick for a few days so we can pamper you." Mrs. Yates started her case.

"Sorry, Mom. Right now I just want to go home and lie in my bed and wonder how my day got so screwed up. I don't need pampering. I don't need anyone to hold my hand. I got myself into a mess and now I have to deal with it." She kissed her mother's cheek. "All grown up, Mom. Sorry I worried you, though."

Mrs. Yates appealed to Carter. "Please talk sense into her."

"Mom, don't put Carter in the middle," Myles said. "You know how Lila is. She's always been stubborn."

"Shut up." Lila turned on Myles. "Look who's calling me stubborn."

"Kids." Rick held up his hands. "No bickering. After what you've been through, Lila, I suspect you're very tired."

"Yes, I am, and I just want quiet. Thank all of you for caring so much about me. I'm a mess right now and will probably ask for your forgiveness later."

"Oh, baby." Mrs. Yates hugged her daughter. "Please

take care of yourself and come out to the house if you get lonely. You're always welcome. You know that."

"I love you, Mom." They hugged tightly and then Lila turned to Myles. "I'm sorry I'm so short-tempered."

He kissed her forehead. "I'm just worried about you. Anything could've happened to you today."

"I know."

"Please try to stay upright for the next few days."

She swatted at him with her fist and he laughed as he went out the door. Mrs. Yates and Rick followed without making another case for Lila to go home with them.

The nurse brought the discharge papers, and Carter and Lila walked out to his car. "You sure you don't want to go to your mother's for a day or two?"

"I'm positive." She slid into the passenger side.

"Where's my purse?" she asked when Carter got into the car.

"I never saw your purse. Where did you leave it?"

"In a chair in front of the secretary's desk."

Carter thought back. "The chairs were all empty."

"It has to be there. That's where I left it and it has my credit cards and personal info in it. The hospital had my medical info on record and I didn't need it."

"Do you feel up to swinging by there?"

"Yes, but I'm not getting out. I never want to see that place again."

Once they'd arrived at Rossini Realty, Carter hurried to the offices upstairs. Mona was getting ready to leave for the day and the receptionist was, for once, at her desk.

"I'm looking for Ms. Colton's purse," he said to Mona.

"I haven't seen a purse."

"She said she left it in one of these chairs."

Mona looked around but didn't find anything. "It's not here."

"It was. Now where is it?"

Mona looked at the receptionist and back at Carter. The girl was thin, painfully thin. Her hair was a blond-orange color from being dyed so many times and there was a purple streak on the right side. Her blue eyes were dull as she stared back at him. He'd seen that look many times. Drug addict.

"Where's the purse?"

"Why do you assume I have it?"

"Where…?"

The door opened and a woman in her fifties walked in. Her blond hair was styled in a short bob around her face. Suave and sophisticated from her high heels to her jewelry to her expensive brand-name purse, she looked like a woman in charge. She hoisted the purse strap higher on her shoulder.

"Why is everyone standing around?"

It took Carter a second to figure out that the woman was Mrs. Rossini. He stepped forward and shook her hand.

"Carter Finch."

"Oh, yes, the man who helped to arrest my husband. I'm Sharon Rossini." She glanced around the room. "Mona, what's going on here?"

"Uh…uh…" Mona stuttered. Obviously, the secretary was nervous around the woman. Mona cleared her throat and replied, "Ms. Colton was here earlier and she left her purse and now we can't find it."

Mrs. Rossini turned to the receptionist and held out her hand. "Where is it?"

The receptionist opened a drawer on her desk and pulled out the purse.

"Go to Accounting and pick up your check. You're fired."

The woman disappeared out the door without a word. Sharon Rossini handed him the purse. "I'm sorry that happened here, but it won't again. I'm taking over the business." She headed for the door to the bigger office. "Can I see you for a minute, Mr. Finch?"

She took a seat at the big leather chair and asked, "How long will my husband be in jail?"

"I don't know. That's up to a judge, but he'll probably be released on bail soon."

"Not if I can help it. I'd just as soon they kept him there. I finally reached a breaking point of the embarrassment, the affairs and the countless ways he has wasted our money. It ends today. His lawyer is on his way back from a trip, but I will speak to him before Lou can."

"Good luck with that, Mrs. Rossini. Your husband has hurt a lot of people. I hope you get your wish."

As she talked with resentment and bitterness, it came to him that she might know a lot more about the fire. "Do you know anything about Lou's activities?"

"You mean the fire?"

He nodded.

"I hired a PI and I know what Lou does every moment of the day, but if I told you, they would say it's only an angry tale of a discarded wife."

"Not if you have photos."

She leaned back in the chair and crossed her legs, and he could see she was clearly thinking like a woman with revenge on her mind. "I'll have to think about it. I have my kids to think about, too." She leaned forward and wrote something on a pad and handed it to him. "That's my private number. Call me if you know Lou is going to be released on bail and we might be able to make a deal."

"I don't have that kind of power. The DA does and that's who you should be talking to."

"I say who I talk to and what I will divulge."

She had about twenty years of pain and suffering building in her from Rossini's treatment and Carter didn't blame her for wanting revenge. He would find a way to work it out with Mrs. Rossini, but he didn't have a lot of time.

"This case hinges on revenge? We know your husband and Walter Fox hired someone to torch the gallery. Make it easy for the DA, Mrs. Rossini, and your life will be a lot easier, too. You have the upper hand and can decide the rest of Rossini's life. That would be called satisfaction."

Lila ached from head to toe, and when she got home, the first thing she did was take a shower. She would hate tobacco smell for the rest of her life. She even washed her hair to get rid of it. She dreaded the night ahead. Nightmares would plague her and there was no way to stop them.

She put on her comfy T-shirt and dried her hair. Afterward, she crawled into bed and welcomed the relief of home and safety. She never would understand why home never appealed to Carter. She couldn't expect him to feel the same way she did, though. She drew a long breath and was grateful that he was here at this point in time. After being in the closet so long, she welcomed the joy to move freely. She never wanted to be locked up again. Freedom was a wonderful blessing, and she never realized that until the darkness shut out the world. It would take a while for her to get over it, but she knew she would.

Tomorrow she wanted to face Rossini and Fox. She wanted them to say to her face why they chose such a diabolical way to hurt her. She didn't know either of them that well, but tomorrow she would have her say and then she would start to put her life back together again.

"Are you awake?" Carter asked as he walked in.

She pushed up in bed. "Yes. I probably won't be able to sleep. I'm afraid to close my eyes."

He sat on the bed as she scooted up against the headboard. "I have some news that's interesting." He told her about his talk with Sharon Rossini.

"She might have photos?" Lila couldn't believe her ears. She curled into a sitting position, needing to know more.

"I'm guessing she does. But she's not willing to show them until she knows Rossini goes away for a long time."

"That must've been a terrible marriage."

"Most of them are..." He put a finger over her lips as she made to protest. "Listen to the news. Read the newspapers. Most marriages don't last. I think it's something you have to work at like everything in life. If you care about it, you will give it one hundred percent. Look at Myles and Faith."

"Don't you dare say anything about them." She

couldn't hold her temper in check. "They love each other and eventually will get back together. They needed a break."

He didn't say anything else, just stared at her with those gray eyes that were dark and challenging.

"Okay. No one has a perfect marriage and I agree you have to work at it. Your problem is that you expect it to be perfect. There is no such thing. You have to be able to love, compromise and always be there for the other person. No two people are alike, either. Someone has to change to make a relationship work."

"I have to leave day after tomorrow," he blurted out, as if she needed to know.

"I'm aware of that."

"And you need to get some rest."

"I'm going with you tomorrow to talk to Rossini. Please don't argue." She scooted under the covers.

"I've tried that. It never works. Seems I'm the one changing."

She laughed. She couldn't help it. It gave her a lift that she needed badly.

"How are you feeling? Does your skin burn?"

"Whatever they put on at the hospital has done the job. I'm kind of hungry. What about you?"

"What would you like, my lady?"

They were so good together. Why couldn't they have a lasting relationship?

"Pizza and salad."

Later they sat on the sofa and ate from the coffee table and talked about the case. "We should know who the arsonist is by tomorrow, or if Rossini actually set the fire himself." Lila had her fingers crossed.

She'd been through a terrible ordeal and tomorrow it would end.

"Rossini and his lawyer will be looking for a deal. We have too much evidence. If Mrs. Rossini will co-operate, we might have the nail to close the coffin for good. And then you can get your insurance money and plan your future."

Yeah. Future. Her future sat beside her. He was a paradox and thought he could explain everything. It was true that many marriages didn't make it. But his conclusion was unacceptable for Lila.

That night, Lila woke up screaming and Carter had her in his arms before the fear could take over. Her body shook and her breath came in gasps.

"Hey, hey, you're dreaming."

She clutched him. "I can't see. I can't move. Hold me."

"I have you. Relax."

They eased down into the sheets and Carter pulled the comforter over them. "Just relax."

"Don't leave me."

"I'm not going anywhere."

Oh, but he was, and she started to pull away to keep from getting in too deep. It was too late, though. She'd been all in from the get-go.

"Are you okay? I'll go back to my room."

She slid her arms around his neck, loving the feel of his masculine skin. "I don't want you to go to your room. I want you to stay."

He pulled back to look at her face, which he could see only by the moonlight. "Are you sure?"

"Positive." She brought her lips to his and forgot

about everything else. This was what she wanted...
to feel like a woman and to be secure in a man's love.
She wanted it all, but she would settle for now.

Chapter 17

Carter woke up to an empty bed. He could hear Lila moving around downstairs. He leaned back and thought of last night. It was perfect. For him. How could he be so selfish? For Lila it would be a different story. It seemed to be that way for them from the start. Their need for each other overshadowed everything else.

He swung from the bed and took the stairs two at a time. She was at the coffeepot filling a cup; her long dark hair flowed down her back, just the way he liked it. In slacks, a multicolored blouse and flats, she looked as beautiful as ever. No evidence of trauma from yesterday. But sometimes the trauma came from within.

"You're up early," he said, watching the way her hair swayed around her hips.

"I'm excited about today. You want a cup?"

He nodded. *"Excited?"*

"Today we're going to find out who set fire to my gallery and today I'm not the one who's going to be hurt. I want to hear Rossini say why the money was so important to him that he set the fire with us in the building. That has to be a crime and I will be there every day of his trial. Then he gets locked in a room as small as a closet."

"Take a deep breath," he urged. The terror was still evident in her, but he had no doubt she could handle it.

"You take a deep breath." She poked him in the ribs, a sly grin on her face. "I'm going to fix my hair." As she passed him, she said, "If you're thinking last night was a mistake, it wasn't. I was weak and needed you. That's all I'm going to say. That's all that needs to be said."

Lila Colton would be fine, and if she needed someone, she had a big family to help her. He just wished those guilty feelings about leaving tomorrow would go away. His cell buzzed and he dashed up the stairs to get it. It was Richards.

"The ADA called and Sapp wants to talk. I'm guessing he wants to make a deal. I told her about your involvement in the case and she said it would be okay for you to sit in."

"Let's go, Lila," Carter shouted. "They're bringing Sapp over from the jail to the courthouse. He wants to talk."

She stuck her head around his doorway. "I'm dressed. You're not."

"Give me ten minutes."

"Ten minutes, Finch."

In exactly nine minutes and fifty-eight seconds,

they were in the car. Carter stopped for coffee and sweet rolls, and then they made their way to the courthouse. They met Richards outside an interview room. He glanced at Lila.

"I didn't realize you were coming, Ms. Colton. I thought you would be resting for the day."

"This concerns me and I should be here to listen to what the scumbag has to say."

"Any arguments?" Carter asked Richards.

"No, but the ADA might."

A middle-aged woman with blond hair and sensible shoes came around the corner. "What might the ADA do?"

"Ms. Colton would like to sit in on the interview," Richards told her.

"Do you think that's wise, Ms. Colton? I've read every word of the file, and if I were you, I would be sitting at home waiting for a phone call. It would be better on your nerves."

"I'd rather be here. Sitting at home just doesn't work for me."

"Okay. You can't sit in, but you will have to watch through a two-way window."

"Thank you."

The ADA spoke on the phone and then said, "They're bringing him over. Ms. Colton, you can sit or stand around the corner in front of the window. Your choice. But please don't talk where Sapp can hear you. Understood?"

"Understood."

Carter gave her a brief smile and filed into the interview room with the others. Soon Sapp was brought in with handcuffs locked around his wrists as well as his ankles. An officer pushed him into a chair.

The ADA sat in the center of the table and laid a small tape recorder on it. Carter and Richards flanked her. Sapp sat on the other side, facing the ADA.

A young man with spiked hair and a tight skinny suit rushed in. "I'm Sapp's attorney. Sorry I'm late." From his youthful appearance, Carter assumed he was court appointed. Gambling and women must have left Sapp broke.

"What's on your mind, Mr. Sapp?" the ADA asked.

"I want out. I'm about to go crazy in here."

He was a shell of the man who had been arrested. His arrogance had been tested by sleeping a few nights on a cot, having company like roaches and rats and eating substandard food. He was used to the finer things in life and a jail cell was not one of them.

"I'm innocent. I didn't plant that device."

"Who did?" Richards asked.

Sapp hunched forward. "I heard Rossini was arrested."

"Yes," Richards replied. "We don't have all day. If you know something and want to clear your conscience, start talking or you're going to spend a lot of time in this place."

"I owed Rossini money," he said. "A lot of money."

"How much?" The ADA opened her notebook and had a pen ready.

"Ten thousand. I lost it to him in a poker game and he told me not to worry, that we would work something out. He showed up in my office one day and told me he needed a favor for the money I owed him. He wanted me to torch the gallery. He said the Colton woman was always complaining about the wiring, and before she called an electrician, he wanted the gallery gone. I told him I didn't do things like that and he told me to find someone who did. Since I own an electrical business, he assumed I knew those kinds of people. He told me I didn't have any choice. Either I give him the money I owed or find someone to get the job done.

"I didn't do anything for several days and he showed up in my office again with a magazine. It had guns and bombs in it. He showed me a tiny pipe bomb that could be converted and would start any fire. And he ordered me to either purchase it or make one. I bought the parts and made it, but I didn't give it much power. It would only burst into flames with hardly a sound. If the building had blown up, it would have hurt a lot more people. After that, I told him I was out. That was all I was going to do, and as far as I was concerned, my debt to him was paid."

"You seem to know a lot about bombs." The ADA looked right at him. He didn't move a muscle or appear nervous.

"My grandparents lived on a farm and I would visit them during the summers. My grandpa had a lot of tree stumps and wanted to get rid of them so he could farm more land. His neighbor told him his grandson had instructions for a small bomb but wasn't having any luck putting one together. I helped him figure out how to make it. We dug a hole in the center of the stump and pushed the device inside. Of course, we didn't have electricity, so I couldn't use a timer. I used a fuse instead. It worked. I haven't done anything like that since."

"What's your grandfather's name?" the ADA wanted to know.

"Edward Sapp. He passed on a few years ago."

"Mr. Sapp, does your grandfather have any stumps on his property today?" Richards asked.

"No. It's all been cleared."

"So you would say that you're very familiar with making small bombs?"

He moved restlessly in the chair. "Yes. Those kinds."

"And you used the same kind for Rossini?"

"Yes, but smaller."

"Where did you make the bomb for Rossini?" the ADA jumped in.

"In the working area of my electrical business. After I finished it, I gave it to Rossini, and I don't know what he did with it afterward. I didn't ask him and stayed away from the poker games. I didn't have any money anyway. But I'm not the one who put the device in the electrical socket."

"Why did you send Boyd to put in new lighting?"

"I knew Philip had a record and I gave him a job because Rossini told me to. Rossini called me and said to send him to install a light in the gallery. The Colton woman was driving him crazy. She was going to hire an electrician on her own and he couldn't have that because they would find the faulty wiring. Rossini didn't count on Philip having scruples."

Carter glanced to the window where Lila was listening. Everything was falling into place and hopefully she would get her answer.

"May I ask a question?" Carter asked.

"If it pertains to this case," the ADA replied.

"It ties into the forgery."

"Okay, but I will stop you if I need to."

Carter turned his attention to Sapp. "Where did the discussions for the gallery and the forgeries take place?"

"The poker games. It started with Walter Fox looking for someone who could forge a painting. And Rossini was always complaining about the gallery and Ms. Colton and her fixation on getting the wiring repaired. The lights would blink when she had a show and she wanted something done."

"How many people knew about these discussions?"

"Just me, Fox and Rossini. Of course, Rossini's girlfriend was always around because the games were usually in a hotel suite. She served drinks and appetizers and Rossini called her the hostess. After a game, we were drinking one night and Fox said an insurance investigator was on his tail and he had to get rid of the paintings. But he'd already offered them to Ms. Colton, who was going to hang them for a show. He'd look stupid if he asked for them back. Rossini was a little drunk and he said we should just torch the whole place. I thought he was joking, but the next day he showed up in my office."

"Mr. Sapp." Carter scooted forward with his forearms on the table. "I know you're trying to be honest—or at least, I hope you are—but Fox recruited Tony long before the fire."

Sapp placed his hands over his face, the steel handcuffs starkly standing out. "It's hard to keep all this straight. Yes, Tony started working for Fox about a year ago. I was trying to get him out of my apartment. He was always there painting something and the smell was terrible. I told Wendy I wanted him out, and then at a poker game Fox mentioned needing a forger and it was a godsend, except Tony never moved out. But he had money to go out to restaurants and to pay rent."

The ADA picked up the tape recorder and clicked it off. "Mr. Sapp, I will have this typed up and an officer will bring it to you to sign. Once that is done, I will meet with you and your lawyer and we will go over a deal."

The whole time Sapp's attorney sat there occasionally making a note. "Are you kidding me? He needs to be set free. He's done nothing wrong except help his friends."

The ADA held up two fingers. "There were two people in the gallery when the fire started. I have attempted murder on the books. I'm willing to take that off and make as low a sentence as I possibly can once we prove Rossini set the fire. But, Mr. Sapp, if your lawyer insists on going for dismissal, you had better talk to him. That's all I have to say."

"You're fired," Sapp said to the lawyer.

The man got to his feet. "You win some, you lose some. Have a good day."

"Where do they find these public defenders?" The ADA stuffed papers into her briefcase.

"Obviously, from Disney World." Carter chuckled as they walked out.

"We have an interview with Fox at one and then Rossini," the ADA said. "It all comes down to what Rossini has to say. He had the device. Now will he admit to pushing it into the electrical socket? We'll have to wait and see."

* * *

As they got into the car, Carter said, "I think I'll pay Mrs. Rossini a visit again She might need a little more incentive to help us. She might be our last hope."

"I think everything Sapp revealed was true," Lila said.

"Me, too."

"Every time I complained about the wiring, Rossini took one step closer to burning it down. I should've left it alone."

"Now, don't get weak on me. Rossini's been breaking the law for years. He got comfortable in his no-strike zone and thought no one would ever have enough courage to challenge him. Bribes were a way of life for him and now he has to face everything that he's done."

"But will he?"

"That's why we're talking to Mrs. Rossini."

Carter turned to Lila. "Are you sure you want to go back in there?"

"That was just a moment of weakness. I don't ever plan to let it cripple me. I would love to meet the woman who married Mr. Rossini. She's probably been downtrodden all her life."

"You'll be surprised."

And she was. Sharon Rossini was not the woman she was expecting. She was impeccably dressed in a white sleeveless shirtdress. The large buttons were brown on the front and matched her heels. The bracelets on her wrist jingled as they shook hands.

"You're the woman who rents the gallery and who was locked inside during the fire?"

"Yes," Lila replied. "Carter and I were inside when the fire started. It was a scary time."

"I can imagine. Have seats, please, and you can tell me why you're here."

"To talk about your husband," Lila told her.

"Not my favorite subject." She wiggled her nose as if she smelled something bad.

"It comes down to this, Mrs. Rossini…"

"Please call me Sharon."

"Okay, thanks." Carter seemed a little rattled. "It comes down to this. For a conviction, the DA's office has to put Rossini in the gallery, and they can't. Nor can they place him with the device, even though Sapp will testify to giving it to Rossini. A jury will have to choose who to believe. And that's leaving it to something like a coin toss. If you want to keep Rossini in jail, now is the time to come forward and help the cops make this a slam-dunk case."

"Are you married?" The question was directed to Lila.

"No."

"I met Lou in college and we got married when I was twenty-two. It was the best time of my life. My dad had money, but he wanted me to learn about money and how to control it and not let it take over my life. Lou and I lived in this little one-bedroom apartment and lived off of McDonald's. My dad gave us an allowance and we had to live on it. We would save our pennies so we could go to the movies on the weekends. I wished our lives could have stayed that way. When I turned twenty-five, I received my inheritance from my parents, which was the bulk of Dunbar Realty. Lou graduated and started working for the company. A few years later, my dad became ill and Lou took over completely, renaming the company Rossini Realty. I had planned to work in the business, too, but Lou decided I needed to stay home and take care of our children. Never let a man take away your power, Ms. Colton."

The words settled on Lila's skin like flakes of ice. "Lou took everything from me, even my pride, but he's not taking anything else. I spoke with a judge yesterday and the board of directors. I've taken over ownership of the company and closed all of our banking accounts. Everything is now in my name and Lou can't get to anything. He will be furious and expect me to give over to him. That day is long past."

"If you feel this way, why won't you help us?" Lila pointed to the closet and a chill shot through her. "He put duct tape on my wrists, ankles and mouth and shoved me into that closet. I couldn't breathe. I was so scared, and my stomach churned with nausea. I thought I was going to throw up and die lying on the floor. He's an evil person and needs to be stopped. I hope you will help us."

Sharon picked up the gold paperweight. "I gave this to him for our twenty-fifth wedding anniversary, knowing he had a mistress. I was such a gullible fool, but not anymore." She glanced up. "When do you have an interview with Lou?"

"This afternoon," Carter answered.

"Do you have enough evidence to get a conviction?"

"As I told you earlier, we have evidence but not enough to be positive about the conviction. It will take more."

"Why can't you help us?" Lila asked, not understanding the woman. She wanted Rossini to be put away a long time, yet she paused at giving information that could make that happen.

"You have to be a mother to understand."

"What are you talking about?" The answer made no sense to Lila.

"I left Lou the first time I found out he was having an affair. He talked me into coming back. We had two small children and I wanted them to be raised in a family atmosphere like I was, so I went back to him and got pregnant again. The two older children know about their father and his many affairs and have no respect for him, but I kept it from the younger daughter. She's Daddy's little princess and she loves him, and I find it very hard to break her heart. She'll be devastated."

"Then why hire the investigator?" Lila asked, not pulling any punches. "If you really want out of your rotten marriage, your children have to be with you. They have to know everything, and that includes the younger child. How old is she?"

"She just turned eighteen and graduated high school."

"She knows."

Sharon frowned. "What?"

"My dad had many affairs and even as a young child I knew he was cheating on my mom. They argued a lot and children pick up things. He didn't stay home some nights and I knew he was with some other woman. Take it from someone who lived through it. Your daughter knows. She just doesn't want to admit the truth or hurt your feelings."

"How do your other children feel?" Carter asked.

"My son, who is the oldest, wanted me to kick him out years ago. He has very little respect for his father. My older daughter is at the University of Chicago and lives in one of our apartments. She has her own life and wants nothing to do with her father. She's known for some time and tries to avoid family functions."

Sharon got up and walked to the floor-to-ceiling windows. "It's not an easy decision to make."

"You made the decision when you hired the PI," Lila said. "You wanted evidence, probably hoping deep down that there wasn't any. But I'm guessing you found more than you wanted. Use it, Sharon. You'll be grateful afterward. My mother was."

Sharon turned around to look at Lila. "Your mother left your father."

"Yes, years ago. The moment she knew for sure that he was cheating, she took me and my brother and left without much of anything. It was hard for her at first, but now my mom is happy. She found a great guy to love her and to be a father to us. Sometimes when I hear her singing or humming in the kitchen, I'm grateful for the decision she made, not only for herself, but for my brother and me, as well."

"You're part of the Colton family that has been in the news," Sharon stated as Lila's name seemed to finally click in her head.

She didn't flinch or give an inch. "Yes. I've had my fair share of gossip and media, so be warned. Luckily, there will be another news story coming along."

Sharon walked to the desk. "It's not only that. I'm afraid for my own life and what Lou might do when he finds out I've taken over the company. He knows a lot of bad people."

"Sharon, you have money and can hire round-the-clock bodyguards for you and your children." Carter got to his feet. "Give it some thought, but you don't have much time. The interview will probably start about two in the DA's offices. The ADA would love any help to put Rossini away."

"Don't expect a miracle. Lou is notorious for having the police under his thumb and probably the DA's office, too."

Lila reached for her purse, knowing that nothing they said would sway her. She had to make her own decision.

"I'm sorry for all that you've been through," Lila said. "The only thing that's going to ease your pain is to show Rossini just how strong a woman you really are. Stand strong and he can't hurt you anymore."

"That's what I'm doing in this office, Ms. Colton. My father built the business and now I'm taking it back for my own peace of mind."

They walked out of the office, down the stairs and to Carter's car. "What do you think?" Lila asked.

"We have to wait and see what decision she makes, and it is her decision."

"Yeah. That's the hard part."

"Let's eat lunch before we go back," Carter suggested.

"That sounds good, even though I'm not hungry."

"You need the strength. This'll be the first time you get to see Fox and Rossini after their arrests."

"I can't wait."

Lila's cell buzzed and she grabbed her purse, hoping Sharon had made up her mind. The caller ID gave her pause. It was her father. Should she answer or call him back? Maybe he'd heard about the so-called kidnapping and wanted to know how she was. *Gullible, thy name is Lila.* She answered anyway.

"Hey, Dad."

"What do you think you're doing?"

"Excuse me?"

"Your grandmother is livid. The other Coltons got information from a friend of yours and the judge is now pushing the court date back until experts can thoroughly examine the will. You have betrayed the family. How could you?"

"Don't you want to know if the will is a forgery?"

"Hell, no. Mom wants that money and she better get it or we'll never speak to you again."

"I have no control over that."

"Well, you seem to have control over other things."

Tears were threatening to squeeze from her eyes, but she was strong enough to hold them back. He didn't ask about her kidnapping, as the media was calling it. He didn't care about her. How many times had she told herself that, and today she believed it for the first time. It finally sank in.

"By the way, I'm fine. I didn't have to spend the night in the hospital or anything. It's amazing how strong a person can be at times."

"What are you talking about?"

"The kidnapping."

"Oh, that. Mom said you faked that to get attention."

"No, Dad. The knot on my head is very real and the fear in my heart was very real. Nice talking to you. Give my regards to your mother."

She held the phone tight in her hand. A tremor ran through her. Carter was right. There was no happiness in a marriage or home and family. There was no happiness anywhere.

Chapter 18

Carter paced as they waited in a small area. The ADA was running late. Richards came in and took a seat. No one spoke. This was the end of the line for the truth and Carter prayed the truth was all dressed up and ready to be exposed.

They were called back and gathered in a large interview room. Lila had talked to her dad on the phone and she seemed upset. The excitement of the morning was gone and replaced with the seriousness and determination he knew well. Nothing would keep her from having her say.

They made room for the ADA. Richards was on one end and Lila and Carter were on the other. The ADA would sit between them, and Carter hoped they could get this over with quickly.

The ADA rushed in with an armful of files, a laptop, a briefcase and a purse slung over her shoulder. "Good afternoon, everyone." She laid everything carefully on the table and took a deep breath. "They're bringing Walter Fox in. The forgery is a done deal. My concern now is the arson charge."

"Why?" Lila asked. "Sapp says he was in on it."

"I intend to take this slow, Ms. Colton. I'm allowing you here because it was your place of business that was destroyed. I feel you have a right to face them. Just let me handle this."

"Yes, ma'am."

Lila's expression was tight. She was upset, but he had a feeling it wasn't about Fox. It was about something else.

He reached out and touched her arm. "Relax."

The door opened and Walter Fox in jail attire and handcuffs was escorted in by an officer and a lawyer. Fox was a small man, probably five feet seven inches, and always dressed as if life was an occasion. Carter thought he probably lived it that way, too, needing money and more money to fit his lifestyle. Now it had all come crumbling down and his demeanor was one of a broken man.

Today there was no hat and no bow tie and no three-piece suit to grab one's attention. He was just a man looking for forgiveness.

"Mr. Fox will plead guilty to the forgery charge, but he had nothing to do with the arson." His lawyer took up the cause.

The ADA placed the tape recorder on the table. "We have a witness who will testify that you and Rossini talked about burning down the gallery, which Rossini owns."

The lawyer whispered to Fox and nodded for him to speak. "I talked about wanting to get rid of the paintings because I knew Mr. Finch was coming to town and I would get caught selling forgeries."

"May I ask a question?" Carter asked.

"Go ahead."

"How did you know I was coming to Chicago?"

"Just a friend who works in the art industry."

"What's his name?"

The lawyer and Fox whispered again and then the lawyer spoke. "That has nothing to do with the arson case and my client has no reason to answer it."

"I agree," the ADA said. "You're a good detective, Mr. Finch, and I know you can figure it out on your own. Let's move on."

Damn! He was hoping to get a little help, but she was right. He would find it in the archives of people who wanted to get even for putting them in prison. It could wait until another day. This day was for finding the arsonist.

"Mr. Fox, our witness says that you talked with Mr. Rossini about torching the gallery. Mr. Finch could verify the paintings were fakes and the only way to save yourself was to get rid of them. Am I correct?"

"My client…"

"I'm willing to tell you my part in this—" Mr. Fox interrupted "—for a lesser sentence."

"I'm listening."

"Yes, Lou and I talked about it. He wanted to get Ms. Colton off his back before she called an electrician. We agreed to pay half if we could find someone to do it."

"What is half?"

"I paid five thousand and Lou paid five thousand."

"Who did you pay this money to?"

"I gave my share to Lou and he would give his share to the person he hired."

"Who did he hire, Mr. Fox?" Richards asked.

"I don't know. He never told me."

"So you just gave him five thousand dollars?"

"Yes. He promised to give me thirty thousand when he got the insurance money for the building."

"Thirty thousand? For what?" Carter asked.

"So I can get the full amount for my paintings."

Rossini didn't even need Fox. There was something that wasn't ringing true about the stories.

"Mr. Fox, did you ever receive any money from Mr. Rossini?" Richards wanted to know.

"No. That's why I went to his office to find out what was going on. I needed my money." He turned his gaze to Lila. "I'm so sorry for what happened to you. I didn't mean to hurt you."

"But you did hurt me to keep from getting caught. And you stole from Homer Tinsley to feed your gambling habit. He trusted you and that trust meant nothing."

"Where did you get the gun, Mr. Fox?" The ADA took control again.

"It's a small Smith & Wesson. I bought it for protection after poker games. It went off in the car when I tried to take it away from Lou. I didn't mean for anything like this to happen. I'm sorry."

The ADA clicked off the tape recorder. "Mr. Fox, I will talk to your lawyer later. I will definitely have a deal for you if you will testify against Rossini."

"Yes, yes. I would be willing to do that."

The interview ended and Fox and his attorney left the room. The ADA looked at her watch. "I have to go to my office and make a phone call. Rossini should be brought over in about fifteen minutes. The girlfriend is here and trying to bail him out, but Rossini just learned that his wife put a lock on everything he owns. He's not happy and the girlfriend is demanding to see me. Oh, what a wonderful day."

"I have to check in at the office," Richards said and walked away.

Lila and Carter made their way to the waiting area and a young girl brought them coffee. "Thank you," Lila said. "That's very nice of you."

"You're welcome."

"Are you okay?" Carter asked as they sat down.

"Why wouldn't I be okay?"

"You talked to your dad on your cell and I could see it upset you."

"He and my grandmother found out about the experts looking at the will, and the hearing has been pushed back till a judge can rule on the expert's findings. They're very upset and said it was all my fault."

"It's not. Lila—"

"I know it's not my fault. My fault is loving too much and believing that one day my father would love me the way most fathers love their children. I realize that's never going to happen, and even though I know it's true, it still hurts."

"I'm so sorry he hurt you again. I wish I had more time to—"

"You were right all along. Love hurts, and having a home and a family does not make it better. It is not the solution to everyone's problem. I can see that now.

Marriage has to be a personal commitment that you're willing to make. It's a risk that you have to be willing to take. Sometimes it works out and sometimes it doesn't."

"Please don't change into a bitter person who doesn't believe in love. I know that it exists. How do I know? I see it every time I look into your eyes and I see it in the way you deal with life and your family. That's love. Don't throw it all away because of my jaded ideas."

Richards slid into a chair across from them. "They're bringing Rossini over. Showtime."

Carter pulled out his phone and sent a text to Sharon. *The interview with your husband and the ADA is about to start. Just thought you might want to know.* He slipped his phone into his pocket and hoped she showed up. If not, there was a very good chance Rossini's attorney could get him out on bail.

He turned to Lila. "Ready?"

"Ready."

They sat in the interview room once again in almost the exact same positions. Rossini was shown in with his lawyer, who was cursing and yelling at the top of his lungs.

"This is ridiculous. I demand that Mr. Rossini be released."

"Sit down, Mr. Harris, and if you don't change your attitude, I will have you removed from the interview."

"You can't do that."

"Try me. This is not a courtroom. I'm just trying to see if we have enough information to take Mr. Rossini before a judge."

"You don't." Mr. Harris set his monogrammed brief-case on the table. "Can you place him at the fire?"

"No. But his fingerprints are all over the place."

"He owns the building."

"I'm aware of that. I'm just letting you know."

"You can't put my client anywhere near that build-ing on that night."

"No, not at this point."

"What do you have?"

"For starters, the kidnapping of Ms. Colton and being held against her will." The ADA held up two fingers. "Two witnesses who say that Rossini talked about setting the fire. One made the device for him and the other actually gave him money to destroy the paint-ings in the gallery. Mr. Rossini offered him thirty thou-sand dollars after the fire from his insurance money."

"Why would Mr. Rossini offer anyone thirty thou-sand dollars after the fire?"

"For his silence, Mr. Harris," Carter replied. "Si-lence is worth a lot of money."

"That's hogwash. You'll never get a jury to believe that. Mr. Rossini is well-known around this city and is a respected businessman. This is a witch hunt, and a jury will never believe this insane nonsense."

Voices outside distracted the meeting. The ADA motioned to Richards. "See what's going on?"

He was back in a second. "Ms. Wilcox is demand-ing to see Mr. Rossini and she's taking offense at your attempt to keep her out."

Carter leaned over and whispered to the ADA. Lila could hear him, as he had to speak over her. "Let her in. She was at the poker games and knows more than she's saying and she might accidentally let something slip."

The ADA gave it some thought. "Let her in."

Ms. Wilcox charged into the room like a bull into an arena full of energy. With a twist of her head, she tossed back her long dark hair, daring anyone to question her presence here. Richards brought another chair and she sat close to Rossini, stroking his arm. "Don't worry, baby. We'll get you out of here."

"Ms. Wilcox." The ADA's voice rose. "Sit back and listen or I'll have the officer remove you."

"I'm only trying to help Lou."

Mr. Harris leaned in and spoke to Rossini. "Tell her I can handle this."

Rossini patted Tanya's hands. "Just be quiet, baby."

Tanya crossed her legs and scooted back in the chair with a smug expression.

Lila stared at the woman and something clicked in her mind. "You're the woman who called me from Rossini's office and wanted my signature on a piece of paper that concerned the safe's contents."

"Yeah, that was me." She twirled a strand of dark hair around her forefinger. "Mona's always trying to get the best of me. I offered to take it to you, but she said I didn't have enough sense to do that. I showed her."

"How many times have I told you not to come to my office?" Rossini's anger sparked.

"Don't yell at me! I heard you come into your office and had to leave quickly. I took it back later that afternoon when no one was there. I just laid it on Mona's desk with a sticky note attached. I drew a smiley face on it."

Mr. Harris cleared his throat to get the interview

back on track. "You don't have enough evidence to charge Mr. Rossini with anything. I demand a bail hearing so he can be released."

"Attempted murder, kidnapping and arson are not crimes I dismiss without a lot of thought," the ADA told him.

"You can't be serious."

"Don't push me, Mr. Harris. Rossini was caught at the airport fleeing our jurisdiction. He is not going to be granted bail."

"Mr. Rossini did not set the fire and did not know two people were in the building. Mr. Rossini did not build the device to set the fire. Mr. Rossini has done nothing wrong. He is innocent and I demand that he be taken before a judge."

Lila looked down to see Carter reading his phone. She read it, too. It was from Sharon. She couldn't embarrass her children. Lila's heart sank. She'd made it to the courthouse, but then changed her mind. After all they'd been through, it came down to a wife who didn't have the courage to stand up to her abusive husband. Rossini was going to get away with it.

She glanced at Carter and she could see the same thoughts were running through his mind. Lila got to her feet. "Excuse me, please."

"Lila…"

"Is there something you'd like to share?" the ADA asked.

"No. I just have to make a quick call. It's private."

Lila left the room and expected Carter to follow her, but he didn't. She hurried to the big foyer and asked the receptionist if she'd seen anyone waiting. The girl pointed to the front doors and Lila ran for her life, trying to catch Sharon. She stopped and caught her breath as she saw Sharon standing there with her car keys in her hand and the strap of a big purse over her shoulder.

"Sharon!"

The woman turned toward Lila's voice, and in a split second, Lila thought she was going to run, but decided otherwise and walked toward Lila. "I'm sorry, Lila. I'm just not a hero."

"I bet your children think otherwise. From everything that you've told me, I'm assuming your life was miserable. Even expensive clothes and a fancy house can't disguise that. Your children know the pain you've been through—at least, the older ones." Lila touched the big bag on Sharon's arm. "You probably have enough evidence in there to put him away for a long time."

Sharon clutched the purse a little tighter.

"You don't have to use it if you don't want to. You can just walk away and your husband will, too, as well as his girlfriend. She came to his rescue and she's in there, sitting right by his side, thinking he has millions of dollars to share with her." Lila gave her a minute and then added, "Maybe he does. Maybe he knows you better than you do."

Sharon clenched her jaw but didn't say anything.

Lila went back into the building and she didn't know how she was going to handle Rossini being released. Scream. Cry. Kick the furniture. Probably none of those. She would wait patiently until they found more evidence that pointed to him. She wondered if they sold patience at the pharmacy.

She slipped back into the room and whispered to Carter, "Tell you later."

"Do you have anything to share, Ms. Colton?" the ADA asked.

"No, ma'am."

"Okay, Mr. Harris, you get your arraignment. The judge will decide bail, but I'll fight it."

Tanya jumped out of the chair and leaped onto Rossini, almost knocking him out of his. "Oh, baby. We'll be in Hawaii in no time." She held out her left hand. "And I'll be wearing a beautiful wedding ring. You said they couldn't touch you and you were right."

"Shut up, Tanya."

"It's best if we go." Mr. Harris spoke up.

The ADA's phone buzzed and she took it. "Yes, send her in." She placed her phone on the desk with a thoughtful expression. "It seems we have more information, so please keep your seats."

"What?" Rossini was on his feet, his earlier happy expression marred by a scowl. He looked at his lawyer. "We don't have to put up with this, do we?"

"Yes, you do." The ADA was quick to correct him.

"Who is this person that has information?" Mr. Harris asked.

"Mrs. Rossini."

"My wife?" They now had Mr. Rossini's full attention.

"She can't testify against him. They're married." Relief was evident on Mr. Harris's face.

The ADA picked up her phone and touched a couple of numbers. The door opened and Mrs. Rossini walked in dressed in a navy sheath with short puffed sleeves. She was every bit the businesswoman she opted to be.

"What the hell is she doing here?" Rossini wanted to know.

"Everyone take a seat," the ADA ordered. "And I will speak to Mrs. Rossini." They went into the hallway and the others sat there, not saying a word.

Carter glanced at Lila and she gave him a thumbs-up, hoping Sharon's appearance meant exactly what she wanted it to.

In a few minutes, the two women came back. The ADA folded her hands over a large folder she'd brought in with her. "Mr. Rossini, do you have anything to say before I start?"

"No. I'd just like to get out of here."

The ADA looked at Tanya. "You mentioned Hawaii and marriage. Are you aware that Mr. Rossini is married?"

"Of course." She flipped her dark hair over her shoulder. "He's divorcing her as soon as he can and then we're getting married in Hawaii, just like he promised."

"Mr. Rossini promised you marriage?"

"Yes."

"For what?"

Tanya blinked. "What do you mean?"

"Why couldn't he divorce her six months ago, a year ago or even two years ago? All he had to do was ask her for a divorce, but he didn't. Why all of a sudden is he going to ask his wife for a divorce?"

"Because he realized how much he loved me and not that old crow." Tanya glanced at Sharon, but she remained stone-faced.

The ADA pulled a file from a folder and slid it across the table to Tanya. "Sharon Rossini filed for divorce yesterday, and to have all the evidence she needed, she hired a PI to follow Mr. Rossini for the last four months." She held up a CD. "On this CD is just about everything he's done during that time."

Tanya paled significantly. "What…? What…? Lou?"

"Don't worry, baby," Rossini told her with a sneer on his lips. "I got this. My wife, or soon-to-be ex-wife, is not intelligent enough to outsmart me." He faced his wife. "You know that PI you hired? I offered him a lump sum of money for his information and he took it. He wasn't very loyal to you. So, my sweet wife, you have nothing and you'll be out of my office by tomorrow."

"This is highly irregular," Mr. Harris complained. "And I will be talking to the DA."

"Go ahead, but first, let's go over some things. Mr. Harris, you've been asking me if I can place Mr. Rossini at the gallery. No, I can't, but I can place someone he's very close to there."

Tanya stood. "I really have to go…"

Richards jumped up and blocked the doorway.

"Sit down, Ms. Wilcox," the ADA said. "I'll show you some interesting pictures and videos."

"What's going on?" Rossini asked.

"You'll find out soon enough."

The ADA removed the CD from its holder and pushed it into the recorder beneath the TV. Picking up the remote control, she went back to her seat. Everyone scooted their chairs around and Richards stood at the door.

"I haven't seen this before, but I'm assured of what's on it." She clicked the remote control. Nothing happened. She clicked it again. Nothing but a whirling sound.

Rossini laughed, a sickening sound. "It's blank. I

told you, you stupid cow. I bought everything he had. You have nothing. You'll never outsmart me. You're just a dumb bitch who's worth nothing and…"

Carter got up and grabbed Mr. Rossini around the neck and squeezed as hard as he could. The man's face turned red and he spluttered.

"You say one more word and I'll snap your neck." Carter released him.

Rossini rubbed his neck. "That's police brutality. I'm suing the Chicago Police Department and Mr. Finch."

"Mr. Finch does not work for the Chicago Police Department," the ADA told him. "I'd advise you to tone it down." She turned her attention to Tanya. "Ms. Wilcox, are you sure Mr. Rossini has plans to marry you?"

"Of course he does. We talk about it all the time. He hates his life with her." She pointed to Sharon.

Sharon sat between Lila and Carter. Her head was bent, and she gripped her hands tightly in her lap. It was the final blow in her life with Rossini. She finally stood up for herself and he had humiliated her beyond belief. Lila wanted to touch her hands or something to make her realize she wasn't alone. But she didn't want to embarrass her more.

"This has all been very interesting," Mr. Harris said, "but can we move on and get to a hearing?"

Sharon moved and Lila thought she was leaving the room, but she reached down and pulled out a big folder from her purse. She held it in her hand as she started to speak. "It seems very ironic that no one has thought of the real motive for the gallery fire."

Real motive? That puzzled Lila. How many motives could there be?

"It was because of the wiring," Richards said.

Sharon shook her head. "That was only part of it. Lou bought the building many years ago. The roof had a leak, but Lou never fixed it. There were steel beams in the roof to make the dome of the gallery. Chicago has lots of rain, and water leaked onto the beams, causing them to rust. Lou decided to sell the place, but it didn't pass inspection because of the rusted beams and the wiring. The inspector put a lock on the door. Until the repairs were done, Lou couldn't sell the place. So Lou does what he always does. He hired an inspector for a false report and rented the place to Ms. Colton."

Lila listened to this in shock. "No, that can't be right. I had an inspection done before I rented and the guy said everything was okay. I have the report in my files."

"I'm sorry, Lila. It was another fake inspection. When the wiring problem came up again, I decided to look for the first file and found Lou hadn't done any of the repairs as he'd told me and the city of Chicago." She waved the file toward the ADA. "It's all in there."

"You mean the roof could have come crashing down at any moment?"

"Yes, I'm afraid so."

A chill ran through Lila. So many people could have been hurt, some killed. It was a horrible thought.

Sharon reached for her purse and took out something that looked like a photo. She walked to the ADA and slipped it inside the file. "In case you need it." She then eased her purse strap over her shoulder and stared at her husband. "Lou wanted the building gone, but he didn't have the guts to do it himself. He tried to frame Sapp and Fox. He finally found the perfect pigeon to do his dirty work." She glanced at Tanya and walked out of the room with her power intact.

"What did she mean by that?" Tanya asked. She got up out of her chair as the truth hit her. "Oh, no, no! I'm not taking the blame for this."

"Sit down, Ms. Wilcox," the ADA ordered.

"I'm not going to be set up."

"Just shut up, Tanya," Lou said. "Trust me on this."

"If you have anything to tell us, you better tell us now. I tend to be lenient when people are honest."

They waited, but Tanya didn't budge.

"This might help." The ADA laid the photo in front of Tanya. Carter and Richards got up to view it and the lawyer and Rossini leaned over, as did Lila. It didn't take long for Lila to figure it out. There was a large photo of three children on a dresser, and in front of the photo lay a steel-like object about two and a half inches long and bigger than a tube of lipstick. Rossini stood at the mirror putting on cuff links.

"Mr. Rossini, can you identify the children in the photo?"

"They're mine."

"Where was the photo taken?"

"Looks like our bedroom."

"Who took the picture?"

"I have no idea. This is the first time I've seen it. Obviously, some of Sharon's handiwork," Rossini said.

Carter pointed to the person who could be seen in the mirror lying in the bed. "Who is that?"

Rossini swallowed. "You know who that is."

"Say it."

"It's Tanya."

Carter placed his finger on the object in front of the photo. "What is that?"

"You don't need to answer," the lawyer whispered.

"No, he doesn't," the ADA said. "Donald Sapp made it and I'm guessing he knows what it looks like."

"I'll have all of this thrown out," the lawyer said.

"I don't think so, Mr. Harris." She tapped the device on the photo. "I can almost put it in his hands. Wait— no. He put it into Ms. Wilcox's hands for a promise of marriage. Am I right, Mr. Rossini?"

"I refuse to answer."

"Do you have plane tickets to Hawaii? Do you have a wedding ring?" The ADA directed the questions at Tanya.

It took a moment for the answers to sink in for Tanya. She leaped toward Rossini and slapped his face and kept on slapping until Richards and Carter pulled her off. "You bastard. You used me. I'll bury your ass."

The ADA motioned for Richards to get Rossini out of the room. He read him his Miranda rights as he arrested him, leading him out the door.

As the room emptied, Rossini shouted to Tanya, "Babe, don't tell them anything. It's you and me, babe, all the way."

For the next thirty minutes, Tanya told her story. She'd placed the device for Rossini on the promise of marriage and a future. She'd done it during the showing when it was busy. No one had noticed her. An officer led her out, no sass left in her. The ordeal was over.

Lila hugged the ADA. "Thank you. And thanks to Sharon. We could have never proved that Tanya was the one who set the device."

"You're right about that." The ADA gathered her things. "It's been the weirdest interview I've ever taken and I never want to have one like that again. Have a good evening."

Lila and Carter walked to the car without saying a word, both shell-shocked at the outcome of the interviews. Now she had to concentrate on the morning and Carter's leaving. That would be even more gut-wrenching.

Chapter 19

When they reached the town house, Carter grabbed bottled water for himself and Lila. They sat on the sofa, both consumed with what had happened today.

"I would never have guessed that it was Tanya." Lila took a sip of cold water.

"I thought Rossini had hired someone, but he knew Tanya would do anything for him at the mention of marriage. He tricked her and she'll spend a lot of time in prison for that."

"How much time do you think Sapp will get?"

"Not over two years and he might get a probated sentence. He got used, too."

"It's really sad. So many people got hurt because Rossini is a cheapskate. If he had just paid the money to fix the roof and the wiring, no one would've gotten hurt."

Carter studied her face. She appeared calm and serene, like she had the first time he'd met her. Maybe the wounds would disappear, too. "How are you feeling?"

"Great. We finally know who the arsonist is, and that's a load off of my mind." She sat up straight. "Damn. I had my chance and forgot to jump on Rossini for locking me in the closet."

"I think he got the message. Don't mess with Lila."

Her cell buzzed and she got up to get it out of her purse with a smile on her face. She winked at him. "You got it."

He listened as she talked. It was mostly, "Sure.

"Okay.

"It was awesome.

"That sounds like fun. I'll see you then."

"Are you going somewhere?" He bit his tongue, but it didn't stop the words from spilling out.

"Savon and I are going out to celebrate."

"Shouldn't you rest?"

Lucky for him, her phone rang again. "Savon must've forgotten something."

It wasn't Savon. He could tell by her demeanor and her serious voice. She was happy to talk to this person and her voice echoed that. It took him a few minutes to figure out it was Heath.

"That was Heath," she said as she sat on the sofa. "He had good news about the will. It's the same as my dad told me. The experts found evidence of doctoring of the named heirs. The judge granted more time to investigate, so the trial date has been extended, and Heath and his family are happy about that. It's giving the other Coltons a little longer to hold on to their father's legacy. He said to tell you thank you."

"I hope it works out the way *you* want."

She looked down at the phone in her hands. "I would just like some peace between the families. And if the will is a fake, then we all have to be prepared for that. If it's real, we have to be prepared for that, too. Now—" she got to her feet "—I need to take a shower and get dressed for an evening out. I'm not going to think about the arson or the will. I'm just going to have fun and drink a little and smile a lot."

"What about your dad?"

That stopped her in her tracks. "My relationship with my dad is what it's always been…not much. I do all the calling, but I won't be doing that anymore. I have to step back from the relationship. He's never going to change and I've finally accepted that." She headed toward the stairs and turned back. "I guess you'll be packing?"

"I don't really have that much, but yes, I'll be getting my things together. My flight leaves at eleven."

She held up her hand. "I know. You like to be there early."

Sitting on the sofa with an ankle resting on a knee, he felt more alone than he ever had in his life. He thought she would be upset. Maybe a little sad at his leaving, but she seemed fine. And he wanted her to be. It was just that…loneliness pressed down on his chest. Was this love? Was this what a man experienced when someone he loved moved on?

Why hadn't she asked him to go out with them? After the high tension of the day, he would have welcomed an evening out with her.

And there it was.

He would be leaving in the morning.

And she would be here alone.

He couldn't ask that of her. This had been a special time in his life and he would remember her forever.

She came downstairs talking on the phone and he just stared. The outfit was definitely a party dress. The black skirt looked satiny, as did the black-and-white-striped top. The silver heels made her look taller and her legs longer. A black jacket rested over her arm. Attraction stirred in his gut and made him very aware that every inch of her was woman.

She slipped the phone into a silver purse she was carrying. "I'll see you later."

"If you need someone to pick you up, just call."

"Problem solved. We're taking a cab and calling one later. We played it smart this time. Bye," she called as she dashed out the door to the waiting cab.

He watched until it was out of sight and then he closed the door and went to the refrigerator. It was empty again. He had to get something for supper. To keep his mind busy, he ran upstairs to change into shorts and a T-shirt. Then he hit the street, the same route he'd taken the first time he went jogging with Lila. He'd like to eat one more hot dog before he left. But it wasn't the same sitting there at the table without her. Nothing was ever going to be the same again... without her. He finally realized that.

It was dark when he made his way back to the town house. With the many streetlights, it didn't make a difference. Streets were lit up, just calling for people to come out and play. A small grocery store was one street over and he crossed without a problem. He was getting to know Chicago. He bought the usual stuff for breakfast and snacks for the night. He planned to watch a movie or something to kill time.

When he got back, he packed everything except his shaving kit, and then he took a shower and dressed in pajama bottoms and a T-shirt. Lying on the sofa, watching a movie he couldn't get interested in, he jumped at every sound, thinking she was home. But she wasn't. The last time he looked at the clock it was 1:00 a.m. She wasn't going to miss him at all. She had a full life and he was happy about that. He just couldn't understand why he was conflicted about leaving.

When Lila got home, she was very quiet, not wanting to wake Carter. Then she saw him sleeping on the sofa. What was he doing downstairs? The TV was on and she walked over and turned it off. Carter stirred.

"You're home."

"Yes, and why are you here and not in your bed?"

He yawned and stretched, and she watched the play of muscles as they lit a flame deep inside her. "I was watching a movie." He got to his feet. "I better go to bed. Did you have a good time?"

"We had a great time." She sank into a chair and pulled off her heels. "I'm probably going to have sores on my feet from dancing so much."

He frowned. "You and Savon danced?"

"No, silly. Richards was there with one of his detectives. They stopped by our table for a drink. We talked about the case and just had a good time. Richards is a good dancer and a nice person once you get to know him. He's not so brusque."

"And are you getting to know him?"

His voice bordered on jealousy and she didn't like

it. "For the record, Richards and his wife are separated and he's ready to go home, but he doesn't know how to go about it. I gave him some advice. That's all."

"Like what?"

She drew a deep breath and started to tell him it was none of his business, but they both were edgy and she should give him credit for that. "I told him to buy something that she really likes, take it over and tell her you would like to talk without the resentment. I guess we waited for about thirty minutes for him to figure out something that his wife liked. He doesn't know anything about her. We laughed at him and he finally said jelly beans. His wife loved jelly beans. He left to go buy jelly beans, and it was almost midnight. Imagine a husband not knowing anything about his wife. Richards is a total cop."

Carter didn't say anything and his flash-in-the-pan jealousy seemed to be gone. He picked up the pillow from the sofa. "Why didn't you ask me to go tonight?"

She was shocked and had to swallow a couple of times to speak. "Excuse me? You're leaving in a few hours. That should have said it all."

"What are we doing, Lila?"

"I'm trying to get through this night the best way I can." She charged up the stairs and slammed her bedroom door. She didn't want to spend this night with him, with memories of what they'd shared all around them. She wasn't that strong.

The next morning, she overslept, the dancing and the laughter having taken all her energy. It was 8:30 a.m. and she rushed into the bathroom, wanting to be gone by the time Carter had everything packed. She heard him in the shower. Her plan hadn't worked. She would have to face him once again.

She changed into shorts and a T-shirt and sneakers. Her mom had called last night while she was in the cab and invited her for lunch. Myles and Jackson would be there and she wanted both her kids to be home. She said Jackson would be excited. He would have someone to play with in the dirt. Myles wasn't too fond of playing in the dirt. But Lila would welcome it. For the distraction.

"Breakfast is ready!" Carter called from downstairs.

What? He had cooked breakfast? Where did he get the food? Instead of running out the front door, she played the good-girl part and went down to eat breakfast with him one more time.

"You didn't have to do this," she said as she took a seat.

"I'd rather eat something here than at the airport."

She sipped her coffee and decided to be an adult about this. "I'll miss you. I don't know how our stars crossed here in Chicago, but I'll never forget you."

"I'll miss you, too," he replied, his voice hoarse. "I never dreamed that when I came here I would meet the most gorgeous woman in the world. I'm sorry if you're hurt. I never meant for that to happen."

"It's my own fault. You told me up front that marriage wasn't for you and happy-ever-after wasn't in your DNA. You'd rather be on the road traveling. You told me all that and my heart still got involved." She tilted her head to look at him closely and her heart beat a little faster at the sculptured features and beautiful gray eyes. "You saved my life a couple of times and I will always be grateful for that."

She got to her feet and carried dishes to the sink. "You know, I might spend the night at my mom's. I'm going to pack a bag." It would be good to spend time with the family, especially with Jackson. If she stayed busy, the first week wouldn't be so bad. She just didn't know how to remove the love from her heart. Carter seemed to have no problem. But it wasn't love for Carter. She was just a girl he'd met along the way.

Carter had everything in the car. He had to go back and say goodbye, and it would be difficult. Lila deserved all the best things in life and he couldn't give her that. He found her sitting on the bed and waiting for him to drive away. Her eyes glistened and he knew they were tears. He swallowed the constriction in his throat.

"This isn't easy for me, either."

Her eyes met his. "I know, so don't feel bad about it. You can't produce love by snapping your fingers. It just wasn't meant to be for us. Call me every now and then if you get a chance. But it's not mandatory."

"Are you going to open another gallery?"

"I think I'm out of the gallery business, but only time will tell. I have an appointment with the insurance agent next week and I should get my money soon. By then I should know what I want to do."

"Hmm…"

"I wonder if the insurance company will pay out to Sharon."

"I'm sure lawyers will tear into it like vultures and she'll probably get half of what the building is worth. But I wish her the best. She really came through when we needed her."

"She's a nice lady. The nice ones always get stuck with the jerks. My personal opinion."

"Is that aimed at me?"

"I wish I could dredge up that much anger, but I can't. Have a good life, Carter."

He leaned over and kissed her forehead. He couldn't resist. He wanted to keep his lips against her warm skin, but time had run out for them. "You, too." Then he added the hardest word in the English language. "Goodbye."

Don't cry. Don't cry. Lila sat on the bed with that resolve in mind, but her strong willpower couldn't stop a tear from slipping out and running down her cheek. She reached for a Kleenex on the dresser and wiped away the emotions of the past couple of weeks. He was gone and soon he would be just a memory, a very good memory of a special man.

The front door opened and she paused. Was that Carter? Had he forgotten something? She threw the tissue in the trash can and waited for him to enter the room.

The lines on his face were drawn and his gray eyes were dark and troubled. "Did you forget something?"

"I couldn't start the car."

"Oh. I'll take you to the airport."

He shook his head. "I didn't mean that."

"What did you mean?"

"I couldn't physically make myself start the engine. Everything I love is here and I can't walk away from it. I can tell myself all kinds of stories, but they even ring hollow to my ears. If you're not going to open another gallery, come to London with me."

What did he say?

She shook her head to clear it of cobwebs. "You want me to go to London with you?" She said the words slowly to get it right.

"Yes."

"And then what?"

"We live our lives the way we want…together. If you get homesick and want to come home, we'll come home."

Her heart was beating so fast she had to stop and take a deep breath. "Is marriage on the table?"

"If you want it to be."

She ran a hand over her hair. "Carter, you're blowing my mind. Just a few minutes ago you said you had to go. You've been saying that since you've been here. Marriage, home and family weren't for you and all that stuff. What changed your mind?"

"You. I know you love me. I can see it in your eyes every day and yet you're willing to let me go because you think that's what I want. Slowly you've been changing my mind. I like waking up with you and fixing breakfast. I love everything about you. I was too stubborn to admit it. Just now I couldn't start the car. I couldn't forcibly make myself do it because I was leaving behind everything I wanted. Besides, what kind of woman would tackle a criminal for me—someone who loves me. I love you, Lila Colton. Come spend the rest of your life with me."

She placed her hands on her hips, trying to balance herself, trying to believe everything he was saying. "Where would we live?"

"Anywhere you want to. We would have to sort it

out down the road. I can't leave Neil on the spur of the moment. We have to talk about a lot of things."

"I'm listening."

"You could be my assistant searching out art fraud. We would be together a lot, but I don't think that's a problem."

"I'd like that. But I want you to be very sure about changing your mind."

"I am. I knew something was missing in my life and now I know what it was. It was you."

Not able to stand it anymore, she practically jumped into his arms and held on for the bliss that was to come. "I love you," she whispered. "For a lifetime."

He held her face in his hands. "I love you, too. I'm thinking about what kind of house we would like."

She buried her face in his neck and breathed in the masculine scent of him. "Let's leave that until later. First, you have to tell my mother you're taking me far, far away."

"That might be my biggest challenge."

She jumped back. "Oh, Carter, your plane is leaving at eleven. You have to hurry."

"I canceled the flight and now I have to make a new one. I just wanted to make sure you'd say yes."

"Yes. Definitely yes." She put her hand over her mouth. "First problem."

"What?"

"I planned lunch with my mom, and Jackson will be there. He knows I will be there. I can't break his heart. What are we to do?"

He pulled out his phone. "Let me see when I can get the latest flight out. You do have a passport, right?"

"Yes. I'll get it." She hurried upstairs, found it and

rushed back to Carter. "It's up to date." Her heart was about to burst with happiness.

Carter laid his phone on the bar. "How does eight o'clock tonight sound? First-class."

"Wonderful. Thank you." She slid into his arms.

An hour later, they were in the car and on their way to the suburb of Wheaton.

"You're a long way from your mother," Carter remarked.

"Sometimes that's a plus." She winked at him. "My mom tends to still baby me, and I'm the oldest—at least, by a few months. Myles and I have always been close. I just wish he and Faith would get back together."

"They'll work it out."

"Turn right."

"Is this it?"

"Yes. The big building is the nursery and the house is in the back. It's a two-story green Craftsman with tons of light and fresh flowers and airy windows. They sell everything from fresh flowers to fruit trees to prickly cactus, which I have a few scars from."

"I'll check later."

She chuckled. "You already have."

"This is a big place."

"Landscapers buy a lot from them and they're busy all the time. They work hard and that is just one of the little things I love about them." She pointed to an area near the house. "Park there."

They went into the house arm in arm. "The smell is intoxicating," Carter said.

Her mother met them at the back door with hugs. "I thought Carter was leaving?"

"Mom, I have some news." She told her about London.

"That's so far away. I'll never get to see you."

Rick placed an arm around his wife's shoulders. "Now, honey, she's grown. Let her live her own life. We'll miss her, but we'll celebrate twice as hard when she comes home." Rick shook Carter's hand. "It will just take some adjusting."

Myles walked in with Jackson, who had two big trucks under his arms. "Look, Li, I brought trucks to play with."

Lila rubbed his hair. "Yes, you did. We'll do that after lunch. Grandma is waiting for us to eat."

"Okay."

They gathered around the dining room table and Lila breathed in the scent of fresh flowers that were sitting in the center of the table. That would be a memory of home for the rest of her life. Her mom always had flowers on the table when they ate. The whole house smelled like a broken perfume bottle. That was what she used to think. Now she thought of how lucky she was to have that treat in her life.

Her mom and Rick brought the pot roast and all the trimmings to the table. Two chocolate pies were on the buffet.

"Everyone is very quiet," Myles said.

Rick told him about London. "Your mom is a little down."

"Mom." Myles shook his head. "How old is she now? It's time to let go."

"Where she going?" Jackson asked.

"London," he told his son.

"Is that far away?"

"Yes, it's far away."

Jackson's face crumbled into a baby-cry expression. "I don't want her to go."

Lila pulled him into her arms. "I'm not going to be gone forever. I will call you and talk to you on the phone. And we can see each other on the iPad. We can do all sorts of things. It's just like talking in person."

"Can I get a cell phone of my own?"

"You walked right into that one," Myles said to Lila. "And the answer is no, in case you're wondering."

Lila made a face at her brother.

Her mother began to remove the plates and Lila hurried to help. She put an arm around her mother. "Why are you so upset? Don't you want me to be happy?"

Vita turned and hugged her. "Of course I want my kids to be happy. Myles and Faith are separated and you're moving away. I feel like an old woman clinging to my babies."

"You love too much."

"Yes, I do, and you're a lot like me. I'm just hoping your feelings for this man are real, the lasting-forever kind."

"They are, Mom."

She reached for a dish towel and wiped her hands. "I felt the same way about your dad. It didn't take me long to figure out he wasn't my knight in shining armor. I don't want you to get hurt."

"Carter?" Lila called.

He came into the kitchen looking a little startled. She was startled, too, at her mother's reaction.

"Tell Mom our future plans."

"Um… We're going to London so I can validate a painting, and from there I suppose we'll come back to

Chicago so Lila can finish up all the paperwork with the fire. Lila's going to be my assistant and we'll be working together like you and Rick. Eventually we plan to build a home somewhere in Chicago or somewhere close to her mother."

Her mother's whole demeanor changed. "You're coming back?"

"Yes," Carter replied. "What did you think?"

"I thought you would be living there."

Carter shook his head. "No, ma'am. Lila's roots are here and I would never take her away from that. We'll be in and out for the next couple of years."

Her mom patted his cheek. "Oh, you sweet boy."

Myles poked his head around the door. "All clear?"

"Yes," her mother said. "Now let's eat chocolate pie. Where's Jackson?"

Jackson wolfed down his pie and then played with his trucks.

"Heath called me, Myles. I haven't had a chance to tell you."

"I already know. Dad called. Carin called. Enough said."

"How do you feel about it? Dad said it was all my fault because I told Heath about the experts. And ruined his life. He won't be invited to any poker games because of what I did. Carin is very distraught and upset, and I'm supposed to call and apologize."

"Are you thinking about that?"

"No. I want to know if the will is a fake or not. I think we'll sleep better if we know. That's just my opinion, it seems."

Myles wiped his mouth with a napkin. "Sometimes I think about how good it would be to have that much money. Faith and I are arguing about money and how important it is to me. She thinks family is more important. If I inherited a lump sum of money, it would certainly make my life easier. But then I remind myself that Carin has never given me or you anything that I can recall. She's not going to share that money with anyone."

"You would side with Carin for the money?" Lila was appalled.

"I said *sometimes* I think about it, especially when I'm really down about Faith. That's it. Let me be clear in case you're not. I don't plan on sharing anything from the grandmother from hell. I haven't forgotten that she said I would never amount to anything and she wasn't going to spend one dime on a needless education."

Lila placed her hand on Myles's. "Money is not going to solve your problem. Only you can."

Jackson came into the room with trucks in his arms. "Is it time to play?"

"Yes, son."

For the next hour, they all sat out in the backyard watching Jackson play. He had a motorized dump truck that he could drive. He would fill it up with the smaller truck and dump the dirt to help Rick. Sometimes he wanted Lila to help put dirt in the truck with her hands.

"Carter, come play with us," Jackson shouted.

Without pausing, Carter removed his shoes and socks and rolled up his slacks. And then he pulled off his dress shirt and laid it on the porch.

"We have to load my truck with dirt."

They played in the sand, moving it from one spot to

the other. Finally, Carter put his truck and sand in the bed of Jackson's truck. Lila followed suit.

Jackson got out of the truck shaking his finger at them. "You're doing it wrong."

Carter got to his feet and chased Jackson around the yard. "I'm doing it wrong? Wait until I catch you." Jackson's screeches echoed around the neighborhood. They laughed and played and it was a nice family afternoon.

Her mom had a gardenia bush blooming at the end of the house. The decadent white blooms were heavenly. She sat in a swing with Carter since Jackson was busy avoiding them.

"I've never seen a place like this. It looks all dressed up and just waiting for somewhere to go, but it has that feel of home. Raising a kid in an apartment in New York wasn't my parents' best idea. Kids need to be raised here in the open with all the flowers and the trees and lots of space."

She leaned over and kissed him. "It's getting late and we better go. I have to pack a few more things."

They got to their feet and Carter found his shoes and socks and put them on. They hugged and kissed everyone.

"When you coming back?" Jackson asked.

"Soon, and I'll bring you a gift."

"A gift?" He clapped his hands and then looked at Myles.

"Okay."

Her mom insisted they have another piece of chocolate pie before they left. They were sitting at the kitchen table when a young girl walked in with a red clay pot in her hands.

Her mom waved her over. "Sara, come on in."

"I didn't know you had company."

"That's okay. I'd like for you to meet my beautiful daughter and her boyfriend, Lila and Carter Finch. And this is Sara Sandoval. She's helping with marketing."

The pot crashed to the floor, splintering into many pieces. "Oh, I'm so sorry."

"Calm down," Rick told her, and he had the mess cleaned up in no time.

"Did you need something?" her mother asked.

"Oh, yes. A truck driver came into the office and said he has five hundred of—" she glanced down at the floor "—those and wanted to know where to put them."

"I'll take care of it," her mother said. Then she hugged Lila so tight she could barely breathe. "Take care of yourself. I love you, baby."

The trio made it out the door, and the young girl looked back and said, "Nice to meet you."

Lila and Carter made it back to the car.

"You seem deep in thought," Carter said.

"That girl. Who did my mom say she was?"

"Sara Sandoval."

"She seemed nervous. Did you think that?"

"A little. I think it was just seeing strangers when she only expected your mom and Rick."

"It's a little strange that Rick hired her. Rick says he'll hire family if he needs help. We have all worked there from time to time when we were in college or needed money. He was adamant about outsiders for some reason. That girl looked vaguely familiar."

Carter reached over and took her hand and squeezed it. "Let it go. Your mom will tell you if she's someone you need to know. Let's think about our future. It's going to be the best times of our lives."

"An adventure." She squeezed his hand, and every problem she ever had vanished with the feelings inside her. Life with Carter Finch would be an adventure.

* * * * *

Don't miss the next
Colton 911: Chicago story:

Colton 911: Desperate Ransom
by Cindy Dees

Available from
Harlequin Romantic Suspense!

"You doing okay?"

"Yeah. I'm fine."

Ace's gaze searched Veronica's face. "I wasn't trying to
scare you earlier."

"I didn't think that. At all. It doesn't seem real, but I
know that it is."

"I know my family has seen more than its fair share of
bad happenings around here and I'm not asking for trouble,
but there was something off about that guy. I'm not going to
ignore it or pretend my gut isn't blaring like a siren."

Ignore it? Had she been so wrapped up in her frustration
that she'd given him that impression?

"Once again, my inability to speak to you with any
measure of my normal civility left the absolute wrong
impression. I'm grateful to you."

Those sexy green eyes widened, but he said nothing, so
she continued on.

"You were watching out for me and I couldn't even manage the most basic level of appreciation." She stood, suddenly unable to sit still. "I am grateful. More than you know. I just—"

Before she could say anything—before the awful, terrible words could spill out—Ace was there, those big strong arms wrapped around her.

Just like she'd wanted all along.

"What happened?"

Her face was pressed to his chest, but it gave an added layer of protection to say what she needed to say. To let the terrible words spill out. Words she'd sworn to herself she'd never say again after she got through the horror of police statements and endless questions by drug company lawyers and even more endless questions by insurance lawyers.

She'd said them all over and over, even when it seemed as if no one was listening.

Or worse, that they even believed her.

But she'd said them each time she'd been asked. And then she'd sworn to bury them all.

His arms tightened, his strength pouring into her. "You can tell me."

"I know."